TOMORROW'S WISH

"*Go home, muñequita,*" *he whispered hoarsely.*

"No." Faith shook her head. "I'm not a 'little doll.' I'm a woman and I need—"

"I know what you need," he interrupted harshly. "But you won't get it from me. Not here. Not now. You are Faith Jennings. Not a whore to be taken in the dirt."

Faith jerked as though slapped, and Cord immediately regretted his harsh words. Maybe he had spoken a truth she wasn't prepared to hear.

She turned her back to him, and Cord felt a wrenching pain in his gut. God! He had never meant to hurt her. "Faith?"

She whirled to face him, and instead of the tears Cord had expected, he saw the light of triumph in her eyes. "You want me just as badly as I want you, Cord McCamy. You just proved it."

Yesterday's Promise

DiAnna June

LEISURE BOOKS   NEW YORK CITY

For Mabel Owenby, who never lost her faith.

A LEISURE BOOK ®

February 1991

Published by

Dorchester Publishing Co., Inc.
276 Fifth Avenue
New York, NY 10001

Printed in the United States of America.

Prologue

1857

The Texas plains were awash with moonlight as the young man drew his horse to a halt on the crest of a rise. The night air was cold and coyotes howled their lonely songs in the distance, but he paid no heed. He was at home in the vast open country and accustomed to worse conditions. Much worse. He had not rested nor eaten for a very long time, but this too was something he was used to.

The young girl who slept so soundly within the circle of his arms stirred in her sleep and snuggled closer to his bare chest. He had held her close for many long miles but he scarcely felt her weight. He looked into her sleeping face and felt a great surge of love and protectiveness. The child trusted him to take care of her and keep her safe. This he was sworn to do.

They were going home, and the journey was far from over.

PART ONE
Muñequita

Chapter 1

1871

The powerful stallion tossed its head and pawed the ground restlessly, but the lone rider held it in check as he kept watch on the scene below.

She was home.

He watched silently as she rode the pinto mare into the ranchyard, closely followed by her two-man escort. Even from his position on the distant hill, he could see the bright glow of happiness on her face and the golden highlights of her rich brown hair.

He had known she was coming. He had been expecting her. But he was unprepared for the actual sight of her and even more unprepared for the force of emotions that assailed him.

His eyes followed her movements as she dismounted and turned the mare's reins over to a gawking cowboy. She stepped away, then paused and looked around the ranchyard as though searching for something—or someone.

Her eyes lifted to scan the distant hills, and his breath caught as her gaze seemed to find him. He knew she couldn't see him, but for an endless moment he could have sworn he felt the warmth of her soft brown eyes on his skin. A bolt of white-hot desire shot through him to settle in his loins, and without conscious thought he lifted a hand, as though to caress her creamy cheek. Then she turned away and the spell was broken.

His hand dropped slowly to rest on his thigh as he watched her throw her head back and laugh at some comment made by a ranchhand. The sound, soft and musical, was carried to him on the warm still air.

A few moments more and she entered the ranchhouse and was lost from his sight.

He had seen her, and for now that was enough. He turned the impatient stallion and rode away.

Faith Jennings had returned to Texas. She was home, where she belonged.

Faith Jennings leaned back in her chair and massaged her temples. She had been poring over the ranch ledgers for so long that all the numbers had begun to run together.

Mindful of the need to familiarize herself with ranch business, but unwilling to be closeted indoors on such a lovely day, she had carried the heavy books outside, to the table in the central courtyard.

With a weary sigh, Faith closed her eyes and tilted her head back. It felt so good to be home at last. True, the ranch was a home she had not seen since she was eight years old, but it was nevertheless home.

Over the years, as she had grown from rough-and-tumble tomboy to accomplished young lady, Faith had often felt compelled to return to her Grandfather Jeremiah's ranch for a visit. Jeremiah, however, had preferred to visit Faith in New Orleans, or New York, or Paris, or London, or wherever her peripatetic Aunt Nicole had decided they should live for a short while. He had never come right out and said so, but Faith had always got the distinct impression that her grandfather had not wanted her at the ranch. Not from lack of love on his part, but from some deep-rooted concern only he could understand.

How ironic then, and how sad, that it was her grandfather's death that had at long last brought her back to Texas.

Faith had loved her grandfather deeply and would have postponed the journey home until her grief had lessened, but the letter from Matthew McCamy, Jeremiah Jenning's attorney, had urged her to come right away. She was needed.

Faith heard a soft rustle and opened her eyes to see the housekeeper, Emily Stubbs, standing beside her.

"Can I get you anything, Miss Faith?"

Faith opened her mouth to reply, but before she could speak, a voice called out from behind them, "How about a cup of coffee?"

Startled, both women turned to see who had spoken.

He stood at the entrance to the courtyard, a tall silhouette outlined by the sunlight. As he stepped forward, he removed his hat to reveal hair the color of golden desert sand and eyes of a startling green. His lips curved upward into a brilliant smile as he dangled his hat on one finger and lifted one broad shoulder in an apologetic shrug.

I know him, was Faith's first thought. An image, brief and fleeting, flashed through her mind but was lost before she could grasp it.

She stared openly at the stranger. He was so completely and intriguingly male, so alive and bristling with warm masculinity, that even across the expanse of the courtyard, Faith could feel his vitality. Her eyes absorbed each detail, from the blond hair long enough to brush his collar to his black three-piece suit and polished black boots, but the memory of who he was would not come.

"Mr. Matthew," Emily scolded, "you gave us quite a fright."

"I'm sorry. I would never intentionally startle two such lovely ladies, but if I could trouble you for a cup of coffee, I'd be obliged."

"No trouble at all, Mr. Matthew. I'll bring it right away." To Faith's surprise, the elderly housekeeper blushed as she hurried to the kitchen.

The man turned his charming smile on Faith,

and for a brief span of seconds she once again felt a sense of déjà vu.

"I assume you are Faith Jennings." At her affirmative nod, he continued, "I'm Matthew McCamy. Your late grandfather's attorney."

"It's a pleasure to meet you, Mr. McCamy." Faith's voice was soft and musical. Her upbringing had involved living in a variety of cultures amid a myriad of languages and dialects. Her slight accent therefore was entirely her own.

Matthew held up a hand in protest. "Matthew, please, and the pleasure is all mine."

"Will you join me . . . Matthew?" She gestured to the chair adjacent to hers.

"Thank you." Matthew placed his hat on the table as he took the proffered seat.

Outwardly, Matthew McCamy was calm and composed, but inwardly he was completely awed. Faith Jennings was even more beautiful than he had expected. Her deep brown eyes were framed by thick black lashes, her lips were a lush rose-petal pink, and her waist-length brown hair shone with a golden fire. Her skin looked as cool, smooth and creamy as fresh honey, and when she spoke he was captivated by the melodious tones of her voice.

Matthew cleared his throat. "I'm sorry about your grandfather. He was a good man."

Faith closed the ledgers and pushed them aside. "Thank you. Did you know him well?"

"He was a good friend. As a matter of fact, when I opened my law practice two years ago,

Jeremiah was my first client."

"Here we are," Emily sang out as she returned with a pot of coffee and two cups. She placed the cups on the table and filled each with the strong black brew. "Would you care for something else, Miss Faith? Mr. Matthew?"

"No thank you, Emily." Faith smiled at the gray-haired woman. "Just leave the pot."

"Okay. I'll be in the kitchen if you need me."

Matthew waited until Emily had left before he resumed the conversation. "I'm sorry I wasn't here to greet you yesterday when you arrived. We weren't expecting you quite so soon."

"I left the same day I received your letter," Faith replied as she lifted her coffee mug. "I saw no reason to delay."

"I understand you've been living with your late mother's sister, Nicole de Beauharnais. Did she accompany you?"

Faith shook her head. "No. I was alone at our house in New Orleans when your message arrived. Aunt Nicole had gone upriver to visit friends. She may—or may not—join me later." She shrugged slightly. "According to her whim."

"I take it your aunt can be rather impetuous," Matthew ventured.

Faith smiled as she thought of her Aunt Nicole . . . of the lazy summer days they had spent at Faith's maternal grandparents' home in France, of shopping sprees in London and Paris, spring afternoons in New Orleans, Christmas snow in New England, impromptu adventures in Spain and Italy. During the Civil War, Faith and Nicole had lived in Paris, as both waited anxiously for news of Jeremiah's safety and the war's end. Despite their penchant for traveling, both women preferred America. Faith was American by birth, Nicole by choice.

"I prefer to think of her as a free spirit," Faith replied.

They chatted easily for a while as they exchanged gossip about mutual acquaintances in New Orleans. Finally, as Matthew poured himself a second cup of coffee, he got around to the purpose of his visit. "I suppose we should get down to business."

Faith pushed her empty mug aside. "Yes."

Matthew removed a sheaf of papers from his inside pocket and scanned them briefly. "Jeremiah's will is fairly cut-and-dried. You are his sole heir. The ranch, land, house, cattle and horses are yours, as well as the income from his European investments."

Faith smiled politely. "Surely, Mr. McCamy, you didn't require my immediate presence in Texas just to tell me the contents of my grandfather's will."

"You're right," Matthew agreed. "Tell me, how well do you know Diego Montez?"

"I've never met him," Faith replied, "but I've heard Granddad speak of him. He's the son of Granddad's younger sister Hannah, and the last I heard, he was living in Spain."

Matthew nodded. "Did you know he owns a ranch that borders on yours?"

"Yes. Granddad said he gave the property to Great-aunt Hannah as a wedding present."

"Diego was born here in Texas, on the Montez ranch," Matthew told her. "His parents took him to Spain for a visit when he was a young boy. Shortly after their arrival, they were killed in a carriage accident and Diego was taken in by his father's family. Diego remained in Spain, but the ranch has continued to be managed in his behalf for the past thirty years."

Faith smiled. "I assume this little foray into the Montez family history is leading up to something."

Matthew nodded. "Diego Montez is here in Texas. He arrived at his ranch about six weeks ago."

Faith arched a brow in question. "And?"

"And"—Matthew's expression bespoke a person forced to perform an unpleasant task—"he is contesting your grandfather's will."

A jolt of anger surged through Faith, only to be wiped away by disbelief, quickly followed by hurt and confusion. Had she heard correctly? "I'm afraid I don't understand." Faith's voice was calm and composed despite her inner turmoil. "Why? On what grounds?"

"He questions your parentage."

Faith was shocked. Surely she had misunderstood. "I beg your pardon."

Matthew spread his hands palm upward in apology. "I'm sorry to be so blunt, but there you have it."

Faith waved her hand in a dismissing gesture.

"Don't apologize. I prefer you to be straightforward."

The courtyard was surrounded on three sides by the house itself, but the fourth side was bordered by a low adobe wall. Faith stood up and walked to the waist-high wall. She folded her arms atop the wall's cool surface to stare out over the ranchyard.

Matthew approached her. "Are you okay?"

"Of course." Faith managed to smile. Despite her distress, she felt a frisson of warmth at his nearness. "I simply fail to understand what prompted a man I've never met to make so outlandish a claim."

"Not so outlandish from his point of view," Matthew pointed out. "In his eyes, he is the rightful blood heir and you are the interloper. After all, you have no certifiable proof that Thomas and Angelique Jennings were your parents."

Faith regarded him with narrowed eyes. "Whose attorney are you?"

Matthew chuckled softly. "Yours, of course. I was simply pointing out the strengths of his suit."

. "I know who I am."

"So do I, and more importantly, so did your grandfather." Matthew quelled the urge to enfold her in a comforting embrace, rightly guessing that it would not be entirely welcome. "With your cooperation, I plan to fight him on this."

"Of course you have my cooperation. I'm afraid it just comes as quite a shock to discover that some relative I've never even met wants to take my inheritance away."

"I understand." Matthew smiled reassuringly. "Now, do you feel up to answering a few questions?"

"Of course." Faith returned his smile. "Do you mind if we walk as we talk? I don't think I can sit still right now."

Together they passed through the courtyard gate and strolled across the ranchyard in the direction of the stables.

"First of all," Matthew began, "do you have any memory at all of the years you lived in Texas as a child?"

"None." Faith sighed softly. "Aunt Nicole has taken me to doctors all over the States and Europe, and they all say the same thing. My memory may never return, or it could come back partially, or I could just wake up some morning and remember everything. In the meantime, there is nothing anyone can do to help me regain my memories."

Matthew frowned slightly. "It would, of course, help if you could remember something, but we will have to manage without it."

"My earliest memories are of being with Granddad and Aunt Nicole in New Orleans," Faith said. "Nicole has told me the story of my childhood many times, but Granddad never mentioned it."

"Could you tell me what your aunt told you?" Matthew asked. "It might help."

"There's not much to tell. My mother was

captured by Comanches when she was six months' pregnant with me, and though my father spent years searching, he never found us. He died trying to find us. When I was about eight years old, I was delivered to my grandfather along with the news that my mother had died. I could have been anyone, but Granddad never doubted who I was. He said I had the Jennings look." She laughed softly. "Whatever that means.

"Granddad loved me," Faith continued, "but he was a man living alone and found himself at a loss as to what to do with a half-wild little girl who could speak very few words of English. My mother's older sister, Nicole, was living in New Orleans at the time, so he took me to her."

"And that's everything you know?" Matthew asked.

"That's it," Faith replied. "No one knows what happened to my mother and me during our years with the Comanche. No one but me, and I can't remember."

Matthew paused in thoughtful silence for a moment. "We do have one thing strongly in our favor. Your grandfather knew who you were and acted accordingly."

They turned and began the walk back to the house.

"Montez is a strange one," Matthew said soberly. "Shortly after he arrived he visited your grandfather. Jeremiah told me that Diego was a big disappointment. He had expected his sister's child to be a better person. He didn't tell me, though, what Diego had said or done to make him feel that way."

"Granddad was always a shrewd judge of character," Faith said as they approached the courtyard.

"One more thing," Matthew said as he retrieved his hat and prepared to take his leave. "I've recently met Diego Montez and the small army of cutthroats in his employ. He is a hard and ruthless man, Faith, and he has greed for motivation. I would not rule out foul play on his part."

"Would he actually try to harm me?"

Matthew shrugged. "Let's just say we can't be too careful while we wait for the circuit judge. In the meantime, I've made some arrangements for your safety."

Faith nodded. She felt suddenly drained and at a loss for words.

Matthew placed his hat on his head and checked his gold pocketwatch. "I need to get back to my office, but if you need me for anything, anything at all, don't hesitate to send for me."

Faith walked Matthew to his carriage and stood, watching, as he rode away.

As she turned back to the house, she felt suddenly, overwhelmingly, alone.

Chapter 2

The sun was a golden ball suspended low over the eastern horizon and dew still glistened on the courtyard greenery, but life at the Double J was in full swing. Cowboys saddled their horses amid sounds of laughter and good-natured curses, while in the distance a calf bawled loudly for its mother. A buckboard rattled and squeaked as it was driven across the dusty ranchyard, and the air was redolent with the aroma of baking bread.

The sounds and smells carried through the warm, still air and suffused Faith with the desire to be out and about. She ate a hasty breakfast, despite Emily's attempts to foist a heartier meal on her, then hurried outside to the corral, which appeared to be the hub of the morning's activity.

A group of vaqueros—Mexican cowboys— stood near the railed enclosure where José, the domador, was working with a new stallion. Faith knew that all of the Double J vaqueros had been chosen for their exceptional skill with horses, for Jeremiah Jennings had been exceedingly proud of the high quality of his horseflesh.

Faith called out a greeting as she approached, and Paco, the lead vaquero, tipped his hat. "Good morning, Dona Faith. Have you come to watch José tangle with Diablo?" Paco was young and quite handsome with glossy black hair and dark laughing eyes. He had been one of the men assigned to escort Faith from town the day she had arrived, and she had felt a liking for him almost instantly.

Faith's eyes swung to the prancing, snorting stallion inside the corral. "Is that the horse you were telling me about?"

"Sí. He is a most fierce beast. I fear even José despairs of breaking him."

Faith's attention had focused on the wild mustang when a voice spoke softly from behind her. "Some horses are not meant to be broken."

She turned to see which of the vaqueros had spoken and found herself staring into the greenest eyes she had ever seen. For an endless moment she felt herself being drawn forward into twin pools of emerald green. She was filled with a surging warmth that left her feeling both exhilarated and unnerved. By sheer force of will, she was able to give herself a mental shake and take a step backward.

The slight distance enabled Faith to take in the

man's appearance in a single glance.

A pale blue shirt, grown soft and faded from numerous washings, was stretched across his hard-muscled chest and broad shoulders. His hat and vest were black, as was the bandana around his neck. His buckskin pants were tucked into knee-high moccasins. Slung low on his hips was a holstered .44 revolver. And the hair that curled slightly over his collar was the color of golden desert sand.

My God! She knew him. The feeling was stronger than before. So strong, in fact, that for a few seconds she had to fight against the urge to throw herself into his arms. She clasped her trembling hands together and took a deep calming breath. "Matthew?"

The man smiled but without humor. "No. Not Matthew." Did she have any idea how incredibly beautiful she was he wondered? Her soft brown eyes were wide with confusion and her cheeks were becomingly flushed. He longed to pull her into his protective embrace. To hold her and explain, but knew he couldn't. With a will of iron, he kept his hands on his hips.

"But you have to be Matthew," Faith said. "No two people look this much alike . . . unless . . ."

"Unless they are twins. I'm Matthew's brother, Cord McCamy."

"Sí," the momentarily forgotten Paco chimed in. "Did you not know there are two Senor McCamys?"

"No." Faith's eyes never left Cord's face. "I didn't know."

Cord returned her gaze, but allowed his eyes

to drop as he boldly assessed her slender body. She was clad in worn riding boots, a divided riding skirt and faded green blouse. Her silky brown hair hung loose to her waist and a flat-brimmed hat dangled down her back from the cord around her neck. To Cord she was absolutely perfect.

Paco, knowing when his presence was unnecessary, bid them adios, and hurried away to join his compadres.

"I'm sorry if I shocked you." There was a husky note in Cord's voice. "I thought you knew about me."

Faith took a step forward, her gaze still locked on his handsome face. "No, but you seem so familiar." She lifted a hand as though to touch him, but quickly pulled back. "Will you be staying here at the Double J?" She clasped her hands together again, surprised at herself. What had come over her?

Cord felt a stirring of disappointment when Faith drew her hand back, but as was his way, he pushed the emotion aside. "Yes. I'll be here for as long as you need me."

"Need you?" Faith's brow dipped in confusion, and for the first time since she had met Cord McCamy, she allowed her eyes to stray from his incredibly handsome face. "I don't understand."

Cord merely smiled his humorless smile and smoothly changed the subject. "Have you ever seen a horse-breaker at work?"

Completely bewildered, Faith could only shake her head.

Cord extended a hand and she automatically slid her fingers into his firm grasp. The result was electric. Faith felt a warm tingling begin in her palm and work its way rapidly up her arm to spread through her body. Her eyes widened as her gaze flew first to their linked hands, then back to Cord's face.

His mouth spread into a grin that transformed the harsh lines of his face and lent sparkle to the brilliant green of his eyes. He gave Faith's hand a reassuring squeeze.

She returned his smile without hesitation. It felt right somehow—so incredibly right, her hand in Cord's. The two of them together beneath the early morning sun.

"Come on." He tugged gently on her hand and she followed, unresisting, as he led her the few remaining steps to the corral.

After a moment's hesitation, Cord released her hand to lean his arms on the top rail of the corral. Faith was shocked by the sense of loss she felt when the simple contact was broken. More than a little confused by her own reactions to a man who was little more than a stranger, she struggled to push her feelings aside and turned her eyes to the action inside the corral.

"The stallion José is working with is a 'Bayo-Cobos-Negros,'" Cord explained, "a dun with black legs, black mane and tail, marked with a black line down its back. He's not a thoroughbred, but these horses are known for their stamina and endurance. Necessary qualities for a cow pony."

Faith nodded, only half comprehending his words, but she stayed as close to him as she dared. Scant inches separated them as they stood side by side to watch the domador at work. For reasons beyond her comprehension, the thought of moving even a few feet away from Cord McCamy was devastating.

José had a rope around the animal's neck and was attempting to advance, hand over hand, up the rope to the head. When the elderly domador had accomplished this feat, Cord explained patiently, he would then blindfold the stallion to make it more docile.

Just as José appeared to be making real progress, the stallion's eyes began to roll wildly. Emitting a harsh, frightened whinny, it reared onto its hindlegs and began to slash the air with its powerful forefeet. Caught unaware, the old man lost his grip on the rope and fell backward to land on his back in the dust.

Before anyone else had a chance to react, Cord vaulted over the fence and caught the trailing rope in his hands. Without hesitation, he began advancing hand over hand toward the stallion's head. Faith watched in fascination, her gaze captured by the rippling flow of muscles beneath the pale blue of Cord's shirt as he kept the rope pulled taut.

In a matter of moments, Cord was holding the rope beneath the stallion's chin with one hand and stroking its sleek, trembling neck with the other.

With Paco's help, the somewhat dazed José

hobbled from the corral. After throwing a few well chosen curses at the unruly beast that had caused his disgrace, he limped over to join Faith.

"Are you all right?" she asked the elderly man.

"Sí, senorita. I suffer only from bruised pride." José smiled sheepishly. "But watch Senor Cord. I'll wager the wicked beast will not get the best of him."

Faith watched as Cord continued to stroke the horse, speaking softly until it appeared to calm. Inching even closer, he breathed into the stallion's nostrils, then stepped back and removed the rope. With swift fluid movements, Cord threw the rope aside and swung himself onto the animal's bare back.

The horse balked at first at the unaccustomed weight. It tossed its head and pranced sideways until Cord leaned forward and spoke a few words near its ear. It calmed almost immediately and, guided by the hand that gripped its mane, allowed itself to be ridden around the corral.

"Did I not tell you, senorita?" José grinned. "No one is better with horses than Senor Cord."

"Amazing." Faith shook her head. "How did he do it."

José shrugged. "In the way of the Comanche."

Before Faith could question José's strange answer, Paco appeared. "Come on, old man." He grabbed José's arm. "We'll get Senora Stubbs to check your ribs. You may have cracked a few in that fall you took."

Still pondering all she had seen and heard,

Faith watched the two men walk away. With a shake of her head she returned her attention to the corral, only to discover that Cord was nowhere in sight. The newly docile stallion was being led away by one of the vaqueros, but Cord McCamy had disappeared.

Her eyes instinctively scanned the ranchyard for some sign of him, until at last she caught sight of his broad back as he entered the stables.

For reasons even she couldn't understand, Faith followed him.

The stable was a long narrow building on the far side of the corral. Wooden stalls lined both sides, and the doors on either end were open to receive the sunlight. Leather bridles and halters hung from pegs on the wooden support posts, and the air was pungent with the scent of horses and hay.

Most of the stalls were empty, but one contained the most beautiful white stallion Faith had ever seen. Inside the stall, brushing the horse's magnificent floor-length mane, stood Cord.

Faith stepped onto the stall's lowest railing and leaned her crossed arms on the top. "He's beautiful. Is he yours?"

Cord showed no surprise at Faith's appearance. He spoke without bothering to look up from his task. "No. Bright Star belongs to no one. He allows me to ride him because he and I are friends."

"Oh."

"Hand me that brush."

Faith passed the indicated brush, then continued to watch him silently.

When the stallion was groomed to his satisfaction, Cord turned to Faith. An amused light gleamed in his eyes as he instinctively reached out to brush a stray lock of hair from her face. She was so lovely. So full of life. Just as he had imagined she would be.

Faith felt a warmth deep in her stomach as Cord's callused fingertips brushed her cheek. She looked into his eyes and felt herself drawn by their brilliant green depths. What power did he possess to affect her so strongly? He was a stranger to her, yet she felt so secure in his presence. She turned her eyes from his mesmerizing green gaze and stepped back from the stall. "How did you calm that wild stallion down so quickly?"

Cord shrugged his broad shoulders. "He trusts me."

"So do I." Faith bit her lip. The sentiment was true enough, but she had never intended to say it out loud.

Cord swung the stall gate open and moved to stand in front of Faith. "Do you?"

Faith tilted her head back to look into his face. "Trust you? Yes."

"Why?"

"I don't know," she answered honestly. "It's just something I feel. Deep down inside."

He stretched a hand forward to gently caress her cheek. "Brother Matthew would probably warn you against placing your trust in me."

Unconsciously she pressed her cheek against his hand. "But why? You're his brother."

Cord laughed, harshly, without humor. "Because I'm considered to be the black sheep of the family."

Faith stepped closer to him as his hand moved to her shoulder. "I'll trust my instincts."

Cord's eyes searched her upturned face. "Good. You need to trust me if I'm to take care of you."

"Take care of me?"

"That's why Matthew sent for me. I'm here to protect you from Montez and his henchmen."

"You're here to protect me? Why you?"

Cord's expression was grim. "My reputation with a gun. Most people are afraid of me."

Faith moved even closer until her hands were pressed flat against his hard-muscled chest. "I'm not afraid."

Cord's arms encircled her to draw her closer still. It felt so good to hold her, to see her huge brown eyes gaze at him so trustingly.

Faith leaned against him. Allowed him to support her weight.

He lowered his head, and Faith waited breathlessly to feel his lips pressed to hers.

Suddenly Cord stiffened and jerked his head back. What was he doing? He gripped Faith's shoulders and moved her away from his chest.

Bereft, Faith could only stare at him.

"Do you still trust me?" he demanded.

She nodded.

"Good. Just do as I say and everything will be

fine." He released her shoulders and without further words turned and walked out of the stables.

Faith watched him go, but this time she did not follow.

Chapter 3

The ranch office, like every other room in the sturdy, single-story ranchhouse, opened onto the central courtyard. With the doors opened to admit any breeze inclined to enter, Faith could sit behind the massive oak desk and look out past the low courtyard wall into the ranchyard. She watched for a while as two vaqueros put their horses through a series of intricate paces. The horses' powerful hooves raised small clouds of dust and earned the men a scolding from Emily, who was struggling to hang the day's wash on a crude rope clothesline.

With a sigh, Faith wrenched her gaze from the outdoor scene and allowed her eyes to scan the interior of the office. It was her favorite room, for the office, more than any other place on the ranch, reminded her of her grandfather. With its leather-upholstered armchairs, heavy oak desk and cluttered bookshelves, the room stirred faint warm feelings of nostalgia. She sometimes felt her memory was there somewhere, locked away in a desk drawer, or perhaps tucked away among the clutter of leather-bound books.

Jeremiah Jennings had never allowed Emily, or anyone else, to clean his private office. He had preferred his own sort of "organized" disarray.

The room was so masculine, so entirely Jeremiah's that Faith felt almost like an intruder in her own home. But still, she felt compelled to look through her grandfather's private papers, not only to learn more about the workings of the ranch, but also to discover more about her parents and maybe even herself. She took a deep breath and opened the top drawer.

At first glance the drawer appeared to contain nothing more than a multitude of receipts—some as much as two years old—from places such as Mullins General Store and Bettendorf Feed and Livery, but beneath the haphazard stack of papers lay a leather-bound appointment book. Faith placed the slim volume on the desktop and began to leaf through the pages.

The date was neatly printed at the top of each page, and appointments were written across the bottom in Jeremiah's bold scrawl. The first entry had been dated almost a year earlier, and notes appeared on almost all of the following pages. Events for each day were carefully scheduled, from routine reminders such as "check with Bettendorf about new buckboard" to more businesslike tasks such as "Cattlemen's Meeting, seven o'clock." As she read through the book, Faith could sense the purposeful, no-nonsense way her grandfather had approached ranch business. Each appointment and task, no matter how seemingly insignificant, was carefully recorded. His careful attention to detail was partially responsible for the Double J's success, and at odds with the apparently careless way he kept his office.

Near the end of the book, Faith found an entry dated just one week before Jeremiah's fatal heart attack. "Meet with Matthew at noon" was written across the center of the page, and in the lower right-hand corner the aging ranch owner had written "Cord" and underlined it three times.

Faith's brow wrinkled in thought. She could understand her grandfather scheduling a meeting with his attorney. But why had he written Cord's name? And underlined it?

As Faith studied the strange notation it occurred to her to question Matthew about it, but she quickly dismissed the thought. After all, lawyer-client relationships were confidential. Her mind drifted quickly to the other McCamy brother. She had seen Cord only from a distance since their fateful meeting, and she had wondered, more than once, if he was avoiding her. Matthew she had spoken to only briefly since the day, a week earlier, when he had told her the contents of Jeremiah's will.

How could twin brothers be so completely different? Matthew had a ready smile and charming, easygoing manner, while Cord was more intense, more withdrawn. He brought to mind a tightly coiled spring ready to fly into action at the least provocation. Faith felt irresistibly drawn to both McCamys, but Cord stirred something deep inside her. Feelings she had never been in touch with before.

Faith made an unsuccessful attempt to remove the McCamys from her mind. When they refused to budge, she shrugged and decided to work around them.

She turned to the next page in the book only to discover that it as well as the following three pages were blank. It was unusual to see so many blank spaces, but judging from the previous entries, Jeremiah had completed spring roundup shortly before his meeting with Matthew. Perhaps he had allowed himself some leisure time. The next entry had been made a week later and said simply "send letters to Faith and Nicole." Letters? As far as Faith knew, neither she nor Nicole had received a letter from Jeremiah in months.

Faith flipped to the next page and noticed something strange. An entire week was missing from the book. The dates jumped from May 15 to May 22. On closer examination, she saw that the pages had been neatly cut away.

She felt a sinking sensation in the pit of her stomach. Her grandfather had died on May 22.

The entire week preceding his death was missing!

Had Jeremiah cut the pages from his own datebook? If so, why? And if Jeremiah hadn't, then who had?

Faith stood up and walked to the window, the book clutched in her hand. It was mid-June. A month had passed since Jeremiah's death. Ample time for someone to slip in and remove the pages. But why destroy just a few pages? Why not the whole book? And for what reason? There had been no foul play involved in the elderly man's death. Jeremiah had died of a heart attack. Hadn't he?

The sound of a horse and buggy arriving drifted through the open office door and alerted Faith to the fact that she had company. She moved to the desk and returned the book to the top drawer. Having drawn no logical conclusions, she decided to make no mention of the datebook. To anyone. Not yet anyway.

Faith left the office and crossed the courtyard just in time to see Matthew enter the parlor. At least she was fairly certain it was Matthew.

She stepped through the open doorway and allowed her eyes to slide admiringly across the wide expanse of his back. He was clad in an obviously custom-tailored suit of dark gray. His boots were polished to a high gleam and he held his hat in his hand. It was Matthew.

"Hello."

Matthew turned around and flashed his trademark smile. "Faith, you look lovely. As always."

"Thank you." She returned his smile as she stepped forward and they clasped hands in greeting.

Warmth emanated from Matthew's palms, seeping into Faith's hands and working its way through her entire body. She felt flushed and just slightly disoriented by the contact.

She pulled away. "Why don't you sit down and I'll fix something cool to drink."

Matthew's emerald green eyes sparkled with amusement. "If it's no bother."

Faith was already moving toward the kitchen. "No bother at all. Is lemonade all right?"

"Sounds wonderful."

They chose to drink their lemonade in the courtyard, seated on opposite sides of the round wooden table, in the shade of the marble fountain.

"Are you getting settled in?" Matthew asked.

"Yes, thank you. I find myself feeling quite at home here already." Faith felt more at ease with the table between them. She had not expected to feel a reaction to Matthew's touch. It had unnerved her. She placed her glass on the table and folded her hands primly in her lap before asking bluntly, "Why didn't you tell me about your brother?"

"Cord?" Matthew's brow creased in a slight frown. "I thought I did."

"Not quite. And needless to say, it came as quite a surprise when I met him."

"I apologize if Cord's presence has distressed you in any way, but I did tell you I had arranged for your protection."

"Yes, but I assumed you meant legal protection. Not a gun-toting twin brother."

Matthew leaned forward in his chair. "Do you have objections to Cord?"

"No. Not at all." Faith felt a blush stain her cheeks. He might as well have asked if she had objections to sunshine. "I just like to be kept informed."

Matthew settled back into his chair. "That's why I'm here. To keep you informed. I just came from a meeting with Montez."

"About my inheritance?"

"Yes. He has 'generously' offered to drop the entire suit if you will sell the Double J to him."

"Never."

"That's what I told him."

Faith looked at him through narrowed eyes. "I beg your pardon."

"I rejected the offer. I told him you would not sell."

"Without first checking with me?"

"Yes." Had Matthew known Faith better, he would have recognized the tone in her voice and chosen his words more carefully, but being ignorant of her moods and personality, he blithely forged ahead. "I knew you had no wish to sell, and besides, the sum he offered was a mere pittance. Hardly enough to buy the parlor furnishings, let alone the entire ranch."

"MISTER McCamy." Faith's voice was as smooth and as cold as ice. "When I gave you leave to act as my attorney, I did not grant you permission to make my decisions for me. You had no right to reject Don Diego's offer without first consulting me."

Matthew was taken aback by the thread of steel in Faith's voice. She spoke in a controlled and even tone and her eyes had changed from their customary warm brown to icy topaz. She was serious. "I'm telling you now," he reminded her.

"After the fact. You should have discussed the offer with me before giving Montez an answer."

"What difference does it make?" he snapped. He would never admit it, but the entire conversation was beginning to make him uncomfortable.

"A great deal of difference," Faith told him. "You would never have presumed to speak for my grandfather or any of your male clients. I deserve the same consideration."

"I promised Jeremiah that if anything happened to him, I would look out for your welfare."

"My grandfather would have been the first to point out that I am a reasonably intelligent adult and quite capable of making my own decisions. I own the Double J, and in the future I will expect you to consult with me on all important matters. Do I make myself clear, Mr. McCamy?"

"As crystal, Miss Jennings." Matthew glared at her from beneath lowered brows. Like it or not, he had just been put quite thoroughly in his place. And she had never once raised her voice. Suddenly he began to laugh. He threw his head back and laughed so long and so loud that Emily rushed outside to see what was going on.

"Will Mr. Matthew be staying for supper?" the housekeeper asked tentatively.

A smile tugged at the corners of her mouth as Faith regarded her lawyer. "Would you care to stay for supper, Matthew?"

The laughter had finally ceased, but Matthew's grin was back in place. "I'd love to, but I can't. I'm late now for a meeting in town."

"Some other time perhaps?" Faith offered.

"I'd like that."

Emily returned to the kitchen, but every few steps she would glance back over her shoulder at Matthew, as though not quite sure what to make of his behavior.

"I believe I have just been given a proper set-down," Matthew said. "You would make one hell of an attorney."

"Thank you. I'll remember that if I ever find myself in need of employment."

"I apologize for not consulting you, but believe me, I won't underestimate you again."

"See that you don't."

Matthew stood up and prepared to leave. "Still friends?"

"Of course."

"Good. I'll probably drop by again in a few days."

Faith walked Matthew to his buggy. "Matthew, it has occurred to me that Don Diego and I have never met. Perhaps if I could meet with him, face to face, I could convince him to drop the entire matter."

"No!" Matthew saw Faith's spine stiffen and hastened to add. "I wouldn't advise it. Montez is not the type of man you can reason with."

"I could try."

Matthew was overwhelmed by the urge to grab Faith by the shoulders and give her a good shaking, but he suppressed the impulse. "Listen, Faith, I'm not trying to tell you what to do. I just don't want to see you hurt. I'm speaking now as a friend as well as your attorney. Stay away from Montez."

Faith merely smiled. "Good-bye, Matthew, I'll see you in a few days."

Matthew looked at her for a few moments as he tried to ascertain if she had accepted his advice. Her face was a cool emotionless mask and he could read nothing in the velvety soft-ness of her eyes. Finally he swung into his buggy and drove away.

Unable to sleep, Faith left her bedroom to sit in the cool, moon-washed darkness of the court-yard. Seated on the edge of the marble fountain, she gazed up into the awesome beauty of the Texas night sky. Thoughts of Jeremiah's appoint-ment book still plagued her and she longed to find the answer to her questions.

Faith didn't know how long he had been there before she felt his presence. She simply knew he was there. Even before she turned her head and saw him. "Hello, Cord."

Cord smiled, his special secretive smile that

pulled one corner of his mouth upward. "Couldn't sleep?" He had been leaning casually against the far wall, but as he spoke he straightened and walked toward her.

Faith felt her heart lurch in her chest as she shook her head. Her hair, which hung loose down her back, rippled across her shoulders and appeared to capture moonbeams in its silken strands.

Cord sat down beside her. He had known she was troubled. Had known she needed him. So he had come. Even though he had cursed himself for a fool, he had come to her. "Want to talk?"

"Yes . . . no . . . I don't know." Faith laughed softly. "Yes. I would like to talk, but not about me." It had returned. That feeling of instinctive trust she felt in his presence. Despite the fact he wore a gun, even now in the middle of the night, she trusted him. "Where were you? Before?"

"Before?"

"Before you came to the Double J. You said Matthew sent for you."

"California."

"I've never been there."

Cord reached out to clasp her hand. "I know." He held her hand lightly in his larger one, turning it over to trace the lines of her palm with a callused fingertip.

Faith felt her heart begin to flutter wildly in her chest. A delicious tingle began in her hand and picked up speed as it traveled through her body. "Is that where you live? California?" She managed to sound only slightly breathless.

"Sometimes." He released her hand and Faith felt almost devastated at the loss of contact. "What's wrong?"

How did he know? Could he see into her mind? Read her very thoughts? Faith shrugged. She trusted Cord completely, but she didn't want to tell him about the datebook. Not yet. "I had a disagreement with Matthew."

Cord nodded. "Knowing Matthew, that's not surprising."

"He can be a bit overbearing."

"To put it mildly." Cord smiled. "Did you leave Brother Matt with any shred of his masculine pride intact?"

"What makes you so certain I won?"

Cord shrugged. "Just a hunch."

"Well, there wasn't a winner because we didn't argue. We discussed."

"Uh-huh."

"There is no reason for mature adults to get into a screaming match just because they happen to disagree."

"Uh-huh."

"There was no reason to fight."

"So you say."

Faith Jennings, who never in her life had raised her voice in anger, who even as a child had never had a temper tantrum, came very close to losing her composure with Cord McCamy. She rose to her feet. "I think I'll return to my room now," she said evenly.

Cord laughed softly as he reached out to grab

her wrist and pull her back down beside him. "Can't you take any teasing, muñequita?"

Faith felt a thrill race through her as the endearment fell softly on her ears. Muñequita, Spanish for little doll. "I thought I could."

"Tell me what you and Matthew disagreed about."

"He made business decisions without consulting me."

"And you took objection?"

"Of course." Faith sniffed. "He also told me to stay away from Diego. I think Diego and I should meet, face to face, and discuss our differences."

"Hold on, little wild cat," Cord admonished. "Matthew happens to be right about Montez. You should stay away from him."

"Why?"

"Because Diego Montez is one dangerous hombre. He would chew up a little handful like you and spit you out."

"How do you know?" Faith demanded.

"I know."

Faith rose to her feet again. "Just what I need, another overbearing male."

Cord stood and gripped her lightly by the shoulders. "Not an overbearing male, muñequita. Just a man concerned for your welfare."

Faith's eyes, usually so soft and warm, began to glow with an inner fire as Cord's gaze swept over her, lingering briefly on the slim column of her throat and the gentle swell of her breasts.

As his arms moved to encircle her and draw her close, Faith lifted a hand to caress Cord's stubbled cheek. He turned his face to place a kiss in the palm of her hand and Faith felt her knees grow weak. She pressed herself against him, safe within the circle of his strong arms. Cord held her close as he rained tender kisses on her temples, her eyelids and the pulsepoints beneath her ears.

Faith moaned deep in her throat. She was pressed tightly against the hard wall of his chest, but she longed to be even closer. She couldn't get close enough.

Cord stifled a groan. Faith felt so wonderfully right in his arms. So soft. So sweet. His hands tangled in her silken hair as his lips blazed a path across the satiny warmth of her neck.

A moan escaped Faith's lips, and Cord, already rock hard with desire, stiffened as a new wave of sensations surged through him. "No." He broke contact with a suddenness that left Faith stunned. "No, niña." He stepped away from her and took several slow, deep breaths.

Faith watched Cord as she too breathed deeply in an effort to gain control of herself. She knew she was out in the open air wearing only a thin cotton nightgown. And she knew she had practically thrown herself at a man she barely knew. But no matter how hard she tried, she could find no shame or embarrassment within herself. Anything that felt so incredibly right could not be wrong.

"What was that?" she asked in a breathless whisper. "What came over us?"

Cord reached out as though to touch her

again, but instead dropped his hand and turned away. "Desire, sweetheart," he said softly. "It was desire."

Without a backward glance, he walked away, into the darkness beyond the courtyard.

Chapter 4

Seated at the dressing table in her bedroom, Faith stared out the window at the open range. The Double J Ranch consisted of thousands of acres, and the more Faith learned about her new home, the more she felt the pride of ownership.

She had spent the previous week learning all she could about the inner workings of the ranch. She had spent two days reviewing ranch records with Ross Fulton, the Double J foreman, and had listened tirelessly as he explained all aspects of cattle ranching. She had ridden out on the range with Paco Lopez and taken a look at the cattle close up, while the vaquero explained the ranchhands' jobs and responsibilities. José had filled her in on the details of horse-breaking and had taken her on a tour of the ranch buildings. Faith had also met Max, the elderly man who tended the vegetable garden, hogs, chickens and milk cows in addition to cooking the ranchhands' meals.

Everywhere Faith had gone, she had looked for Cord, but she quickly discovered that Cord McCamy was seen only when and where he wanted. He had shown up twice, without warning, at the breakfast table, where he had proceeded to charm Emily and tease Faith.

Faith had accepted his teasing with good humor while silently she had implored her heart to slow its too-rapid beat. The sight of Cord's handsome face across the breakfast table had conjured too many fantasies in her fertile mind.

Matthew had returned in midweek with papers for Faith to sign and had remained for supper. It was during the meal, as Matthew was explaining the details of one of Jeremiah's investments, that Faith had experienced the first glimmering of her idea. By the time Matthew had ridden away, the idea had solidified and she had already decided on a course of action.

With a heavy sigh, Faith turned to the mirror and attempted once again to twist her hair into a fashionable arrangement. Despite her many talents, hairdressing was one thing at which she had never been adept.

"Here now," Emily said as she sailed into Faith's bedroom. "Let me do that. You're making a mess."

"Thank you, Emily." Faith smiled at the housekeeper's bluntness. "I'm afraid I'm all thumbs this evening."

"As well you should be," the older woman snapped. "This whole thing is a mistake and you know it."

"I know no such thing," Faith returned.

"Hmph!" Emily looked skeptical, but proceeded to expertly arrange Faith's hair nonetheless. "What do you suppose Mr. Cord and Mr. Matthew are going to think about this?"

"It doesn't matter what they think. This is my ranch and my life. The McCamys are not my keepers."

"Maybe not," Emily conceded, "but they care for you, just as I do, and they're not going to be very happy when they hear about this little scheme of yours."

"If they don't like my actions, then it's their problem. I have to do what I think is best."

"So you say, but don't discount the people who care about you. Have you considered how we'll feel if something happens to you?"

"Oh, Emily." Faith smiled. "I appreciate your concern. I really do. But what could possibly happen to me?"

"I don't know," Emily admitted, "but I don't trust Don Diego any farther than I can throw him. Your grandfather never discussed his personal business with me, but I do know he had no love or trust for that Montez man. Despite the fact that he was his nephew." She gave Faith's hair a final pat. "Mr. Jeremiah wouldn't approve of this at all."

Faith surveyed her artistically arranged curls in the mirror before turning to face the motherly housekeeper. "You have to trust me. I know what I'm doing . . . I think."

The gown Faith had chosen to wear had been specially designed for her in Paris. Made of deep red silk, with a daringly low-cut bodice, she had never worn it before, but had been pleasantly surprised to find it packed in the trunk her Aunt Nicole's maid had shipped to her from New Orleans.

Once dressed, Faith added a garnet necklace and matching earrings, then turned to Emily. "How do I look?"

"Pretty as a picture and much too good for the likes of him," Emily sniffed, "but if you're determined to go through with it, I might as well go set the table." Grumbling beneath her breath, the housekeeper left the room.

Faith was in the parlor when her dinner guest arrived. Instead of entering through the court-yard like most visitors, Diego Montez came to the seldom-used front door. While Emily—still grumbling—went to admit him, Faith quickly checked her appearance in the mirror. The deep red silk of her gown highlighted her own natural coloring and lent added sparkle to her velvety brown eyes. The simple jewelry added just the right touch and, she hoped, gave her the appearance she had been striving for. That of a sophisticated woman of the world.

Faith turned just as Diego entered the parlor. He was tall and slim with narrow shoulders and he sported a pencil thin mustache beneath his hawklike nose. He shoved his hat into Emily's hands as he swept into the room. "My dear, I can't tell you how pleased I was to receive your dinner invitation."

"Don Diego." Faith smiled warmly as she extended a hand in greeting. "How wonderful to meet you at last."

Diego bowed low to kiss Faith's proffered hand, and she was surprised to feel a slight revulsion at his touch.

"Hmph!" Emily placed Diego's hat none too gently on the parlor table. "Dinner will be served shortly."

"Thank you, Emily." When the housekeeper showed not the slightest inclination to leave the room, Faith glared a warning at her. With a fatalistic shrug, the older woman retreated to the kitchen.

"Would you care for a drink before dinner?" Faith offered her guest.

"Your beauty, senorita, is intoxicating enough. I dare not imbibe more." Diego spoke to Faith, but his black-eyed gaze raked over the parlor furniture in an appraising manner.

"You flatter me, sir." In truth, Faith found his manner more than a little confusing. "You speak English remarkably well. I was given to understand you were raised in Spain."

"But educated in England," Diego replied smoothly. His voice was deep and cultured with only a slight accent.

Emily returned to announce dinner, and Faith allowed Diego to escort her to the courtyard. "It's such a lovely evening, I thought we would have dinner outside."

"A marvelous idea, my dear, but I fear even the stars will be outshone by your presence."

Faith swallowed a laugh. Diego Montez was certainly giving her a full dose of his oily charm.

Emily had prepared the table with extra care. A white lace tablecloth set off the china and silverware to perfection, and two silver candlesticks sported slim white candles at the table's center.

"How very European," Diego commented as he held out a chair for Faith. "You must miss France a great deal."

"Not at all," Faith said truthfully as she poured the wine. "I miss my grandparents, my mother's parents, but I have always preferred America. Especially Texas."

"Oh yes, your mother was French, wasn't she?" As Diego spoke, he held one of the forks up and examined it, as though assessing its possible value.

"Yes," Faith replied. A tiny frown creased her forehead as Diego replaced the fork and focused his attention on the exquisite silver candlesticks. "Her parents still live in France."

"Tell me, niña, why have you asked me to dinner tonight?" Diego asked, abruptly changing the subject. "I assume you have decided to accept my most generous offer."

"No. I have no wish to sell the Double J," Faith told him. "I simply thought that if we could meet, face to face, we could work out our differences."

Diego regarded her with narrowed eyes. "I

can't understand a well-educated, European lady such as yourself preferring the wild West to the civilized culture of Europe."

"You forget, I am not European, but American. I find the savagery of Texas to be quite beautiful."

"But then, you were raised by savages, weren't you," Don Diego sneered. He was enraged. He had accepted Faith's invitation only because he had been certain she had decided to sell. But the ridiculous girl had obviously hoped to sweet-talk him into leaving her alone. Was she really that naive?

Faith felt a shudder of fear at the look of icy contempt in Don Diego's eyes. At that moment, she understood why Cord and Matthew had called him a dangerous man. "Since you are family, I will try to ignore your last remark," she said as calmly as she could. "I asked you here tonight to try and work things out between us."

"But," Diego said with barely veiled hostility, "we are not family. I am a Montez. Product of the joining of the Jennings and Montez families. You are most likely the result of a liaison between your slut of a mother and some red-skinned heathen."

Faith came to her feet. "Leave my home!" she said evenly. "Now."

Diego rose and allowed his gaze to flicker briefly over the expanse of flesh exposed by Faith's low-cut bodice. "Gladly. Buying the ranch would have been so much less tedious than a lawsuit, but in light of your ridiculous attitude, I now withdraw my offer. I will see you in court." He took a few steps, then paused. "Thank you, senorita, for a most interesting evening."

"Montez," Faith called to him.

Diego glanced back over his shoulder, a disdainful expression on his face.

"One more thing," Faith said calmly. "If you ever mention my mother again, if her name even passes your lips, I will kill you."

Without deigning to reply to Faith's threat, Diego swiveled around and walked away.

Faith sat down at the table and stared morosely at the remains of the ruined meal. Apparently Diego Montez was every bit as evil as Cord and Matthew had implied. Not to mention heartless and cruel. For the first time in her life Faith had been in the grip of a murderous rage and it had left her emotionally drained. "Well, that was certainly a mistake," she said out loud.

"I agree."

Faith turned to see Cord standing in the shadows. Her heart began to beat triple time. "What are you doing here?"

"Keeping an eye on you."

"Do you think I need a bodyguard?"

"Apparently you do," he spat. "Anyone foolhardy enough to allow a snake like Montez into their home is in need of a keeper. Full time."

Faith laughed softly. "Maybe you're right."

Cord walked forward until he was standing directly in front of her chair. With a lightning-fast move, he grasped her wrist and pulled her up against him. "Just what were you hoping to accomplish?"

Faith gazed into Cord's eyes and was amazed to see the anger they held. He was furious. "Cord, are you angry?"

"Damn right, I'm angry." Cord held her tightly against his chest. When he had walked up and seen Montez seated at the table with Faith he had known a killing rage. It had taken all the willpower he possessed not to charge in and tear him limb from limb. He hadn't been able to hear the conversation, but from the look on Faith's face it hadn't been pleasant. "What possessed you to do something so foolish?"

Faith slid her arms around Cord's waist and snuggled against his chest. She inhaled deeply of his masculine scent. He smelled of soap and horses and his own unique fragrance. "Oh, Cord, I really thought I could convince him that he's mistaken about me. I thought once he saw me that he would realize that I am a Jennings."

"Oh, muñequita." Cord, his anger dissolved, kissed the top of her head. "Montez doesn't care if you're a Jennings or not. He just wants your ranch."

"I realize that now."

Cord's hand slipped behind her neck to tilt her head back and gaze into her face. "Did he touch you?"

"No. Only my hand. And Cord."

"Hmmm?"

"When he kissed my hand, I thought I was going to be sick."

Cord chuckled. "So much for the famous Montez charm."

Faith searched the depths of his emerald green eyes. "Are you still angry?"

"Yes. Yes, I am." Then his mouth descended on hers. He kissed her lips apart and felt the sweetness of her response as his tongue explored the inner recesses of her mouth.

Faith moaned deep in her throat. An inner fire raged through her and turned her knees to water. She leaned more heavily against him, instinctively arching her back to get even closer.

Cord's mouth moved to her cheek and then her neck. "Faith, querida." His breath was harsh in her ears.

Then as quickly as he had begun his sensual assault, he ended it. Setting Faith from him, he took a step back. He was consumed by a lust far stronger than any he had ever before experienced. From just one kiss.

"Cord?" Faith's eyes were soft and liquid with desire. She reached for him.

"No, sweetheart." His voice was raw and husky. "Not now, not yet. I think it's time for you to go to your room."

Faith smiled. She had no idea how sensual her expression was. "Will you come with me?"

Cord bit back a groan. It took every ounce of willpower he possessed not to sweep her into his arms and carry her off to the nearest bed. "No."

"I'm not a child."

"No. You're definitely not a child." Cord smiled grimly. "Trust me. Go to your room. I'll stay here until you're safely inside."

Faith glared at him for a few moments. When she saw he wouldn't change his mind, she stepped forward and stretched on tiptoe to kiss his cheek. "Good night." Then she turned and walked away, deliberately swinging her hips in a provocative manner.

Cord watched until the door closed behind her, then turned around and found himself face to face with Emily.

"It's about time, Cord McCamy," the elderly woman snapped.

Cord narrowed his eyes at her, but it did not bother Emily in the least. Humming merrily, she proceeded to clear the table.

Diego Montez slammed the front door behind him and strode straight to the liquor cabinet. He poured himself a shot of bourbon and drank it down in one gulp.

"Apparently dinner didn't go as well as you had planned."

Diego poured himself a second drink, then turned his icy glare on the woman who had spoken.

She lounged indolently in a velvet-upholstered chair, her bare legs draped over the arm. She was dressed in only a short silk wrapper and her long raven hair was unbound. "She won't sell?"

Diego slammed his glass onto the marble cabinet top. "The bitch refused."

Languorously unfolding her long silky limbs,

Luisa Alvarez stood up. She walked over to Diego and twined her arms around his neck. "Will you take her to court?"

"Damn it," Diego growled. "I don't have time to wait for a court decision."

Luisa pressed herself against him. "There are other ways, querido. And more effective methods."

He slipped his hand inside her robe and cruelly squeezed a soft breast. Luisa's dark eyes glittered with pleasure and her lips parted in a feral smile. "Will you use your original plan then?"

Diego's free hand tangled in her hair to pull her head back with painful pressure and look into her eyes. "What do you think?"

Chapter 5

A buggy pulled into the ranchyard, halting Faith on her way to the stables. She stepped forward, a smile on her lips, as Matthew swung down from the driver's seat. "What brings you out on such a beautiful morning?"

"What do you think?" he demanded.

"I'm sure I have no idea," Faith said cheerfully as she turned and continued on her way to the stables. Matthew followed closely on her heels.

"No idea? Then would you care to tell me what went on out here two nights ago?"

"Two nights ago?" Faith entered the stables and went straight to Dancer's stall. She had chosen the spirited pinto mare for her own soon after her arrival. "Are you referring to the night Diego came to dinner?"

Matthew threw his arms wide in exasperation. "What else?"

"Really, Matthew, how should I know?" She slipped soft leather riding gloves onto her hands. "You really should be more specific."

"Okay. How could you invite Montez here after I warned you not to? How's that for specific?"

Faith opened the stall and led Dancer outside. Paco had saddled the mare earlier and it was skittish and anxious for exercise.

Faith swung into the saddle and adjusted her flat-brimmed hat. She flashed Matthew a brilliant smile. "It's a beautiful day, Matthew, and I'm in no mood to argue or listen to a lecture. If you're really spoiling for a fight, perhaps Emily or José will oblige you." Then she was gone, racing away on Dancer's back and leaving Matthew in a cloud of dust.

Faith paused at last by a group of cottonwoods on the bank of a shallow stream. She wasn't sure how long she had been riding, but judging from the sun's position in the sky, at least two hours had passed since she had ridden away from the ranchhouse.

She dismounted and led Dancer to the stream, then walked a short distance along the bank. It was here, out in the open, where she felt the happiest. She felt a peace and contentment on the open range that she had never felt anywhere else.

The rugged landscape stretched before her, and as she gazed at its savage beauty, she felt she could almost reach out and touch her past. She longed desperately to reclaim the lost years. The years she had spent with her mother.

"Faith?"

She turned to see Cord standing a few feet behind her. He had moved so silently and she had been so deep in thought that she had not heard him approach.

"What are you doing out here all alone?"

Faith smiled. She was intensely pleased to see him. She gestured downstream to where Dancer had been joined by Bright Star. "I've been riding. I needed time alone to think."

Cord's brow furrowed into a frown. "It's dangerous for you to be out here all alone."

Faith laughed softly as she stepped closer and tilted her head back to gaze into Cord's face. "Why?"

"Because," he said sternly, "your horse could step in a hole and break its leg. You could be thrown and break *your* leg. You could be snakebit or you could get lost, and if that's not enough, I can give you at least a dozen more reasons."

"I think those are reasons aplenty, thank you," Faith replied, completely unperturbed.

With a shake of his head, Cord sat down Indian-style on the ground. He lifted one hand up to Faith in invitation. "Will you join me?"

She allowed him to clasp her hand, reveling in the warmth of his touch as she sank to the ground and drew her legs beneath her. "What are you doing out here?"

Cord gave her hand a squeeze before he

released it. "I've been to the northern line camp. I was on my way back when I saw you."

"Oh." Faith fell silent. She had half hoped he had been looking for her.

Cord studied her profile for a moment, fighting the urge to trace her jawline with his callused fingertips. He wanted her more than anything he had ever wanted in his life. The mere thought of holding her soft, fragrant body in his arms caused him to harden painfully. "I see you found my favorite spot."

"Yours too?" Faith's musical laughter floated softly on the warm summer air. "It is lovely here, isn't it?"

Cord saw the sparkle in Faith's deep brown eyes, and the soft, becoming flush on her creamy cheeks and felt another powerful surge of desire. Perhaps it was time to go. "Would you like to ride back together?"

Faith felt a stab of disappointment in the pit of her stomach. She had hoped to spend more time with Cord. She didn't completely understand her feelings for him, she knew only that he stirred new and exciting sensations deep inside her. His mere presence filled her with intense longing. She managed to smile as she rose to her feet and moved to where Dancer waited patiently.

"Muñequita?" Cord spoke quietly from behind her as he lightly gripped her shoulder.

Faith's heart began to beat triple time at his touch. Did he always have to move so silently? She turned to face him and her breast brushed lightly against his granite-hard chest.

"Are you in a hurry?"

Slowly, Faith shook her head, her eyes never leaving the sudden intensity of his deep green gaze. She opened her mouth to speak, but his lips were suddenly pressed to hers, his hand leaving her shoulder to cup the back of her head.

Of their own volition, Faith's arms encircled Cord's neck to draw him closer. She raised herself onto her toes and arched her spine in an effort to bring herself closer to the object of her desire.

Cord crushed her lips beneath his own as he encircled her waist with his free arm. He couldn't get enough of her. The taste of her honey-sweet lips sent bolts of white heat rushing through his veins. He had not intended to touch her at all, but she was so lovely, so soft, so sweet and so very desirable. And by God, she belonged to him. Whether she realized it or not.

Faith was lost in a sea of heightened awareness. Nothing existed for her in that moment except Cord and the wonderful feelings he evoked. His hand slid beneath her blouse and she could feel his scorching heat as his rough, callused palm caressed the silky skin of her waist and back.

Just as her legs began to tremble and refuse to hold her, Faith felt a stinging sensation in her left buttock. The pain was so sharp that she arched backward and cried out, "Cord?" She looked at him, her eyes wide in confusion.

"For God's sake, Faith, get down." He pulled her down to lie flat on the grass and stretched himself full length on top of her.

Cord's gun had materialized in his hand, and Faith wondered vaguely how he had removed it from the holster so quickly. Then she heard the sharp crack of rifle fire and the truth hit home—she had been shot!

"Faith? Honey? Can you ride? We have to get out of the open."

She tried to speak but her mouth felt strangely dry. Finally, she managed to nod.

"Good girl. I'll cover you while you make a run for your horse. Then ride hell for leather for home."

Cord rolled away and opened fire, his gunshots as loud as thunder in Faith's ears as she made her way to the horses. Then she was on Dancer's back and racing away across the open range. She heard Cord call out to her, then blackness descended.

Faith's eyes opened to be greeted by a velvety night sky. A yellow crescent moon hung overhead, surrounded by a bright scattering of stars. Her head was pillowed on her saddle and she was wrapped in a rough Indian blanket. She turned her head and saw Cord hunkered down by a small smokeless fire, the horses tethered nearby.

As consciousness slowly returned, she became aware of a painful throbbing in her posterior.

Without a word, Cord rose to his feet and approached her. He dropped to his knees and slid an arm under her shoulder to lift her slightly, then offered her a whiskey flask.

"Better?" he asked after she had taken a few sips of the fiery liquid.

"Yes, thank you." She managed a tremulous smile. "Where are we?"

"Not far from the ranchhouse. You fainted a few miles back."

Faith struggled to remember what had occurred. "I was shot?"

"Yes."

"Who?"

Cord released her and sat back on his heels. "You know."

Faith closed her eyes wearily. "Why didn't you take me home?"

"There are three of them. They circled around in front of us and you were injured. It's safer for us to hole up here until morning." Cord's expression was impassive, revealing no hint of his inner turmoil. He blamed himself for Faith's injury. He was supposed to protect her. Instead, he had allowed his lust for her to take full rein. Had he not been so involved in her seduction, he would have seen or heard the men approach. It galled him too that he had been forced to run. He had never backed off from a fight in his life, but he had had Faith to consider. Her safety came first. Damn it. It should never have happened.

Faith groaned softly. "I hurt."

One corner of Cord's mouth curved upward. "I imagine so. That slug left quite a crease."

Faith's eyes flew open. "You . . . uh . . . dressed my wound?"

"Who else?" Cord's smile grew to a full-fledged grin. "You were unconscious."

Faith glanced down at her body, clad only in her chemise and the Indian blanket, then turned her gaze back to Cord. "I don't know what to say."

"How about thank you?"

"Thank you."

"You're welcome."

He rose to his feet and moved back to the fire. "Emily will send some men looking for you if you're not back by dawn. It will be safe for you to go home then."

"Me? Alone?"

Cord returned the whiskey flask to his saddle-bag. "Not alone. With the ranchhands."

"What about you?"

"I'm going after the men who shot you. I would have already if you hadn't been injured."

"Is it bad?"

"Your wound?" Cord shook his head. "No. Just a crease. Painful but not life-threatening. You'll dance again."

Faith regarded him silently for a moment. "Did you undress me?"

"Do you see anyone else around?"

Despite her best intentions, Faith felt a blush stain her cheeks. She covered her face with her hands.

Cord chuckled softly. "Don't worry. I only

looked at your wound. I had to clean it and dress it."

"I know I shouldn't be embarrassed, but . . ."

Cord knelt beside her and gently pulled her hands away. "Don't. Just trust me. After all, it's not the first . . ." He stopped abruptly and gazed out into the darkness.

"First what?"

Cord turned back to her, but his smile was sad. "Not the first wound I've tended."

Faith yawned hugely as the whiskey began to take effect. Cord tucked the blanket more securely around her. "Try to get some sleep. I'll wake you if anything happens."

But she was already sleeping, her breathing deep and even. Cord felt her forehead for any sign of fever, but she was cool to his touch. Still, he watched her for a long time.

Cord dismounted and continued on foot to the crest of the mesa. If he had read the signs correctly—and he had never been wrong before—the snipers who had wounded Faith were headed for Mexico instead of the Montez ranch. Don Diego must have paid them in advance. Hired guns weren't the type to hang around and answer questions.

True to Cord's prediction, Ross Fulton, Paco Lopez and three of the Double J ranchhands had arrived in camp shortly after dawn. Once Faith's well-being had been ascertained and she was safely on her way home, Cord had set off to search for her assailants.

He was preparing to remount and continue

the hunt when he saw a rider approaching from the south. Cord immediately recognized the horseman by the way he sat his mount. Cord waved a signal, then led Bright Star down the slope and onto open ground.

The rider ran his horse full tilt toward Cord, halting scant inches in front of him, but Cord did not flinch or move away. He knew the man would not run him down.

The rider slid from his horse's bare back. He was dressed in moccasins and buckskin pants topped by a calico shirt. His black, poker-straight hair was waist-length and held back by a beaded headband.

"Fierce Hawk," Cord said, holding up a hand in greeting. "It is good to see my blood brother."

"And you, Wind Rider," the Comanche returned. "Is your woman well?"

Cord regarded his friend closely, but could read nothing in the blank expression or the obsidian eyes. He was not surprised that Fierce Hawk knew about Faith's injury. The Comanche brave seemed to have a way of knowing everything that went on. "Yes. Her injury was not serious."

Fierce Hawk nodded. "It is good."

"I go now to find the men who shot her," Cord said. "Will you ride with me?"

"I would ride proudly by your side, my brother, but it is not necessary."

"I must avenge her."

"There is no need. The men are dead."

Cord stared blankly at Fierce Hawk for a

moment until comprehension dawned. "You killed them?"

"Yes."

Cord felt cheated. He had wanted to be the one to kill the men for harming Faith. He had also wanted to question them about their employer. "It was my right to avenge her. Their blood was mine."

Fierce Hawk's blank expression did not change. "Will you deny that the right was also mine?"

Cord shook his head. He couldn't dispute Fierce Hawk's claim, but he was still filled with unreleased fury. "Did the men speak at all?"

"No, but they screamed like women. They did not die bravely."

Cord stared into the distance for a moment, then swung himself onto Bright Star's back. He had reached a decision. There was still business that needed to be taken care of. "Thank you, Fierce Hawk. Will I see you soon?"

"Yes." Fierce Hawk mounted his horse. "I will be nearby, keeping watch on Little Shadow." The Indian wheeled his horse around and rode off in a cloud of dust.

With grim determination, Cord rode just as swiftly in the opposite direction.

Diego Montez awoke slowly from a deep sleep. He blinked his eyes as he wondered groggily what had awakened him. Then he felt the prick of a cold steel blade at his throat.

"You're a heavy sleeper, Montez," growled a

voice in the darkness. "Not an asset for a man with as many enemies as you."

"Who are you?" Diego's voice was surprisingly arrogant for a man in his position. "If it's money you want, remove the knife and I'll get it for you."

"I don't want your money." A hand gripped Diego's hair to pull his head back and make his neck even more vulnerable to the knife blade. "I want your life."

Diego's mouth felt uncomfortably dry, but he fought the urge to swallow. "What is this all about?"

"Be quiet and listen before I give in to the temptation to slit your throat and be done with it." The knife's pressure increased slightly until Diego could feel a thin rivulet of blood trickle down the side of his neck. "I'm giving you fair warning, if Faith Jennings is harmed again, you won't live to regret it. Any more attempts on her life and I'm coming for you. If she suffers so much as a broken fingernail, I will hold you personally accountable."

"Is that you, McCamy? I'll speak to the sheriff about this. You'll be arrested." Diego's voice bordered on hysteria.

"You can try it, Montez, but you won't be safe from me no matter what you do." Diego's hair was released, but the knife remained at his throat. "Just remember, I don't need the law to solve my problems. I prefer the personal touch."

The knife was removed and the room fell still and silent.

Diego reached for his bedside lamp and, after several minutes of nervous fumbling, finally managed to light the wick.

No sign remained of the late-night intruder. If not for the blood on the collar of his nightshirt, Diego might have thought he had dreamed the entire episode. He thought briefly of rousing his men to go in search of his assailant, but dismissed it. He had the feeling they would find nothing.

Still weak-kneed and trembling with fear, Diego left his bed. He knew sleep would not return to him this night.

Faith awoke to silvery moonlight streaming through her bedroom window and an unfamiliar weight on the bed beside her.

Due to the soreness of her bottom, she had slept on her stomach, so had only to raise herself onto her elbows to see Cord lying next to her. He lay on his back, atop the quilt, fully clothed. He had removed only his moccasins and hat. His gunbelt hung from the bedpost within easy reach.

Faith's first reaction was shock. What on earth was he doing in her bed? But as she studied his sleeping form, she began to feel a wave of tenderness wash over her. He looked so tired. His cheeks were shadowed with two days' growth of beard and dark circles graced his eyes. Even in repose, the tension did not leave his face.

"Morning, muñeca." Cord spoke without

opening his eyes. "Do you always thrash about in your sleep like that?"

"I suppose," Faith murmured. How long had he been awake? "What are you doing in my bed?"

"Sleeping."

"I can see that, but *why* are you sleeping here?"

Cord wearily raised his lids to regard Faith through eyes bright with amusement. "I was very tired."

Faith couldn't resist smiling. Despite the strangeness of the situation, there was something quite pleasant about his presence in her bed. "Obviously you were exhausted, but I was under the impression that you had a bed in the bunkhouse."

Cord rolled to his side and raised himself on his elbow to prop his head in his hand. "I stopped by a little while ago to check on you. I was only going to take a quick peek, but your bed looked so inviting. You don't take up much room."

"Well, I see you made yourself at home."

"Do you mind?"

Faith shook her head. "Not really."

Cord reached out to gently caress her cheek. "How's your wound?"

"Better." She laughed softly. "It's like Emily said. If I have to have a scar, my rear end is the best place to have it."

Cord frowned. "Scar?" He hadn't thought of that.

"Just a tiny one." Faith grinned and her soft brown eyes sparkled with mischief. "Want to see?"

Cord regarded her through narrowed eyes. Her silky hair was loose and flowing over her shoulders, and, raised on her elbows as she was, he was afforded an unobstructed view of her breasts through the round neckline of her gown. He felt himself begin to harden, and the temptation to say yes to Faith's teasing question was almost overwhelming. As a matter of fact, he would love to look at every inch of her lovely body. "Keep this up and you'll end up on the part of your anatomy that is already sore," he warned.

Faith's smile did not falter, but she wisely changed the subject. "Did you find the gunmen?"

Cord reached out and enfolded her protectively against his chest. "They won't bother you again."

Faith snuggled against his hard-muscled length. "Thank you," she said softly.

Ignoring the throbbing in his loins, Cord kissed her lightly on the forehead. "Go to sleep," he murmured, "it's been a long day."

With a sigh of contentment, Faith closed her eyes. In a few moments she was asleep.

Cord lay with her until the pale light of dawn began to fill the room. Then silently, without disturbing Faith, he left.

Chapter 6

Cord's brows drew together in a frown. "So. You're determined to go into town."

Faith placed her flat-brimmed hat on her head and stepped through the gate into the ranchyard. "Yes, I am. I want to send a telegram to Aunt Nicole and I have some shopping to do."

"It's been less than a week since you were shot," Cord reminded her.

"And I feel fine."

"You should wait a few more days at least."

"What ever for?" Faith asked as Paco drove up in the buggy. She preferred to ride horseback, but her bottom was still too sore to sit the saddle.

"Would you like me to drive for you, Doña Faith?" Paco asked as he stepped down to help her into the buggy.

"That won't be necessary," Cord said. He moved in front of Paco and lifted Faith onto the buggy seat. "I'll accompany Miss Jennings into town."

Faith slid over to make room for Cord, but he shook his head. "I'll go with you, but I'm not riding in any buggy."

He walked to the stables and returned a few minutes later on Bright Star's back. "Let's get it over with."

Cord could not tell Faith the true reason for his concern about her trip to town. He was determined to keep her safe, and it was a much simpler task within the ranch boundaries. He hoped his actions had drawn Diego's wrath away from Faith and onto himself. He was accustomed to dealing with cutthroat tactics. She was not. She was just too damn vulnerable.

The town of Sonria, Texas, was large by Western standards. An odd conglomeration of buildings, ranging from board to adobe to log, it sprawled across several acres of the Trans-Pecos region.

Sonria's citizens were an even mixture of Mexicans and Americans. Riding along the crowded main street, Faith saw people of both cultures going about their business, as well as a few Chinese and a family of Indians. Horses graced almost all of the town's hitching rails, and buckboards formed a line at the General Store.

YESTERDAY'S PROMISE

As they passed the Brass Bull Saloon and Dance Hall, fancily dressed saloon girls, lounging in gaudy splendor on the upper veranda, called out lewd greetings to Cord. Shamelessly they blew kisses and leaned over the railing to give a full view of their ample bosoms.

When Cord grinned and tipped his hat to the garishly painted "ladies," Faith felt a swift stab of anger. She shot him a quelling look, which he chose to ignore.

The telegraph office was a small building on the far edge of town, wedged between Dunbar's Tobacco Shop and an adobe building whose sign proclaimed it simply as "Rosa's."

Faith drew the buggy to a halt in front of the office, but before she could step down, Cord was beside her, lifting her from the seat. He set her gently onto her feet and she leaned against him for a moment, grateful for his support. The ride into town had been harder on her than she had expected.

"Are you okay?" Cord asked.

"Yes." She took a step back and regarded him with narrowed eyes. "I can manage my errands on my own if you want to visit your 'friends' at the Brass Bull."

Cord's eyes sparkled with suppressed laughter. "Jealous, muñequita?"

Faith blushed. "Yes. I guess I am."

Cord smiled his special secretive smile that quirked up one corner of his mouth. "Good." He gripped her elbow and, still smiling, escorted her into the telegraph office.

Once Faith had sent a telegram assuring her Aunt Nicole of her well-being, she and Cord walked down the street to Gladys Perkins' Dress Shop, which unfortunately for Cord was directly across the street from the Brass Bull.

Cord waited patiently as Faith ordered several new riding skirts and plump, good-natured Gladys took her measurements. Despite admonishments from both women to leave and come back later, Cord refused to budge from the shop. He would allow Faith out of his sight only long enough for her to go into the fitting room.

Her business completed, Faith had just bid good-bye to Gladys and stepped outside onto the boardwalk with Cord when they heard someone call out.

"McCamy."

Cord reflexively shoved Faith behind him as he turned toward the sound of the voice.

The man was standing in front of the Brass Bull Saloon. He was small in stature with bowed legs and a narrow hatchet face. A dusty hat was pulled low over his eyes and a six-gun gleamed from the holster on his hip.

"Blacky." Cord's voice was edged with steel.

Blacky stepped forward, the jingle of his spurs clearly audible in the silence of the suddenly deserted street. "I'm calling you out, McCamy."

"I've got no quarrel with you, Blacky."

Blacky merely shrugged as though it was of no consequence to him.

"Faith." Cord's voice was low as he spoke without turning to look at her, never for a second taking his eyes from the hatchet-faced Blacky. "Go inside with Gladys and, no matter what happens, stay there until I come for you."

Something in Cord's voice made Faith obey him without question. On legs that seemed to have turned to water, she managed to move to the shop door and slip inside.

"Come away from the windows," Gladys called to her from the back room. "Sometimes a bullet goes wild."

Faith could only shake her head, frozen to the spot. How could she hide when Cord was in so much danger?

The tension in the air was as thick and as visible as the small dust clouds that rose with each jangle of a spur as the men squared off in the street.

Blacky's fingers twitched nervously above his holstered six-shooter and his eyes, beneath a low-slung Stetson, darted about anxiously.

Cord stood ready. His impassive face displayed none of the uneasiness exhibited by Blacky. He wanted only to get it over with. To put the episode behind him—as he had so many others—and see to Faith's safety.

Death hovered overhead. A real and tangible entity that filled the humid air of the street and echoed in the men's eyes.

Blacky took a step forward. A muscle in his jaw twitched spasmodically as a rivulet of sweat slid across his cheek. With a sudden, lightning-fast movement, his hand dropped to his gun.

The heavy silence of the street was broken by

the sound of exploding bullets as two guns burst into action. Red sparks flew. Acrid smoke filled the air. And one body dropped, bleeding onto the dust of the street.

A mass of spectators surged through the saloon doors and into the street, their eyes filled with morbid curiosity. The undertaker, tape measure in hand, hurried forward eagerly to bend over the prone body.

Cord reholstered his gun. He felt no satisfaction or even relief. Only emptiness. He stepped forward and flipped a gold coin to the undertaker. "For the burial." He turned away and moved back toward the dress shop, only to be brought up short by Faith throwing herself into his arms. Her arms twined about his neck as she pressed her face to his hard shoulder.

"I told you to wait," Cord murmured near her ear.

"I know. I waited as long as I could."

Behind them, the undertaker was attempting to sell Blacky's boots and gun to a drunken cowboy.

A grimace of distaste crossed Cord's face. "Come on." He removed Faith's arms from his neck and clasped her hand. "We haven't got much time." He led her quickly up the street and into Rosa's, the restaurant next to the telegraph office.

"Sit," he ordered. Cord pushed Faith into a chair near the window and took the adjacent one for himself. "Blacky has friends. Friends whose pockets are lined with Don Diego's money. Friends who are going to come gunning for me as soon as they drink up enough courage at the Brass Bull."

When Faith would have spoken, Cord stopped her with a look. "Just listen for once, please, sweetheart. I am going to ride out of town alone. You are going to wait here at Rosa's until someone comes to take you home."

"But Cord . . ."

"No buts. Diego's gunmen will follow me out of town, and you will be here. Safe. I will not take chances with your life."

Faith felt a sinking sensation in her stomach. How could a simple trip into town have gotten so out of hand? In a matter of moments the day had gone from good to bad to worse. The thought of Cord, alone, against a group of ruthless killers filled her with icy dread. "I want to go with you."

"No." Cord's tone was such that Faith knew she could not change his mind.

A broad-bellied man with three days' growth of beard and sweat-soured clothes entered the restaurant and approached their table. Faith recognized him immediately as Sheriff Leroy Hobbs.

"I know your type, McCamy," the sheriff sneered. "You're nothin' but a two-bit gunslinger, and I don't allow your kind in my town." He tapped the tin star on his chest with a dirt-encrusted fingernail. "I'm the law here, and you just committed murder in front of the entire town. It is my duty to arrest you." His hand dropped to his pistol.

Cord was on his feet in an instant. He moved with such silent, pantherlike speed that Sheriff Hobbs had not a split second of warning before he found himself against the wall, Cord's forearm pressed painfully across his throat. "I don't have the time to put up with your nonsense today, Leroy." Cord used his free hand to remove the sheriff's pistol and lay it on the table in front of Faith. "Return the fool's gun to him after I leave." He removed his arm from Hobbs' throat.

Red-faced and sputtering, the portly sheriff slid down to sit on the floor.

Cord reached for Faith's hand to pull her to her feet and jerk her tightly against him. "I'll see you in a few days." He kissed her quickly, with a hard, bruising pressure, then he was gone. She watched through the window as he leapt onto Bright Star's back and rode away.

Faith retrieved the sheriff's pistol and walked over to drop it into the still gasping man's lap. "Tell me, sheriff, are you naturally stupid or do you have to work at it?"

"I could arrest you as an accessory," he croaked.

One corner of Faith's mouth quirked upward in wry amusement. "Feel free to try."

Groaning and mumbling beneath his breath, the sheriff got to his feet and stumbled through the door.

The restaurant was bright and cheerful with red checkered tablecloths, colorful Mexican rugs and the warm spicy aroma of good food. Fortunately for Faith, it was also temporarily devoid of customers. She could feel herself beginning to tremble with delayed reaction and she was grateful for the lack of an audience.

She could think only of Cord. The mere thought of harm befalling him caused a wrenching pain deep inside her. Why did Diego want the Double J? Could he really want it badly enough to kill for it?

Rosa herself brought Faith a cup of hot tea. A small woman with a ready smile, Rosa was as cheerful as her restaurant's decor. She spoke reassuringly to Faith in an attempt to ease the younger woman's anxiety. "Do not worry for Senor Cord. He is one hombre who can take care of himself."

When Rosa returned to her kitchen, Faith was left alone to sip her tea and stare out the window. She was considering defying Cord's order and driving herself home in the buggy when she saw Paco standing across the street. He was having what appeared to be an intense conversation with a young Mexican woman. Twice, Paco turned as though to walk away, but the young woman stopped him both times. After a while, they appeared to reach an agreement and parted company.

Faith fully expected Paco to cross the street and enter Rosa's. She assumed that he had come to escort her home. But to her surprise, Paco mounted his horse and rode away. It was the young lady who crossed to the restaurant.

She was a lovely young Mexican girl dressed in a white camisa, red skirt and leather sandals. Her long raven hair was unbound and she moved with a fluid grace as she made her way between the tables. "Mama," she called.

Rosa bustled from the kitchen, her face wreathed in smiles. "My daughter Luisa," she told Faith. "She helps me in the kitchen."

Luisa turned to smile at the posada's sole customer, and Faith was taken aback by the icy contempt she saw in the girl's dark eyes. "Senorita Jennings." Luisa nodded curtly, then turned back to her mother and chattered rapidly in Spanish for a moment before hurrying to the kitchen.

Rosa turned to Faith with a shrug. "The young are always in a hurry." She sighed heavily as she followed her daughter into the kitchen.

Faith had just finished her tea when she looked up to see a man silhouetted in the doorway. Cord! Her heart leaped in her chest. He stepped forward and removed his hat. Matthew. He walked straight to Faith.

"I thought you were in El Paso," Faith said.

Matthew sat down next to her. "I just got back. I ran into Cord a few miles outside of town."

"Then you know what happened?"

"Yes, I've already talked to Sheriff Hobbs."

"And?"

"And a conversation with my horse would have been more productive. The man sees Cord as the only bad guy in the whole affair."

"He's a fool."

"I agree."

"Is Cord okay, Matthew? He's all alone out there."

Matthew smiled grimly, an expression that made his already extraordinary resemblance to Cord even more pronounced. "I can almost guarantee that he will come to no harm. Cord seems to have a knack for landing on his feet."

Impulsively, Faith leaned forward and kissed Matthew's cheek.

His eyebrows shot upward. "Thank you, but what did I do to deserve that? Tell me so I can do it again."

"Just because."

"Ah." Matthew sighed and reached for her hand. "Come on. I'll take you home."

Seated in a velvet-upholstered armchair, Diego Montez stared into the darkness beyond his parlor window. "You really are a most useless individual, Leroy."

Sheriff Hobbs sat on the edge of his chair, nervously turning his hat in his hands. "I tried to arrest McCamy. I really did, but he assaulted me and that Jennings woman sassed me. Then his lawyer brother came in and threatened me with legal action."

"And you folded like a house of cards."

Luisa Alvarez glided into the room and pressed a drink into Diego's hand. "Would you care for a drink, sheriff?" she asked.

Diego regarded the sheriff with icy contempt. "That won't be necessary, my dear. Sheriff

Hobbs was just leaving."

Hobbs licked his lips as he eyed Diego's drink. "Do you have any more instructions for me?"

"Why? So you can botch them up too?" Diego pulled Luisa onto his lap. "Luisa can be my eyes and ears in Sonria. She doesn't spend her days sleeping behind a desk." Ignoring the sheriff's bug-eyed stare, Diego used his free hand to roughly caress Luisa's breasts. "Get out, Leroy. Your presence is no longer required."

Sheriff Hobbs jammed his hat onto his head and, red-faced, shuffled from the room.

Diego jerked Luisa's skirt up and squeezed her soft buttocks. "I have a foolproof plan this time. I will finally be rid of that little trollop and her private guard dog. Once and for all." He laughed softly. "And as her only remaining Jennings relative, the Double J will be mine."

Chapter 7

Cord continued to stare, unmoving, into the campfire as a lone figure entered the circle of light and sat down across from him.

"Little Shadow seems well. She recovers quickly," Fierce Hawk said.

"She is too stubborn to do otherwise."

"She is your woman now?" the indian asked.

"No."

"I know it is what you wish. Will she not accept you?"

"It is not yet time."

Fierce Hawk snorted. "It is long past time. Why do you not tell her?"

"It is not yet time," Cord repeated.

"You are afraid she will run from her past. I do not believe this is so."

Cord could only shake his head wearily. "I will know when the time is right."

"Do you hold back to spare Little Shadow or yourself?"

Cord remained silent, for in truth he had no answer.

"Is Montez still a threat?" Fierce Hawk changed the subject.

Cord nodded. "For some reason, he's determined to gain possession of the Jennings ranch. He won't give up easily."

"Why do we not kill the Spaniard and end this foolishness? I would kill him gladly to protect Little Shadow."

"It is a tempting idea and I have already given him fair warning, but we can't kill even a snake like him in cold blood."

"White men have strange rules," Fierce Hawk grunted.

Cord could only nod in agreement.

Faith saw him as soon as her horse topped the rise. She had felt drawn to the spot by some deep instinctive feeling. The same feeling that told her Cord was there waiting.

Cord rose to his feet as Faith entered the makeshift camp. "You shouldn't have come." But he was oh so glad she had. He had ached to see her for the past two days. Longed to touch her silken hair, to feel her warm satiny skin.

Faith slid from the saddle and moved to stand in front of him. "I had to." Her eyes feasted hungrily on the sight of him. His golden hair shone in the morning sunlight and his emerald eyes flashed with green fire. She longed for the touch of his callused hands. She had missed him with a painful intensity.

"You're alone?"

She nodded.

"You took a foolish risk." Cord's voice was harsh, but his eyes told another story as they boldly raked her form. Her rich brown hair was loose and unbound, falling in glorious splendor to her waist. Her cheeks were flushed, her lips slightly parted, and her eyes glowed with a fiery warmth. He could see the pulse beating in the slim column of her neck and the way her breasts moved with her labored breathing.

Slowly, Faith removed her hat and riding gloves and laid them aside. "I've missed you."

Cord stepped closer and lifted a hand as though to stroke her hair. Then, slowly, he curled his fingers into a fist and let it drop to his side. Faith's presence alone had been enough to spark the flames of desire deep inside him. He was already rock hard and throbbing with need. To touch her would be madness. "I've missed you too."

Faith swayed toward him, ever so slightly. Her skin felt hot and tingling and in need of his touch. Her eyes moved over him, measuring the breadth of his shoulders, the narrowness of his hips, the powerful strength of his hands, and she felt a curling warmth between her thighs. She looked up into his face, unaware that her eyes mirrored her longing. Cord was here, and some deep intuitive feeling told her that only he could ease the ache inside her. Only he could still the yearning. She slid her tongue over her suddenly dry lips. "Cord?"

Cord swallowed a groan. Those expressive eyes of hers, her pink tongue gliding over her lips. It was almost more than he could bear. He could feel his member straining against the confines of his pants. "Go home, muñequita," he whispered hoarsely.

"No." Faith shook her head. "I'm not a 'little doll.' I'm a woman and I need—"

"I know what you need," he interrupted harshly. "But you won't get it from me. Not here. Not now. You are Faith Jennings. Not a whore to be taken in the dirt."

Faith jerked as though slapped, and Cord immediately regretted his hard words. Maybe he had spoken a truth she wasn't prepared to hear.

She turned her back to him, and Cord felt a wrenching pain in his gut. God! He had never meant to hurt her. "Faith?"

She whirled to face him, and instead of the tears Cord expected, he saw the light of triumph in her eyes. "You want me just as badly as I want you, Cord McCamy. You just proved it." Her gaze dropped to the considerable bulge in his pants.

A muscle tensed along Cord's jaw, and he closed his eyes for a moment in an effort to regain full control. "You told me once that you trust me. Is that still true?"

"Of course," Faith answered without hesitation.

"Then shouldn't you trust me about this too?"

Reluctantly, Faith nodded her agreement.

"Good. Wait while I collect my gear and we'll ride home together."

The long ride to the ranchhouse was made, for the most part, in silence. Both Cord and Faith were too intensely aware of each other to do more than exchange occasional glances.

Faith didn't know how or why—and at this point she didn't care—she knew only that Cord McCamy had the power to set her soul aflame, to make her want him with an intensity that rocked her to her core. At the same time she felt safe in his presence. She knew she could trust him, heart, body and soul. She was also beginning to suspect that tied in among her feelings of trust and longing and desire there dwelled the more tenderly fierce emotion of love. Deep, everlasting love for Cord McCamy.

Cord's white stallion skittered sideways, kicking up clouds of dust as Cord eyed Faith surreptitiously from beneath the brim of his hat. The past two days without her had been sheer hell, but he had been left with no choice other than to stay away. He had succeeded in his attempt to turn Diego's murderous wrath from Faith to himself, but in so doing he had been forced to put himself at a distance from her. To protect her. To keep her out of the line of fire.

Cord shifted slightly in his saddle in an attempt to ease the pressure on his throbbing loins. He wanted Faith every bit as much as she suspected, but how could he make love to her now? If she accepted him now, would she still want him if and when her memory returned? He watched the sunlight glint off her rich brown hair and sighed. Could he accept her love with the risk that she might someday turn away from him? He didn't know. He knew only one thing for certain. He loved Faith Jennings and he always had.

Chapter 8

With a sigh, Faith left her grandfather's desk and moved to gaze out the office window. She had spent the entire afternoon going through all of Jeremiah's papers, ledgers and books, but had found no clues to explain the appointment diary's missing pages.

She wearily massaged her temples with her fingertips. Perhaps she was making too much of the missing datebook entries, but damn it, it just didn't make sense. It didn't fit.

Faith glanced down at her blue calico skirt and smiled grimly. Her hair was twisted into a single fat braid and her white cotton blouse was smudged with ink. She would have to hurry if she wanted to make herself presentable in time for dinner.

Faith's smile broadened and the grimness left her features. She was looking forward to dinner. She had invited both the McCamy brothers to dine with her and Emily and had planned a relaxing family meal for the four of them.

She shook her head ruefully as she thought of Cord and Matthew. Twins. Physically they were almost identical, but when it came to personalities, they were as different as night and day. With a start, Faith realized she had never seen them together. Seeing them side by side at the dinner table would, no doubt, be a most interesting experience. Humming softly to herself, she went to prepare her bath.

Emily smiled a welcome as she opened the parlor doors to admit their guest. "Mr. Matthew," she exclaimed. "Don't you look fine and handsome this evening."

Matthew bent to kiss the housekeeper's wrinkled cheek. "You're looking fine yourself."

Emily blushed with pleasure. "Come on in and visit with Miss Faith. Supper will be ready soon."

Faith rose to her feet when Emily ushered Matthew into the room. "I'm so glad you came," she said as he kissed her cheek.

"Did you think I wouldn't?"

Faith laughed gaily and shook her head. Matthew too had the ability to make her feel more vibrantly alive. Not to the extent that Cord affected her, but he did have an undeniable attraction. "Would you like a drink while we wait for Cord?"

"Yes, thank you." He moved to the liquor cabinet and poured himself a liberal splash of bourbon. "You're expecting Cord?"

"Didn't I tell you? I've invited you both."

"Both of us?" Matthew laughed softly. "It should prove interesting."

Faith regarded him with mild curiosity, but refrained from questioning his strange comment.

"You two young'ns just relax and have a nice visit," Emily said as she headed toward the kitchen. "I'll holler when supper's ready."

Faith returned to her armchair and Matthew took the adjacent one for himself. "Have you always lived in Sonria?" Faith asked politely.

Matthew shook his head. "I was born in Sonria, but we moved to Savannah when Cord and I were quite young. A number of things happened that made my parents unhappy with Western life."

"Your parents are still alive?"

"And well." Matthew smiled. "My father founded the First Bank of Sonria while we lived here, but I think he's much happier in an Eastern bank."

"And your mother?"

"She never cared for the West but she is quite content in Georgia. It's the type of life she and my sisters prefer."

"You have sisters?" Faith asked in surprise. "Cord never mentioned sisters."

Matthew smiled grimly. "Five sisters, all younger, and it's not surprising that Cord hasn't mentioned his family. Our parents have never forgiven him for choosing the wild West over a more civilized way of life."

"Yet they chose to move West once, and so did you," Faith pointed out.

"It's not the location," Matthew told her. "It's the way of life."

Sensing his reluctance to continue the discussion of his parents, Faith changed the subject. "It must be wonderful to have brothers and sisters," she said wistfully. "I've always wanted a large family, but it's always been just Aunt Nicole and myself with an occasional visit from Granddad."

Matthew studied Faith's profile. She was so beautiful. He couldn't help thinking that he would love to be the one to give her a large family. He cleared his throat. "Speaking of your aunt, have you heard from her?"

"I received a wire yesterday. She's been detained by business but she hopes to join me here in a few weeks."

"I look forward to meeting her. From all accounts she is quite a remarkable woman."

"She is unique to say the least." Unable to contain her impatience any longer, Faith got to her feet and walked over to gaze out the parlor doors and into the courtyard. "I wonder what's keeping Cord."

Matthew shrugged his broad shoulders. "With Cord one never knows what to expect."

Emily bustled into the sitting room. "Supper's ready."

"But Cord's not here."

Emily peered about the room as though expecting to find Cord lurking in a corner. "Where is he?" she demanded of Matthew.

"I'm sure I don't know."

"Well, we can't wait for him," Emily announced. "If that chicken gets too cold it won't be fit to eat."

"Perhaps he will arrive in time for dessert," Matthew suggested.

Faith continued to gaze hopefully outside for a moment before turning back to Matthew. "Do you suppose something has happened to him?"

"I think it highly unlikely."

Faith bit her lip, indecision clearly written on her face. Finally, she sighed and turned to the housekeeper. "Okay Emily. Let's eat."

Faith sat up in bed, a book propped against her knees. She had retired to her room soon after Matthew had taken his leave, but sleep had eluded her. Though she had waited hopefully all evening, Cord had failed to put in an appearance. She was, in turn, infuriated and worried about him.

Matthew had been unfailingly charming and amusing all evening, but he had failed to fill the void created by Cord's absence.

Raking a weary hand through her hair, Faith tried in vain to concentrate on her book.

In the kitchen, Emily Stubbs poured herself a fresh cup of coffee and sat down at the table to wait. After a while her patience was rewarded when the back door opened to admit a tall, broad-shouldered visitor.

"I figured you'd show up sooner or later." Emily reached for the pot and filled the waiting cup with steaming black coffee.

"Was she very angry?"

"Not angry. Disappointed."

Cord released a heavy sigh and joined Emily at the table. "Why do things have to be so complicated?"

"You're only doing what you must in order to protect her."

"Yeah, but will she understand that?"

Emily smiled and gave his hand a reassuring squeeze. "Of course she will. She loves you."

Cord frowned thoughtfully. "I'm not so sure."

"Well, I am," Emily told him. "So quit sitting here jawing with an old woman and go apologize to Faith. I know for a fact she's still awake."

Cord rose to his feet and bent to kiss Emily's cheek. "Thanks for the coffee."

Emily eyed his untouched cup and shook her head. "Get on with you, Cord McCamy. It's late and this old woman is going to bed."

Cord crossed the courtyard to Faith's bedroom door. He slipped inside and stood watching her silently for a moment. She looked so vulnerable sitting up in bed, her fingers threaded through the hair at her scalp, her face a study in frowning concentration as she read by the muted light of an oil lamp.

He stepped farther into the room. "Muñeca?"

Faith's head snapped up. "Cord?" The book

was tossed aside as she gracefully rose to her knees on the bed. "Are you all right?"

He stepped closer until his knees touched the edge of the mattress. "Shouldn't I be?"

Hastily, her eyes raked over him, searching for some sign of injury. "You haven't been hurt?"

"No."

"Then why didn't you come to dinner?"

Cord removed his hat and tossed it carelessly onto the dressing table. "I was held up."

Faith sat back on her heels. "You could have sent word. I was worried about you."

Cord lightly brushed her cheek with his knuckles. "Never worry about me, sweetheart. It's wasted energy."

"Why were you detained?" Faith spoke in a husky whisper.

Cord's hand moved down her neck to her shoulder. "In case you've forgotten, there are a few people out there trying to kill me." His fingers slid beneath the strap of her nightgown.

"Oh." Faith felt a faint fluttering in her stomach as Cord slid the strap off her shoulder.

"I do apologize, however, if I've upset you." His hand moved to her other shoulder and that strap went the way of the first one.

"I'm very angry with you," Faith murmured. She tossed her head to send her waist-length hair tumbling in glorious disarray about her shoulders, but her gaze never left Cord's face.

"As well you should be," Cord agreed, but his eyes were on her breasts, which happened to be the only thing holding up her gown. "Do you know what I think?"

Mesmerized by the resonance of his voice and the green fire in his eyes, Faith could only shake her head.

"I think," he said as he hooked his finger in the neckline of her gown and gave a barely perceptible tug, "that gravity is a marvelous thing."

The nightgown slid down to her hips, baring her breasts to Cord's heated gaze.

Faith realized the impropriety of her situation, but she found herself unable or unwilling to cover herself. She shivered slightly as the cool night air caressed her breasts and she felt her nipples tighten and harden. She regarded Cord with eyes made liquid with longing.

Cord bit back a groan as a surge of pure lust raged through him. His arm encircled Faith's waist to pull her tightly against his chest, while his free hand slid between their bodies to boldly caress a creamy breast. His mouth covered hers, parting her lips to make way for his searching tongue.

Faith moaned deep in her throat as she instinctively lifted her arms to encircle Cord's neck. Never had she felt so alive. Her senses were aflame with wild sensation as Cord's tongue sought out the hidden recesses of her mouth.

Just as Faith began to fear she would faint from sheer pleasure, Cord's mouth left hers and moved to her neck. She threw her head back to allow him free access to that sensitive area as her hands slid upward to tangle in his hair.

Never had Cord felt such burning desire. Such raging need. Or such all-consuming love. His hand moved from her waist to cup her buttocks and pull her against his male hardness while the other hand left her breast to grip her hair. "You are mine, Faith Jennings," he groaned hoarsely. "Mine."

Faith heard the fierce possessiveness of his voice and felt a thrill shoot through her. "Yes," she whispered. "And you, Cord McCamy, are mine."

He raised his head to gaze into the velvety brown depths of her eyes. "I know," he said simply. Then he was kissing her again, and this time he held nothing back as his mouth covered hers and seemed to draw on her very soul.

Faith was left weak and limp from the force of Cord's tender assault. She tightened her arms around his neck and allowed him to support her weight.

"Miss Faith! Miss Faith!"

Cord and Faith became aware of Emily's frantic calling and pounding on the door at the same instant. Abruptly, they released each other.

Brought sharply back to reality by the urgency in the housekeeper's voice, Faith moved to leave the bed, only to be halted by Cord's hand on her shoulder. Wordlessly, he pulled her nightgown up over her bare breasts and returned the straps to her shoulders, then, with a nod toward the door, he released her.

Faith hurried to the door, suddenly aware of

the sounds of running horses and shouting.

"Oh, Miss Faith," Emily gasped as the door opened. "The storage shed is on fire and someone set all the horses loose from the upper corral."

Before Faith could react, Cord bolted past her and the flustered housekeeper, on his way to join the ranchhands who were already fighting the fire.

Emily stood in the doorway, her gray hair braided in preparation for bed, her robe buttoned to her chin. "What should we do?"

Faith could smell the pungent smoke and see the flickering light thrown by the dancing flames. "Let's get dressed," she answered. "And then we can help."

Moments later, the mistress of the Double J and her slightly frazzled housekeeper joined the fray.

Some of the ranchhands, in varying degrees of dress, had already formed a bucket brigade from the pump to the burning shed. Others, lassos in hand, were hurrying after the swiftly departing horses.

Without hesitation, Faith and Emily joined the bucket brigade, passing the brimming pails of water along to the head of the line.

By the time the fire was out, the sun had already begun its ascent in the eastern sky to cast its warm light on the bedraggled crew below.

Faith's arms were leaden weights and her eyes were red and watering from the smoke, but still she felt a sense of satisfaction. The fire had completely destroyed the storage shed, but by working together, they had kept it from spreading to the other ranch buildings. Glancing about the ranchyard, she saw a ragtag group of grimy, exhausted men, their faces and arms blackened from smoke. Spying Ross Fulton, she called to him.

Fulton tipped his hat politely as he joined her—despite the fact he was dressed in only longhandles and boots.

"Do you have any idea what started the fire, Mr. Fulton?"

The foreman shook his head. "No, but my guess is it was no accident."

Faith felt her already sagging spirits sink even lower. She had hoped it would be an easily explainable accident and not another plot by Don Diego. "Why is that?"

"Well," Ross hesitated for a moment. "You see, ma'am, that old shed has stood empty for years. As a matter of fact, I've thought about tearing it down. Then when Cord came to the ranch, he wanted to be close to the main house at night in case you should need him. The bunkhouse is so far away and that shed was so nearby, Cord just fixed himself up a sleeping place there in the shed."

Faith felt a tendril of fear curl in her stomach. "So it was another attempt on Cord's life?"

"That's sure what it looks like."

Faith nodded wearily. "And the horses?"

Fulton rubbed his grizzled chin. "Deliberately

set loose. The gate was opened, it wasn't kicked down the way a randy stallion would do it."

"I suppose we should be grateful that the damage wasn't worse, and especially grateful that Mr. McCamy wasn't in the shed at the time."

"Yes, ma'am." Ross eyed her curiously, clearly wondering how she knew of Cord's whereabouts. "You can thank Paco for the lack of damage. He was the first to see the fire and rouse me and the other men. If we hadn't got to it so quicklike, it would have spread to the other ranch buildings."

Faith turned to see Paco deep in conversation with Cord. She thanked the foreman for his help, then walked over to join Cord and the head vaquero. Other than Cord, Emily and herself, Paco appeared to be the only one fully clothed.

"Paco." Faith greeted him as she slid her arm through Cord's. "Mr. Fulton tells me that you were the first to spot the fire."

"Sí, Dona Faith," Paco answered. "I heard the horses. They sounded upset, so I went to check on them, but before I could get to the corral, I saw the fire."

"Did you see anyone in the vicinity of the shed?" Faith asked.

"No." Paco shrugged. "But it was very dark."

"Thanks, Paco." Cord clapped him on the shoulder. "Why don't you go and get some rest."

With a weary nod, Paco ambled off in the direction of the bunkhouse.

"Cord," Faith said, tilting her head back to

gaze into his face, "the fire was another attempt on your life."

"I know."

Faith slid her arms around his waist and pressed her cheek to his hard chest. "How did Diego's men know you usually slept in that old shed? Even I didn't know." She was silent for a moment. "Do you suppose we have a traitor here on the Double J?"

"It's possible." Cord gently stroked her hair. "But very unlikely." He gestured at the smoldering remains of the shed. "This is why I've spent so much time out on the range. I want to keep the danger away from you."

"I think," Faith said carefully, "that until this business with Don Diego is resolved, danger will be following both of us."

The muscles along Cord's jawline tensed. "Then I think I had best 'resolve' things quickly."

Before Faith could comment, Max began to ring the bell that summoned the ranchhands to breakfast and Emily called for Cord and Faith to come into the kitchen for their own meal.

Chapter 9

Cord crossed the wooden sidewalk and pushed his way through the batwing doors of the Brass Bull Saloon. He knew it was probably a mistake for him to show up unannounced in Sonria, but at the moment it was the least of his worries.

He stood inside the entrance for a moment to allow his eyes to adjust to the dim indoor light.

The Brass Bull was the best of Sonria's three saloons. The bar that lined the east wall was made of the finest mahogany and trimmed with polished brass. The mirrors that graced the wall behind the bar had been shipped, at considerable expense, from a glassworks factory in the East. A genuine crystal chandelier was suspended over the center of the room, and the broad staircase that led to the saloon's upper regions boasted a hand-carved banister.

Poker games were in progress at two of the round wooden tables, while a dapper young man pounded out a lively tune on the upright piano. Scantily clad saloon girls wandered among the tables and sat, elbow to elbow, with the cowboys at the bar.

A sudden silence fell over the room as Cord's presence was noted. All eyes turned to look at the newcomer, and even the piano player halted in mid note.

Cord was given wide berth as he approached the bar. A few of the more timid cowboys made their way hurriedly to the nearest exit.

"Whiskey," Cord told the balding bartender, "and leave the bottle."

The piano player began to play a new tune and the buzz of conversation resumed as suddenly as it had halted.

"Is Peggy around?" Cord asked when the barman had returned with his bottle.

"She's in the office with her bookkeeper," the man answered. "She'll be out here shortly."

Cord nodded, then took his bottle and glass to a table at the back of the room. He sat with his back to the wall, his eyes on the door.

Over the years Cord had grown accustomed to the nervous response his presence evoked in others. He had long ago discovered that the majority of Western men consisted of two types. The first type were the cocky ones, certain of victory. They inevitably called him out. The second type avoided him like the plague. Cord preferred the latter.

Filled with a burgeoning restlessness, Cord had left his parent's home when he was eighteen. He had bought himself a good horse, gun and ammunition and proceeded to drift for a while. Place to place, town to town, he found it impossible to settle down.

All alone on the desert, the vast plains or a rugged mountaintop, Cord would practice with his revolver, drawing and firing until his speed and accuracy were awesome to behold.

Cord's wandering took him all across the West. He spent time as a Comanchero, trading goods with the Comanche. He rode drag on cattle drives and worked as a stagecoach guard for Wells Fargo.

In California, Cord found gold. It was a modest strike but it added considerably to his account in a San Francisco bank. The account that would help him to achieve his dream of a horse ranch.

After his gold strike, Cord went to work for a freight company whose main business was hauling wagonloads of gold out of the mountains. He was hired on as a guard to ride shotgun on the gold shipments. A dangerous occupation, but one in which Cord's prowess with a gun was put to good use. And all the while, his reputation grew and continued to grow until he could hardly ride into a town without receiving a challenge from the local fast gun.

The driver Cord most often had found himself paired with was a grizzled, bewhiskered old man known to one and all as Cotton.

Cotton had been ornery, cantankerous and foul-mouthed, and his body had rarely encountered soap and water. He chewed tobacco and had the habit of allowing brown drool to dribble from the corner of his mouth into his gray beard.

Despite Cotton's many faults, Cord had developed a fondness for the old man. He especially appreciated Cotton's talent for spinning yarns to relieve the boredom of the long and tiring trips.

One day as Cotton, Cord and a second guard named Curly were riding out of a treacherous mountain pass, they were ambushed. Six men had concealed themselves among the rocks and bushes at the mouth of the pass to lie in wait for the freight wagon.

One moment Cotton had been reciting a tale about himself and a well-endowed saloon girl. The next moment he was dead, his head half blown away by a shotgun blast.

Cord and Curly had leapt from their horses and returned fire. They managed to kill four of the ambushers before Curly caught a slug in his belly.

Cord bent over Curly as the remaining two gunmen escaped. Curly was young, only sixteen. He had taken the job to provide for his widowed mother and younger siblings. He was a good kid with high hopes for the future. He took a long time to die.

Cord loaded Cotton and Curly into the wagon

and drove the bulky conveyance to their destination. Upon arrival, he saw to both men's burial. He collected his pay and sent it, along with Curly's, to the boy's widowed and grieving mother. Then he set out after the two escaped ambushers.

Cord caught up with the two men in Wyoming. Sons of a wealthy ranch owner, they had returned to their father's home.

He found them in the small settlement's saloon, guzzling beer and boasting of their exploit. They were painfully young and had been overindulged by their father. After seeing them, Cord had made up his mind not to kill them but to take them back for a trial, but the boys merely laughed.

Smug and complacent on home ground, they had simultaneously drawn on Cord and left him with no options.

When the smoke cleared, the two young men lay dead on the barroom floor. Two more wasted lives.

The boys' father wielded a lot of influence in the territory and refused to believe his sons guilty of any wrongdoing. In an astonishingly short time, Cord found himself to be a wanted man. His reputation, too, had grown by leaps and bounds until even he was astonished by the tales that circulated about him.

"Hello, Cord."

Cord looked up to see Peggy, the proprietress of the Brass Bull, standing next to him. Slim-bodied and heavy-breasted, Peggy had lost none of her beauty over the years. She did, however, dress a bit more modestly than the girls who worked for her.

"Hello, Peggy. You're looking good."

"I could say the same for you, handsome."

Cord motioned to the chair beside him. "Will you join me?"

Peggy took a seat and signaled for the bartender to bring her a glass. "What's up?"

"I guess you know about the problems we've been having at the Double J."

"I've heard talk."

The bartender arrived with Peggy's glass. He shot Cord a wary look before scurrying back to the bar.

"Someone's trying to kill me," Cord said as he poured Peggy a drink.

Peggy shrugged. "Nothing new about that."

"True," Cord agreed, "but they have also made attempts on the life of Faith Jennings. I can handle people taking pot shots at me, but I won't allow anyone to harm Faith."

Peggy regarded Cord with a saddened expression. She had long ago given up hope of any relationship between Cord and herself, but it still hurt to hear him speak of another woman in such a fiercely possessive tone. "Why tell me your problems?" she asked more harshly than she had intended.

"Last night, someone started a fire out at the Double J. They're playing a little too close to home for comfort," Cord told her.

Peggy sighed. "How can I help?"

Cord remained silent until the piano player had finished his latest selection. He frowned threateningly at the dapper young man. Noting Cord's expression, the musician grew quite pale and hastily decided to take a break.

"Sooner or later," Cord began, "everyone who comes into town passes through here. I need for you to tell me who's blown into town lately."

Peggy fidgeted nervously. "It's that damned Montez man, isn't it? Things haven't been right around here since he showed up." She sighed. "First thing Montez did when he arrived was to fire his manager and all the ranchhands. They all come in here, madder than hornets at being out of work, but knowing they couldn't do anything about it."

Peggy downed her whiskey and motioned for Cord to refill her glass. "Next thing you know, outlaws are riding into town and Sheriff Hobbs is turning his back. First ones were the Dolby brothers. They worked for Montez for a while, then disappeared. Rumor has it they were killed by Indians down near the border."

Cord smiled grimly. He knew for a fact that only one Indian had killed the Dolby brothers. Fierce Hawk.

"Then Blacky showed up with his sidekicks," Peggy continued, "but you know about them. Since then . . ." she sighed, "there have been a lot of new faces in town. Some, like Ajax Killion, I recognize. The others, I don't know."

"How many?" Cord asked.

"Hard to say," Peggy replied, "but I'd guess at least a dozen hired guns have drifted into town in the past few days."

"Have any of them been hired by Montez?"

Peggy shrugged. "Who knows?"

Cord got to his feet. "Thanks, Peg." He bent to brush a kiss on her cheek.

Peggy grasped his hand. "Cord, be careful."

Cord nodded, then made his way to the door. He imagined he could hear a collective sign of relief from the Brass Bull patrons as the batwing door swung closed behind him.

Chapter 10

On a grassy rise, the Jennings family cemetery overlooked the ranchyard and corral. Surrounded by a low wooden fence, it contained only three graves.

Faith knelt by the newest of the headstones and placed a bouquet of flowers on the grass-covered mound. She felt her heart twist with grief and longing as her fingers gently traced the engraved letters that marked the site as Jeremiah Jennings' final resting place.

Faith missed her grandfather terribly. She recalled the long letters they had exchanged and the many hours they had spent together during his visits. There was no doubt in her mind that Jeremiah had loved her a great deal. And Faith had returned that love wholeheartedly. Grandfather and granddaughter, sole survivors of the Jennings family, they had shared a special bond.

Why, then, hadn't Faith cried? She had felt torn asunder by the news of Jeremiah's death. She had been overwhelmed by anger and grief, yet she had never shed a single tear.

Faith clenched her hands into fists as she gazed at Jeremiah's headstone. It didn't seem right somehow that she hadn't wept. But how could she? She had never cried in her life. Even she wasn't certain why. She knew only that she couldn't.

Faith rose to her feet and looked at the other tombstones. Jocelyn Jennings—Faith's grandmother—rested by her husband's side. A frail woman, Jocelyn had been unable to withstand the rigors of Western life. She had died while her son Tom was still a baby.

Jeremiah had loved Jocelyn with his whole heart and soul. Left at a loss by his wife's untimely death, he had hired Emily Stubbs to keep house and tend to his son, but as far as anyone knew, he had never so much as looked at another woman. He and Emily were friends, but when people attempted to pair them romantically, Jeremiah would shake his head and say, "She's not Jocelyn."

Grieving for her own late husband, Emily would reiterate with, "He ain't Henry."

It had been a comfortable arrangement for them both.

Tom—Faith's father—was buried next to Jocelyn. Next to Tom was a marker in memorial to Angelique. Faith knew her mother had not been buried on the Double J, but still she drew comfort from the simple headstone.

Faith had never met her father, but she correctly imagined him to be like Jeremiah.

Jeremiah's son Thomas had grown tall and strong beneath the harsh Texas sun. And like his father, Tom had wanted no other life than that of a rancher. The Double J was his world and he was content therein.

Tom had met Angelique on a rare trip to New Orleans. Angelique had journeyed from her parents' home in France to New Orleans to visit her sister Nicole. Tom's and Angelique's eyes had met across a crowded ballroom floor, and instantly both knew they were destined to spend their lives together.

Nicole, ever the romantic, made all the wedding arrangements for the happy couple.

As the newly married Mr. and Mrs. Jennings prepared to board the ship that would take them to Texas, the two sisters hugged tearfully and promised to visit one another often. Nicole stood on the docks and waved until the ship had disappeared into the distance. She never saw her sister again.

Faith closed the gate behind her as she left the cemetery. She paused outside the fence to look at the ranchyard below. She loved the Double J. It was her home as surely as it had been her father's and her grandfather's.

She had never understood Jeremiah's refusal to allow her to live with him in Texas. Not that her childhood had been unhappy. Far from it.

Nicole had given Faith a rare and wonderful childhood that most people would envy.

Nicole Dumont had been very young when she married Pierre de Beauhanais. Pierre's dream had been to found a dynasty in America, so together they had journeyed to New Orleans. In only a few short years Nicole was a fabulously wealthy widow.

Pierre had been an astoundingly intelligent and successful businessman, but a poor gambler and an even worse shot. He had died on the so-called field of honor. On the dawn following an altercation at the card tables, he became the victim of his dueling opponent's superior aim.

By the time Pierre died, Nicole had grown to love America and saw no reason to return to her parents' home in France. The Dumonts were wealthy, but Nicole had become wealthy in her own right.

In desperation they sent their other daughter, Angelique, to convince Nicole to return to France. Instead, Angelique had married an American.

Nicole grieved bitterly when news of her sister's disappearance reached her. Each year she traveled to Texas to check on Tom's progress in his never-ending search. The news was never good, but Nicole grew to like and admire both Tom and Jeremiah and they grew to like and admire her.

The day Jeremiah appeared on Nicole's doorstep with Faith in tow had been one of the happiest days in Nicole's life. Finally, she had someone on whom to shower all the love and affection she could no longer give to Pierre or Angelique.

Nicole and Jeremiah agreed. Faith would never want for anything.

The finest schools, food, clothing and jewelry were Faith's for the asking. Trips to Europe were routine as well as jaunts to such cosmopolitan American cities as New York and Boston. Amazingly, Faith remained unspoiled. A quiet child, she grew up secure in the love of her grandfather and aunt. On visits to her Dumont grandparents' home in France she was treated like royalty by her indulgent relatives, but was happiest when she could slip away for a few quiet hours of fishing with the servants' children.

As Faith grew older she became aware of a deep restlessness inside herself. She felt she was searching for something. Some indefinable thing that she could not quite grasp.

The restlessness had not stilled until she had returned to Texas. At the Double J she had found peace. In Cord's arms, she had found home.

Deep in thought, Faith began to make her way down the slope. She paused when she saw Cord walk out of the stables. He saw her at the same time and walked up the rise to join her.

"Muñequita," he said, pulling her into his arms, "I've been looking everywhere for you."

Faith slid her arms around Cord's neck and tilted her head back to gaze into his deep green eyes. "Is something wrong?"

"No." Cord brushed a stray strand of silky hair from Faith's cheek, then allowed his fingers to lightly trace the contours of her lips. "I just wanted to see you."

Heedless of any ranchhands who might be watching, Cord pulled her closer and lowered his mouth to hers. Faith felt herself grow warm as Cord's mouth slashed across hers. She pressed against him, answering his need with an equally fierce passion of her own.

As suddenly as it had began, the kiss ended. Cord looked into Faith's eyes, a wry smile on his lips. "Take it easy, sweetheart, or we'll end up finishing what the fire interrupted last night."

"Would that be so terrible?" Faith asked in a hoarse whisper.

"Oh, muñeca," Cord groaned, "if you only knew . . ."

"If I only knew what?"

Cord stepped away from her and stared out over the ranchyard. "If you only knew how much willpower it takes to hold back, when I want nothing more than to pull you down onto the grass and make love to you. To bury myself deep inside you and hear your cries of pleasure."

Faith stepped forward to press her cheek to Cord's back and encircle his waist with her arms. His words had sent her heart into rapid motion and her knees felt strangely weak. "It's what I want too," she said in a voice grown shaky with emotion. "So why can't we be together?"

"For reasons you wouldn't understand," Cord replied as he turned, breaking Faith's hold on him. He gripped her hand and began to lead her toward the house. "You'll just have to trust me."

How could he make her understand? Cord wondered silently. He loved Faith and he understood her better than she realized. They couldn't make love now. Whether Faith knew it or not, Cord did. She wasn't ready yet. The time wasn't right.

Emily met them at the back door. "I was just going to call you to supper," she told Faith. "You'll join us, won't you, Cord?"

Cord noted the sparkle in Faith's huge brown eyes. "How could I refuse?"

The three of them ate their meal seated around the kitchen table.

Faith watched Cord from beneath lowered lashes as he ate. He was so handsome with his pale golden hair, emerald green eyes and rugged chiseled features. She loved him. She trusted him, and she was undeniably attracted to him. He made her feel alive in ways she had never dreamed possible.

Her gaze dropped to Cord's hands. He held a knife in one hand as he prepared to cut his beefsteak. Faith's eyes locked on the strong tanned hand that gripped the knife. For some reason, she couldn't tear her gaze away. A throbbing pain began in her temples as in her mind's eye she saw a different place, a different time, a different knife.

The knife and fork fell from her hands to land

with a clatter on her plate. She pressed her fingertips to her temples.

"Sweetheart, what's wrong?" Cord rose from his chair to kneel beside Faith. He cupped her face in his hands. "Are you all right?"

"You look terribly pale, dear." Emily voiced her concern.

Faith closed her eyes. What had she seen? Was it a memory flash or simply her over-active imagination? "I'm okay." She managed a tremulous smile. "Really, I just have a head-ache."

Cord stood up and lifted Faith into his arms. "It's straight to bed with you, young lady."

He carried her to her room as Emily hurried ahead of them to light the lamp and turn down the sheets.

"There is no need for so much fuss over a simple headache," Faith told them.

"Do you think we should send for Doc Fogarty?" Cord asked Emily.

"I'm fine, really," Faith insisted.

"I don't know," Emily replied to Cord as though Faith had not spoken. "Maybe we should wait and see how she feels in the morning."

"Please. I just need to lie down." Faith was growing more exasperated by the moment.

"Are you sure?" Emily asked.

Cord continued to eye Faith speculatively.

"I'm certain."

Cord and Emily finally left, albeit reluctantly, after Faith managed to convince them that all she needed was a good night's sleep.

YESTERDAY'S PROMISE

By the time she had changed into her night-gown and slipped between the covers, the pain in Faith's temples had lessened considerably. Still, it was a long time before she slept.

Chapter 11

Diego Montez opened the front door of his ranchhouse in answer to the sharp knocking. When he saw the identity of his visitor he stepped out onto the porch rather than invite the man inside.

The insult was not lost on the man who had come to call. He narrowed his beady eyes contemptuously at his host. He was a short man with greasy black shoulder-length hair, a crooked scar along his cheek and crossed gunbelts on his hips. "Evenin', Montez," he drawled.

"What do you want, Killian?" Diego snapped. "We were just sitting down to dinner."

Ajax Killian leaned his hip against the porch railing and crossed his arms over his skinny chest. "The boys are gettin' restless. They wanna be paid."

Diego scowled at the gunslinger. "You will all receive payment when the job is completed."

"Yeah?" Killian sneered. "Well, me an' the boys are gettin' mighty tired of hangin' around with empty pockets, waiting for you to plan the job. We got no beef with McCamy or that Jennings woman. We're in this for the money you promised us."

Impatiently, Diego consulted his pocket-watch. "I understand your situation, Killian, but you must also understand mine. I cannot pay for work that is yet to be done."

"Then let's get on with it," Killian snarled. "I'll kill McCamy or the woman or even my own ma, but I gotta get paid."

"Don't be a fool," Diego snapped. "Everything must be carefully orchestrated. I've worked too hard to make a mistake now."

"Oh yeah? Well that's real fine for you, but what'll I tell the boys?"

"Damn it! Tell them I said to be patient."

Ajax Killian laughed. A harsh, evil sound. "I'll tell 'em, but don't expect 'em to take it as good as I did." He stepped off the porch, then paused to look back over his shoulder at Diego. "If I was you, Montez, I'd watch my step."

Barely able to contain his anger, Diego returned to the parlor. How dare that two-bit gunslinger threaten him? As soon as the job was completed, he would see about ridding himself of Killian and his henchmen.

Diego took a moment to compose himself, then entered the dining room to join his invited guests.

"Please forgive me, gentlemen," he said smoothly. "I was unavoidably detained."

"Nothing to forgive, old man," the heavy-jowled Owen Montgomery exclaimed. "Rothschild and I have been enjoying the company of your charming hostess."

Luisa beamed as Diego graced her with a tight-lipped smile. She rang the tiny silver bell by her plate and the housekeeper entered with the first course.

Luisa paid scant attention to the business the men discussed over dinner. She was far too thrilled with her role as hostess to be concerned with such mundane matters. At last she was where she felt she belonged. Mistress of a prosperous rancher, entertaining two fine English gentlemen, and wearing expensive clothes and jewelry. One slim hand dropped to her lap to caress the cool smoothness of her silk gown, while the other hand toyed with the diamond pendant at her throat.

"If you will excuse us, Luisa," Diego interrupted her thoughts. "We gentlemen will retire to my office for brandy and cigars."

Owen Montgomery rose to his feet. "Thank you, my dear, for a most delightful dinner." His heavy jowls quivered as he bent low to brush a kiss on Luisa's hand.

Luisa blushed becomingly as the tall, bone-thin Rothschild added his compliments. "The food was excellent, but I'm afraid your charming presence quite outshone the cook's culinary efforts."

Diego watched Luisa with an appraising eye as she thanked the two gentlemen for their compliments. As the men filed from the room, Diego paused to smile at his mistress. Excited by her triumph at dinner, Luisa failed to notice the cold gleam in her lover's eyes.

Luisa had just finished preparing for bed when Diego entered the huge master bedroom.

Luisa smiled seductively as Diego crossed the room to join her. Clad in a diaphanous peignoir of scarlet silk, she was seated at the massive oak dressing table. "Querido. Are you finished with your business?"

"For the moment." Diego traced Luisa's jawline with his fingertips. "Do you know how significant Rothschild's and Montgomery's presence here is?"

A slight frown marred Luisa's smooth brow. "These men, they are muy importante, sí?"

"Sí," Diego confirmed. "So you will also understand how very important it is for me to keep them happy while they're here."

"They seemed happy at dinner," Luisa ventured.

"Yes, you pleased me a great deal at dinner tonight." Diego's hand moved to the slim column of her neck. "The Englishmen also were impressed by what they saw."

"I am very happy that I could please you."

Diego gripped her throat lightly. "Then, no

doubt, you will wish to please me further."

"Sí," Luisa agreed, despite her growing uneasiness.

Diego used his free hand to grip the hair at the nape of Luisa's neck and pull her head back. "Good, because as I said, Rothschild and Montgomery were quite impressed with you. So impressed, in fact, that they are fairly champing at the bit, so to speak. You have been invited to spend the night with them."

Luisa's eyes grew round as Diego's words sank in. "No, querido. You can't mean it."

"But I do mean it," Diego returned calmly. His grip on her throat tightened perceptibly. "Montgomery and Rothschild have grown bored with the quiet life of the ranch and they are seeking, shall we say, a bit of diversion. With you, my dear Luisa."

"Please. Do not ask this of me." Tears formed in Luisa's dark eyes. "I beg you."

"I am not asking you. I am telling you. Either you can spend the night with our two English guests or you can get out." Diego's voice grew icy. "And you know what that means. No more silk, no more diamonds, and no more me."

Luisa closed her eyes as she nodded her head in acceptance.

"Good," Diego released his grip on her. "They are waiting for you in Montgomery's room. Go to them. Do whatever they wish for as long as they wish. Just make damn certain they enjoy themselves." He pulled her to her feet. "If you please them well enough, I may see my way clear to purchase you a few more trinkets."

Luisa walked to the door, her movements stiff and wooden. She paused as she gripped the doorknob. "If you love me," she said quietly, "you won't ask this of me."

"If *you* love *me*," Diego countered, "you will do exactly as I tell you. Without complaint."

After a moment's hesitation, Luisa nodded, then slipped quietly from the room.

Diego stood in the doorway and listened until he heard Luisa's soft reluctant knock on Montgomery's bedroom door. He heard the men's booming laughter as the door swung open, then the soft click as it closed behind them.

Diego turned back into his bedroom and moved to the nightstand to pour himself a liberal shot of bourbon. A satisfied smile hovered on his lips as he lifted his glass in a silent toast. To himself.

Chapter 12

Matthew McCamy used the back stairs to enter the small apartment over his law office. Once inside, he flung himself wearily into his favorite overstuffed armchair and retrieved the telegram from his vest pocket. Despite his exhaustion, his lips curved into a smile as he reread the message. This was exactly the information he had been praying for. The proof he needed to halt Don Diego Fernando Montoya y Montez in his tracks. He couldn't wait to tell Faith. No. He shook his head. On second thought, better to tell her nothing until he had something more definite. No need to get her hopes up in case the telegram turned out to be a false lead.

Yawning hugely, he got to his feet. No time to

rest now. Stifling another yawn, he went into his bedroom to pack.

Kneeling in front of the brass-bound trunk, Faith slid her hand almost reverently across the lid, then lifted her eyes to gaze around the room that had once, long ago, belonged to her parents.

Shortly after Tom's death, Jeremiah had disposed of most of his son's and daughter-in-law's personal effects. Their bedroom had been cleaned, aired and except for the trunk and basic furnishings left empty.

Faith tried to imagine her parents sleeping in the huge four-poster bed or sitting side by side on the window seat, but her mind could summon no visions of the man and woman whose love had given her life.

With a sigh, she returned her attention to the trunk. Slowly she released the clasps and raised the lid. Lying on top was a quilt sewn in a traditional wedding ring pattern. Faith removed the coverlet and ran her fingers lovingly over the tiny hand-sewn stitches as she imagined the long hours it had taken her mother and grandmother to make the quilt. Vowing silently to someday use the quilt on her own marriage bed, she laid it carefully aside.

Faith felt a lump form in her throat when she once again looked into the trunk and saw the homemade rag doll that lay on top of what appeared to be a piece of folded buckskin. She examined the doll closely before placing it atop the quilt and reaching for the buckskin. Only it wasn't merely a piece of buckskin, it was a dress made from softest deerskin and decorated with fringe and an intricate pattern of beads. Faith lifted the dress and saw that it had been made to fit a young girl. A young Indian girl. Had she herself worn the dress when she lived with the Comanche? For a fleeting second her mind's eye saw a woman holding the dress in her hands. A young woman with soft auburn hair and a smile that was sad. Her mother?

Something dropped from the folds of the dress to land on the floor with a muted thud. Faith looked down and was surprised to see a small bone-handled knife lying near her knee. She picked up the knife and closely examined the small razor-sharp blade. The bone handle felt cool to her warm palm, and as she held it another fleeting vision appeared in her mind. This time it was of a grim-faced young man. White, but dressed as an Indian, he held the knife in his hand.

Faith closed her eyes as pain began to pound in her temples. Had she seen glimpses of her past, or was it her overeager imagination working to fill the painful empty spaces of her memory?

Faith rose to her feet and returned the items to the trunk. All but the knife. For some reason, she could not bear to part with the small weapon. She closed the lid to the trunk and slid the knife into the pocket of her skirt. Knowing it was there, feeling its slight weight, gave her a strange sense of well-being that even she could not explain.

Faith left her parents' bedroom and stepped out into the courtyard, to find herself face to face with her ranch foreman.

Ross Fulton removed his hat. He clutched the worn headgear to his chest and nodded a greeting. "Beggin' your pardon, Miss Jennings ma'am," he mumbled.

Faith arched one perfectly curved brow in inquiry. "Can I help you with something, Mr. Fulton?"

"I just wanted to ask you about the burned-out shed," Fulton replied. "If it's all right with you, ma'am, I'd like to assign a couple of the men to clear it out of there today."

"Of course, Mr. Fulton," Faith agreed. "And I see no need for you to check with me over something so minor."

"Yes, ma'am. Good day, ma'am."

Faith took a few steps toward the kitchen, then paused. "Mr. Fulton?"

"Yes, ma'am?" Ross Fulton halted at the courtyard gate.

"Are we by any chance short-handed? I could see about hiring a few additional ranchhands."

Fulton appeared thoughtful. "Now that you mention it, we could use two or three more men around here."

"Would you like to hire them or shall I?" Faith asked.

"I can take care of it, Miss Jennings," Ross replied. "I'll ride into town right after lunch."

"Fine," Faith said as the foreman hurried through the gate. Ross Fulton was certainly a strange man but he was apparently very good at his job. Jeremiah would have never hired him otherwise.

Faith found Emily in the kitchen. The elderly woman was busy kneading bread dough.

"Emily?"

"Mmm?"

Faith removed the small knife from her pocket. "Have you ever seen this before?"

Emily glanced at the small weapon, then returned her attention to the bread. "Not that I recall. Of course, when you reach my age, your memory's the first thing to go."

Faith returned the knife to her pocket, washed her hands and donned an apron. She sat down at the table across from the housekeeper and began to help form the dough into loaves. "How well did you know my parents?"

"About as well as you can know anyone, I reckon." Emily used her wrist to brush a stray strand of hair from her face. "Fetch me those towels, dear. We'll have to let this bread rise again before we bake it."

The two women carefully covered the unbaked bread, then moved to the sink to remove the dough from their fingers. Faith worked the pump handle while Emily washed her hands.

"I don't think I've ever seen two people more in love than your ma and pa," Emily said quietly as she and Faith switched places. "She was such a pretty little thing. When young Tom first brought her home, I thought she would never make it as a ranchwife. But she fooled us all. She took to the life out here like a duck takes to water."

"Were they happy?" Faith asked as she dried her hands.

"As happy as two pigs in the sunshine," Emily replied. She moved to the stove and poured two cups of coffee. "And when Angelique found out she was pregnant with you, I thought Tom was gonna bust a gut. He was so proud and happy."

Emily took the coffee cups to the table and Faith joined her there.

"But he never even saw me," Faith said.

"No." Emily shook her head sadly. "The Comanche made sure of that."

"What happened?" Faith asked anxiously.

"I don't know," Emily replied. "I'd gone to El Paso to visit my sister. When I returned, Angelique was gone and Jeremiah and Tom couldn't bear to talk about what had happened." Emily took a sip of coffee. "I tell you, my heart almost broke in half just thinking about your ma. Six months' pregnant and carted off by the Comanche that way."

"Did Cord and Matthew live here then?" Faith asked.

"In Sonria. Mr. McCamy was a banker, but he and his missus were good friends of your ma and pa, so I saw them pretty often."

Faith opened her mouth to ask yet another question, but Emily rose to her feet. "You'll excuse me, won't you, dear. I have a lot of work to do."

"I'll help you," Faith offered.

"No need," Emily told her. "Why don't you go rest for a spell? We don't want you having another bad headache."

Faith knew a dismissal when she heard one. She left the kitchen feeling more than a little disappointed. Emily had shed very little light on the past, and Faith felt no closer to regaining her memory than she had before. She couldn't shake the feeling, though, that Emily knew more than she was willing to tell.

Chapter 13

Cord was preparing to leave the stables when Paco approached him. "I have some information for you, amigo," Paco said softly.

Cord nodded and walked outside. He wandered over to the corral and braced his arms on the top rail. Paco joined him a few moments later.

"What have you heard?" Cord asked.

"I know who started the fire. Jack Dorsey and Coot Sykes."

"They're here?"

Paco nodded. "They're the latest scum to join Don Diego's payroll."

"You're sure?"

"Yes. It seems Montez found out about the reward they're offering for you up in Wyoming and he's called in bounty hunters."

"Dorsey and Sykes." Cord's voice was heavy with disgust. "It figures."

"What will you do, amigo?"

Cord's gaze automatically turned to the ranchhouse where he knew Faith would be. "Do you know where they are?"

"Sí. They are hiding out, waiting for new orders from Montez."

Cord's hand dropped to rest lightly on the butt of his holstered .44. "I'm going after them."

Faith gazed up at the portrait of her parents and felt a mixture of grief and déjà vu. Rather than take a nap as Emily suggested, Faith had continued her exploration of the ranchhouse. She had found the painting in her grandfather's bedroom, hanging alongside a portrait of herself at age twelve. On impulse, she had moved the picture of her parents to the parlor and placed it over the fireplace.

She cocked her head to one side and studied the couple in the portrait. Angelique Jennings' hair had been a deep and lustrous shade of auburn, her eyes a gentle gray. Faith had inherited her mother's slightly turned-up nose, generous lips and petite frame, but Faith's hair, eyes and stubborn chin clearly proclaimed her the daughter of Thomas Jennings.

Although Faith had never met her father, she still felt grief for his loss. The grief she suffered for her mother, however, went much deeper. She had spent the first eight years of her life with her mother. Angelique had held her, cared for her, loved her, and Faith could not remember any of it. Angelique remained only a vague shadowy image. She had heard stories about her parents from her grandfather, Aunt Nicole and even Emily, but damn it, it wasn't enough. If only she could remember.

At a sound, she glanced over her shoulder to see Cord standing behind her. He stepped forward and slid an arm around her waist. "You have your mother's beauty and spirit," he said as he looked up at the portrait.

Faith felt some of her frustration slip away for the simple reason that Cord had joined her. "You knew my parents, didn't you?"

"As a child," he replied. "My parents used to bring Matthew and me out here for visits."

Faith sighed. "I wish I had known my father, and more than anything I wish I could remember my mother."

Cord kissed the top of her head. "Maybe someday, muñeca, you will remember. And then you may wish to forget."

"No. For no matter what the memories, it would be better than an empty void."

They stood together in silence for a moment as they gazed up at the portrait.

"I've come to say good-bye," Cord said suddenly. He had not intended to tell her in such an abrupt manner, but he knew no way to soften the blow.

Faith felt an inexplicable fear rise within her. Fear that he would never return alive. "Where are you going?'' The calmness of her own voice surprised her.

"Not far. I'll be back in two or three days."

Faith took one look at his expressionless face and made up her mind. "I'm going with you."

"No, you're not," Cord replied firmly. "You are going to stay right here."

"You need me."

"Always. But you can't go with me." Cord gripped her shoulders and turned her to face him more fully. "I have to go and you have to stay. It's that simple."

Faith's features became shuttered and she turned her face away.

Cord gripped her chin and forced her to face him. "Promise me you won't leave the ranch while I'm gone." When Faith remained silent, he added, "Trust me."

Those words did the trick, just as Cord had known they would. Reluctantly, Faith nodded.

"Good." Cord was relieved. He had half feared she would try to follow him. "I talked to Matthew earlier. He's leaving on the noon stage. He'll be out of town for a few days, but Paco Lopez and Ross Fulton will be here should the need arise."

Again Faith nodded, and Cord felt a needle of fear pierce his heart. Not for himself, but for Faith. His muñequita. The one and only love of his life. If something should happen to her, he would have no more reason to live. He pulled her into his arms and crushed her against the solid wall of his chest. "Don't worry, sweetheart.

Everything is going to be fine." For both of their sakes, he fervently hoped so.

Faith stood in the courtyard and watched Cord ride away on Bright Star. Her lips still burned from his fiery parting kiss and she pressed her fingertips against them as though to hold his essence. She watched until he disappeared into the distant hills, then turned and reentered the house. She knew a part of her had ridden away with Cord.

He carried her heart.

Chapter 14

It took Cord the better part of two days to reach the canyon where the line shack was located. He made camp atop the canyon wall and settled down to wait. He had adequate cover in the form of twin boulders and an unobstructed view of the shack below.

The dilapidated old building appeared deserted, but Paco had said the two men responsible for the fire were using it as their hideout. Cord could see no sign of the men's horses either, but he knew it was a common enough practice to hide the horses in a secluded spot away from the hideout, the better to avoid detection.

Cord's hands unconsciously tightened on his rifle. He should have killed Jack Dorsey years ago. A huge, barrel-chested man, Jack was as mean as a one-eyed snake and twice as deadly. Sneaky and sly, he had an inbred instinct for survival. Coot, on the other hand, was just plain mean and stupid—a dangerous combination. The two of them passed themselves off as bounty hunters, but Cord knew them for what they really were. Hired killers.

Cord sat down on the ground, leaned his back against a boulder, pulled his hat over his eyes and propped his rifle against his knee. It was less than an hour until sunset. He would wait until dark. Then he was going in after them.

A short while later Cord awoke from a semidoze and looked up into the lowering sun. He felt a strange prickling sensation along his spine and knew something was wrong. Very wrong. He raised himself to his knees and once again gazed at the seemingly deserted shack. He wasn't going to wait any longer. He was going in now.

Rifle in hand, holstered .44 at the ready, he made his way stealthily down the side of the canyon wall. He paused at the base to look around. He could see no sign of life, nor could he hear the faintest sound that was out of the ordinary.

His moccasined feet moved slowly and silently across the clearing to the front of the shack. He paused a moment, muscles tense and ready, then with a lightning-fast movement kicked the door open and charged inside.

* * *

Faith was perched atop the corral fence, deep in conversation with the domador, José, when Ross Fulton approached.

Ignoring the elderly man, Ross removed his hat and addressed Faith. "Miss Jennings?"

Faith turned to face him, a smile of greeting on her lips. "Yes, Mr. Fulton?"

The foreman clutched his hat and swallowed hard before speaking. "I've some bad news, ma'am."

Faith's smile faded. It was news about Cord. It had to be. Her heart in her throat, she slid from the fence to stand facing Fulton. José stepped forward and placed a comforting hand on her shoulder.

"It's about Cord. Some of the boys found him a few miles south of the ranch. He's in a pretty bad way, ma'am. Shot up pretty bad, and the men are afraid to move him, but he's . . ." Ross swallowed again. "He's asking for you, Miss Jennings."

The world began to spin out of kilter and Fulton's voice began to sound hollow and distant to Faith's ears. With an effort, she managed to regain control. Cord would not die! He could not leave her. "Take me to him, Mr. Fulton."

"Wait, Dona Faith," José said worriedly. "I will get Emily and Paco and we will go with you."

"There's no time," Faith told him. "Just throw a saddle on Dancer. You can follow as soon as you round up Paco and Emily."

The aged domador agreed reluctantly.

Ross followed José into the stables and emerged a few moments later leading Faith's pinto mare and his own bay gelding.

"Where is José?" Faith asked.

Ross shrugged. "Hunting for Paco."

Despite her quaking limbs, Faith managed to swing herself into the saddle. "Please, God," she prayed silently as she followed Ross Fulton from the ranchyard, "don't let him die." Her mind repeated the prayer over and over as they rode. "Don't let him die. Please don't let him die." And Faith Jennings, who had never, even once, in her entire life cried, felt the new and strange sensation of tears welling in the back of her eyes.

It was late afternoon when Ross and Faith arrived on the banks of a shallow creek. Almost frantic with worry, Faith turned to her foreman. "How much farther?"

A sad, resigned smile curved Fulton's lips. "It appears, ma'am, that we have arrived."

"Here?" Faith asked blankly. She slid from her saddle and walked to the creekbank. "Where is he? Where is Cord?" She saw movement from the corner of her eye and whirled around. Three men on horseback were emerging from a grove of cottonwoods. Was Cord lying beneath one of the trees? She started forward, only to find herself staring into the barrel of a deadly looking rifle.

"Do not move, senorita," the man said silkily. "I, unlike some men, will not hesitate to shoot a woman."

Not doubting for a moment that the cold-eyed man would indeed shoot her, Faith slowly raised her hands. "Ross," she called out to her foreman.

"I'm sorry, Miss Jennings," Ross shrugged, "but these men are employees of Don Diego, and so am I."

Faith felt her hopes sink when she realized that no help would be forthcoming from her foreman. "Cord?" she asked simply.

"Off on a wild goose chase, ma'am, but at least he ain't dead. Not yet anyway." Ever polite, Fulton tipped his hat in farewell, then turned and rode away.

Faith managed to block out her fear with angry resignation as the men rode slowly toward her.

If I live through this, she thought silently as she gazed at the unwavering gun barrel, how long will it take Cord to find me?

Don Diego Montez entered his bedroom and looked down on the sleeping form in his bed. "Luisa," he said softly.

Luisa Alvarez opened her eyes and smiled sleepily. "Sí, querido, I am awake." She sat up and brushed her raven hair from her eyes.

"I have just received word that everything is going according to plan. By this time next week, I should be the proud new owner of the Double J Ranch." He stretched out a hand to gently caress her cheek. "Thanks to you."

Luisa's smile widened. "I was proud to help you, querido."

"Then you will no doubt honor my next request as well."

"Sí, of course."

Don Diego's smile was dark and without humor. "Get out."

"Qué?"

"Get out, Luisa. Out of my house. Out of my life. I have no further need of you."

"No!" She sprang from the bed, winding the sheet around her nude form. "You cannot mean it."

"Oh, but I do mean it." He reached into his pocket and withdrew a small drawstring pouch which he tossed onto the bed. "That should be enough money to keep you happy for a while. So just get dressed and leave."

"You cannot do this to me," Luisa screamed. "I will not be tossed aside. You promised to marry me."

Diego's black eyes glittered with icy rage. "You are fast becoming a bore, my dear."

Luisa was too filled with anger and a bitter sense of loss to take heed of Diego's rising anger. She refused to give up what—in her mind—she had worked so hard for. She advanced on him, her hands curled into talons at her sides. "If you turn me out I will go to the authorities," she spat. "I will tell them everything."

Diego reached out and gripped Luisa by her long hair. "That, my dear, would be a mistake. A dreadful mistake." Then his fist came down to connect with her fragile jaw and pain exploded like fireworks in her head. Mercifully, his second punch rendered her unconscious and she was unaware of the vicious blows Diego continued to rain upon her hapless body.

Chapter 15

Faith sat on the ground, her back against a tree trunk as she studied the rugged landscape by the light of the moon. They had finally stopped to rest after what, to Faith's weary body, seemed an eternity of riding. They had crossed the Rio Grande and headed into the Mexican hills earlier in the day, continuing to ride long after darkness fell. There was no fire. Their meal consisted of dried beef and cold tortillas.

"You must eat, chica."

Faith looked up to see the leader of the small band standing beside her. His name, he had informed her earlier, was Arista. He was tall and broad-shouldered with raven black hair and mustache. His eyes were a smoky blue and his skin had been deeply bronzed by the sun. Despite her predicament, Faith could not deny that Arista was an exceptionally handsome man. "I'm not hungry," she told him.

Arista dropped to his haunches and placed a tortilla in her hands. "You must eat to keep up your strength."

After a moment's hesitation, Faith took a small bite of the flat bread and was surprised to discover that she was hungry after all. It took her only a few minutes to finish it off.

Arista passed her a canteen of water. "See, chica," he said smugly. "I am always right."

Faith took a swallow of the lukewarm water, then passed it back to her captor. Arista was certainly a puzzle. He had kidnapped her at gunpoint, yet, when he spoke, he was unfailingly polite and on occasion even charming. He had bound her wrists together with rope, but had apologized for doing so. He had also allowed her to ride her own horse, but he held the reins. He asked after her comfort, cajoled her into eating and watched her like a hawk.

Faith had watched diligently for an opportunity to escape, but Arista guarded her too closely. Even if she could manage to wrest Dancer's reins from her captor's grip, she knew she would be caught—perhaps killed—before she could ride fifty yards. If she tried to escape on foot, she would be stopped before she could take the first step.

"Is the rope too tight?" Arista asked as he noted her unhappy expression. He reached forward and loosened the binding slightly. "Better?"

Faith shook her head. "I won't feel better until you let me go home."

"You know I cannot."

"Whatever Don Diego is paying you, I'll double," Faith offered.

"Ah, chica," Arista said with a sigh. "What I would like from you has nothing to do with money."

As his meaning sank in, Faith turned her face away, only to have her gaze fall on the other two kidnappers. Manuel was a short, broad Mexican with two missing front teeth. He appeared content with the ceaseless riding and paid Faith scant notice. The other man was called Buck. He was a tall, lanky American with a droopy blond mustache and almost colorless gray eyes. Whenever he turned his cold gaze on her—which was often—Faith could not suppress a shudder of revulsion.

"Buck makes me uneasy."

Arista followed the line of her gaze and nodded. "Yes. Buck is a strange one. But do not worry, chica, no harm will come to you as long as I am near."

Faith stared at him in amazement. Arista had kidnapped her, threatened to shoot her, tied her hands and taken her away from her home. Now he had the nerve to say he would allow no one to harm her! Perhaps that was a privilege he reserved for himself.

"Will you at least tell me where we are going?" she asked.

Arista merely shrugged.

"It makes no difference how far we go," Faith

told him calmly. "Cord McCamy will find me."

"Yes." An odd gleam lit Arista's smokey blue eyes. "He will."

Before Faith could question his strange response, Arista rose to his feet. "Rest while you can, chica. We are leaving soon." He turned on his heel and walked away.

Bright Star was lathered and Cord was hovering on the brink of total exhaustion by the time he rode into the ranchyard. The entire trip had been nothing more than a waste of time. Jack and Coot hadn't been in the shack, and from the looks of the place, no one had been there for years.

As Cord drew Bright Star to a halt near the stables, he saw Paco, his "friend." The man who had lied to him, betrayed him and sent him off on a wild goose chase. He dove for Paco, knocking the smaller man to the ground.

"Cord!" Paco cried out as Cord slammed him into the dirt. "Wait! Hold off a minute!"

"Why should I?" Cord grunted as he straddled Paco's chest. He gripped the younger man's shirt collar and twisted it painfully tight. "Aren't you the same son of a bitch that sent me out chasing a pack of lies?"

"Dona Faith," Paco managed to gasp.

Still holding the other man's shirt, Cord got to his feet, dragging Paco up with him. "What have you done to Faith?"

"Stop it! Stop it right now!" Emily Stubbs yelled as she hurried across the ranchyard. "This is no time to be fighting."

"Where is Faith, and what the hell is going on around here?" Cord roared. "I want answers and I want them now!"

"Turn poor Paco loose," Emily demanded, "then we'll go into the house and I'll explain everything." She turned to the stunned vaquero who had witnessed the scene from the safety of the stables. "Ramon, take care of Bright Star, then saddle a fresh horse for Mr. McCamy. He will be leaving within the hour."

"Where is Faith?" Cord demanded again once they were seated at the kitchen table.

"We don't know," Emily admitted.

"You don't know!" Cord surged to his feet. "What do you mean, you don't know?"

"Don't you glower at me, Cord McCamy," Emily said sternly. "Sit down and mind your tongue. We'll tell you what happened, and then you can go fetch Faith home."

Emily made it all sound so simple that Cord returned to his seat, but the scowl did not leave his face.

"I did not lie to you, my friend," Paco began. "I really believed that Jack Dorsey and Coot Sykes were in that line shack. It is what I had been told."

"By whom?" Cord was still skeptical.

"Luisa."

"Luisa?" Cord's brow wrinkled in thought. "Luisa Alvarez? Rosa's daughter?"

"Sí," Paco sighed. "As you know, Luisa is my cousin. She took up with Montez soon after he arrived here. Even though Tia Rosa and I argued with her about it many times, she continued her affair with him. A few days ago, Luisa came to me. She said she was frightened of Don Diego's temper and that she was leaving him. Then she told me about Dorsey and Coot." Paco shook his head sadly. "Luisa had never lied to me before."

"It was Ross that surprised me," Emily said suddenly.

"Fulton?" Cord was growing angrier and more confused with each passing moment.

"Ross Fulton has been on Don Diego's payroll for weeks," Paco told him. "Also thanks to my cousin. Ross has always been crazy about Luisa. She promised to marry him if he would help Diego."

Cord began to feel the icy fingers of dread grip his heart. "What happened to Faith?"

"Fulton came to Faith and told her you had been injured," Emily said softly. "He said he would take her to you. That you were asking for her." Twin tears rolled down the housekeeper's wrinkled cheeks. "We don't know where he's taken her."

Cord turned on Paco. "Why are you just sitting here? Why haven't you been out trying to find her?" He got to his feet and started for the door.

"Wait, Cord." Emily sprang from her chair and followed him out to the courtyard, Paco at her heels. "Almost all the ranchhands are out searching for her now. Fulton got several hours' lead on us. José was the only witness, and Ross conked him on the head so hard that it was almost a full day before he regained consciousness and was able to tell us what happened."

"When did Fulton take her?" Cord asked quietly.

Paco felt a shiver dance along his spine. He wasn't fooled by Cord's quiet tone. He could hear the thread of steel that lay beneath his words. "Yesterday morning."

Cord's spine stiffened. "Then I had better go. The trail's getting colder by the minute."

"We have something that might save you a lot of time," Emily offered.

Cord swiveled his head around to regard the housekeeper. "What?"

"Luisa."

Luisa lay in the guest bedroom, floating in and out of consciousness. Her face was a rainbow of bruises, her eyes mere slits in a puffy mass of blue and purple. Her entire body had been beaten almost beyond recognition. That she had managed to make her way to the Double J and Paco was nothing short of a miracle.

Rosa Alvarez rose to her feet when the trio entered the room. Paco had sent for her immediately following Luisa's arrival. "She has been trying to speak," Rosa said as she looked down at her injured daughter.

Cord stepped closer and stared at the young woman. My God! Would Faith look like this when he found her? Would she even be alive? "Luisa, it's Cord," he said softly. "Can you tell me where Faith is?"

Luisa moaned softly and turned her face toward Cord.

"Bring her some water," he snapped.

Rosa hurried forward and held a cup of water to her daughter's cracked and swollen lips.

"Can you tell me where Senorita Jennings is?" Cord repeated as soon as Rosa stepped away.

Luisa groaned again, then with herculean effort, her lips formed one word: "Arista."

"You know where to look for her now?" Paco asked as Cord placed his saddlebags on the black mare that had been made ready for him.

"Yep." Cord checked his rifle, then slid it into the rawhide sheath on his saddle.

"You're still determined to go alone?" Paco persisted.

"Yep." Cord tossed his bedroll behind the saddle and tied it into place. "Take care of the ranch, Paco, because as soon as I have Faith back safe and sound, I'm going to kill Montez."

"He's gone into hiding," Paco told him. "Probably in El Paso, but maybe as far away as San Antonio."

Cord swung into the saddle. He had not taken the time to bathe or shave and with his three days' growth of beard, the frown on his face appeared even more menacing than usual. "I'll find him."

The tone of Cord's voice left Paco with no doubt whatsoever that Cord would indeed accomplish all his objectives. "Adios, amigo," Paco called as Cord rode away. "And good luck."

Chapter 16

Tucked away in a narrow valley, Arista's hideout looked more like a small village than an outlaw's lair. A sparkling stream wound its way past the scattering of cabins and into a grove of trees. Deep green foliage and exotic colored wildflowers covered the mountain slopes, and under any other circumstances Faith would have been struck by the beauty of her surroundings. As it was, she spared no thought for the scenery as she and her captors left the twisting mountain pass they had just spent a half day traversing.

Arista drew his horse to a halt and signaled for Buck and Manuel to ride ahead. Manuel spurred his horse and raced away toward the cabins. Buck rode by more slowly, his colorless gaze lingering as long as possible on Faith.

After the two men had ridden away, Arista leaned sideways in his saddle and untied Faith's wrists. "You may go anywhere you like as long as you do not try to leave the valley. This is the only way in or out"—he gestured above them to where two armed men stood on an outcropping of rock—"and as you can see, it is closely guarded."

Faith glanced up at the guards before fixing her gaze on Arista. "I don't know why you are doing this, but I promise you, senor, that Cord McCamy will make you rue the day you accepted Diego Montez's money. If I do not do so first."

To Faith's surprise, Arista smiled, his teeth flashing whitely in his dark face. "Lovely Faith, can you not understand that some things have nothing to do with money?"

Still smiling, Arista led Faith to the largest of the cabins. Before she could dismount, he was beside her, lifting her from the saddle.

Men, women and children of varying ages emerged from the surrounding houses to stare openly at the stranger in their midst. A young boy ran forward and, after chattering rapidly in Spanish to Arista, led the horses away.

"Mi casa," Arista said simply as he gripped Faith's arm and guided her up the steps and onto the long wooden porch. He threw the door open and led her inside. Away from the curious eyes of the valley's inhabitants.

Faith found herself in what appeared to be a large common room. A crude bar, constructed of planks and wooden barrels, lined one wall.

Three round tables with rickety chairs sat in the middle of the floor, and homemade shelves held a supply of mescal and tobacco.

Faith pulled her arm from Arista's grasp and stepped out of his reach.

Arista appeared not to notice. "Bianca," he called.

The door in the back of the room swung open and a woman emerged. She was tall, with olive skin and shoulder-length black hair. Her breasts were large and firm, her hips wide. Dressed in a white peasant blouse and red skirt, she was attractive in an overblown fashion.

"Arista," Bianca cried as she hurried forward. "You have returned at last." She threw herself into his arms and gave him a large, noisy kiss. Arista returned the kiss wholeheartedly as his hands moved to squeeze the woman's ample buttocks.

Faith turned away. She had no desire to witness the couple's reunion. "We have a guest," she heard Arista say a moment later.

Guest? If Faith hadn't been so exhausted she would have laughed at Arista's choice of words. Guest indeed!

Bianca turned flashing eyes to Faith. "Who is this skinny gringa bitch you bring to my home?"

"*My* home," Arista said evenly, "and Senorita Jennings is my guest."

Bianca pulled away from him as though he hadn't spoken and moved to stand in front of Faith. Hands on hips, feet planted wide, she snarled, "Dirty gringa."

Faith was sore, weary and grimy. She had

been dragged away from her home at gunpoint and brought to a place she had no desire to be, and now some woman who was a total stranger had the gall to call her names. She had had just about all she was going to take. "Filthy greaser," she returned calmly.

"Puta."

"Whore."

Suddenly Bianca threw her head back and gave a hearty laugh. "Well, skinny gringa, I think you and I will get along just fine."

Damn! Cord swore silently to himself. He was being followed. He had known it for the past two hours. A muscle tightened along his jaw. He didn't have time to fool with Montez's henchmen. He had to reach Faith before it was too late. If it wasn't already.

Near sunset Cord entered an arroyo and knew he would find no better place. He searched until he found a spot suitable for his horse to climb, then led the mare up to the rim and settled down to wait.

Less than an hour passed before the two horsemen rode into the arroyo. As Cord had suspected, it was Jack Dorsey and Coot Sykes. At least Luisa hadn't lied about the bounty hunters' identities.

Cord waited until the men rode abreast of him before he stood up and made his presence known.

"Hello, boys." Cord's voice was deceptively cool, belying the fact that his rifle was trained on

Dorsey's face. "Nice day for a ride."

The men halted their horses as they turned startled eyes up to Cord.

"Damn it!" Dorsey's scowl darkened his already ugly countenance. "You!" he spat. "I shoulda knowed you'd pull some kinda injun trick."

"Fair's fair," Cord chided him. "You were careless."

"You gonna just shoot us, McCamy? In cold blood?"

Cord appeared to consider the idea. "If that's what you want, I'll be glad to oblige, but I think my idea has more merit." He gestured with the rifle. "Dismount, then drop your gunbelts—slowly."

Dorsey and Coot moved to comply, but Dorsey changed his mind at the last minute and grabbed for the gun in his holster.

Cord shot him between the eyes.

Coot looked first at his fallen compadre, then at Cord, his face waxen. He dismounted and stood by his horse, hands raised above his head.

"Well, Coot," Cord said conversationally, "looks like it's just you and me."

When Coot merely continued to stare vacantly, Cord fired a shot over the bounty hunter's head. That got his attention.

"It's up to you," Cord told him. "My way or . . ." he nodded at Dorsey's body which lay sprawled grotesquely on the hard ground, "Jack's way."

Coot lowered one hand and slowly, oh so

slowly, unbuckled his gunbelt and let it drop to the ground.

"Now your boots."

"My boots?" Coot gasped, incredulous. "What ya want with my boots?"

"Do you want your questions answered or do you want to live?"

Coot's choice was obviously the latter for he sat down on the ground and began to struggle out of his boots.

Cord clambered down into the arroyo, his aim never wavering from Coot. He picked up the boots and shoved them into Coot's saddlebag. "Now. Start walking."

"Ya cain't mean it," Coot whined. "I'll never make it."

"At least you stand a chance," Cord replied coldly, "which is more than you would have given me."

"How 'bout him?" Coot nodded at Dorsey's rapidly stiffening form.

"Leave him for the buzzards." Cord gestured with the rifle. "Go before I change my mind."

Cord could spare no sympathy for the horseless, weaponless bounty hunter. Dorsey and Sykes had slowed him down, and for that, they had paid. Cursing the loss of time, Cord prepared to leave.

Chapter 17

Faith awoke with a start. For a brief fleeting
moment she thought she was back in her own
bed at the Double J. Then reality intruded and
she realized she was lying on a narrow cot in a
tiny back room of Arista's cabin. The only other
furnishings the room could boast were an empty wooden crate and a small cracked mirror.
Across the hall, she had been told, was the room
Arista shared with Bianca.

Faith sat up and attempted to smooth her hair
with her fingers. She felt hot, sticky and dirty
and in desperate need of a bath. Judging by the
sun shining through the window, she had slept
for less than an hour. With a sigh of resignation,
she left her room to search for Bianca.

She found the Mexican girl in the common

room serving mescal to Arista and two other men.

"Arista," Faith said briskly as she approached their table. "Your 'guest' would like a bath and a change of clothes."

"Ah, chica, I see your nap did not sweeten your disposition."

"If you want to be friends, Arista, then send me home. If not, then at least provide me with the basic necessities."

Arista chuckled softly as he turned to Bianca and chattered rapidly in Spanish.

"We have no hot water and fancy bath oils here, gringa," Bianca snapped. "You will have to bathe in the stream."

"Fine," Faith returned evenly. "Just point me in the right direction."

Bianca looked at Arista for a moment, then returned the bottle of mescal to the shelf. "I will go with you. Manuel has a daughter whose clothes should fit you. We will stop at his house first." She disappeared into the back room and returned a moment later with a small bundle. "Come on, gringa. I don't have all day to waste on you."

"Nor do I wish to waste my time with you," Faith returned calmly. She refused to allow the larger woman to intimidate her.

Arista watched them leave, his eyes on Faith's gently swaying hips. Santa Maria, but Faith Jennings was a beautiful woman. Her eyes were as soft and warm as a fawn's, her hair so rich and silky his fingers ached to touch it. Strong, proud and unafraid, with more than a hint of steel in her spine, she was a woman any man would gladly kill for. And she belonged to Cord McCamy. Arista smiled to himself as he returned his attention to the glass of mescal. Yes, she belonged to McCamy. But for how long?

Bianca led Faith through the trees to a place where the stream curved to fall over a series of rocks in a miniature waterfall. Beneath the fall was a natural pool.

Without the faintest show of modesty, Bianca stripped her clothes off and tossed them aside to dive head first into the cool clear water. Faith was more reticent. Her eyes carefully scanned the area first to ascertain that no uninvited spectators lurked in the bushes. Slowly she began to undress, her hand going first to her pocket. The pocket that held the small bone-handled knife. Faith had kept the knife on her since the day she had found it in her parents' trunk. Carefully she placed it in the folds of the peasant blouse and skirt Manuel's daughter had loaned her. Faith was nothing if not sensible. She knew the knife would be less than useless against Arista and his band of armed men, but having the small weapon gave her a measure of security.

Hastily, Faith removed the remainder of her clothes and stepped into the water.

"Here, gringa." Bianca tossed her a small bar of scented soap. "You can use my soap and sleep in my house, but stay away from my man."

"Believe me," Faith replied as she lathered

herself, "I don't want your man."

Bianca turned narrowed eyes on the younger girl. Her huge breasts floated on the water's surface as she placed her hands on her ample hips. "Why not? You think Arista is not good enough for you, gringa?"

Despite her predicament, Faith began to laugh. "Make up your mind, Mexican. First you warn me away from him, now you're angry because I don't want him."

Bianca's single-track mind would not be derailed. "Why do you not want Arista?"

Faith sighed. Despite Bianca's bluster, the Mexican girl had all the intelligence and sophistication of a puppy. "Because I already have a man."

Bianca turned this over in her mind for a moment, then nodded, apparently satisfied.

Faith finished her bathing and swam to the bank. She climbed out of the water and sat on a rock to comb her hair with the crude wooden comb that Bianca had provided.

Warmed and dried by the evening sun, Faith had just decided to get dressed when she felt a strange prickling sensation along her spine. She glanced back over her shoulder and saw Buck standing among the trees, his eyes staring at her nude form. Before she had a chance to move or speak, Buck touched the brim of his hat, gave a barely perceptible nod and walked away.

Faith dressed quickly, cursing herself silently for having temporarily forgotten about the cold-eyed Buck. She slipped her knife into her skirt pocket as Bianca stepped from the water. The Mexican girl did not bother to dry herself. She merely pulled her clothes onto her damp body.

"Come on, gringa," Bianca said imperiously. "It is suppertime."

Faith followed silently in Bianca's wake, her mind occupied with devising a means of escape. She had no doubt that Cord would come for her, but she wasn't content to sit idly and await rescue. Faith glanced up as they passed a cabin and saw Buck lounging indolently on the porch. A shiver danced along her spine as his almost colorless gray gaze touched her. It might take Cord days or even weeks to find her. As much as she loved and trusted the handsome McCamy brother, she knew she couldn't wait.

When Bianca stopped to chat with Manuel's wife, Faith continued to the cabin alone. She wanted as much distance as possible between Buck and herself.

Faith paused on the cabin steps when she saw Arista standing on the porch smoking a slim black cigar.

"Senorita Jennings." Arista swept off his hat as he bowed from the waist. "I trust you find the accommodations to your liking."

"It's not the accommodations I take objection to," Faith replied, "it's the company."

Arista laughed, his white teeth flashing in the rapidly gathering dusk. "Ah, chica, at least you are honest."

Faith stepped onto the porch. "May I ask you something?"

Arista quirked a dark brow. "You can *ask*."

"What is this place and why have you brought me here?"

Arista sighed and tossed his cigar into the grass. "This place is Tierra Oro. My home. As for why you are here—why not?"

Faith's spine stiffened in indignation. "Just how much did Diego pay you to get me out of the way?" she asked coolly. "And why haven't you killed me?"

This time Arista made no reply. He merely returned Faith's even gaze.

Suddenly a light dawned in Faith's mind. "This isn't about Montez, is it? Oh, he paid you and gave you a good excuse, but this is really something between you and Cord, isn't it?"

Arista straightened and his expression grew dark. "Basta!" he snapped. "No more questions." He turned on his heel and strode from the porch.

Faith wasn't certain why, but she felt she had just scored a minor victory.

Chapter 18

Cord swore softly to himself as he dismounted. He lifted the mare's front hoof and checked it, even though he knew what he would find. She had picked up a stone.

He cursed the lost time as he used his knife to remove the sharp rock. Now the mare's hoof would be sore and he would be slowed down even further.

Cord patted the animal's sleek black neck. He had chosen the mare because he wanted a quiet mount. In the dark, a stallion would blow and nicker at the slightest movement, while a mare was calmer and better mannered.

"We'll rest for a little while, old girl," Cord told the mare as he poured the water from his canteen into his hat and offered it to the horse, "but not for long. We have to find Faith."

The mare lifted her head from the makeshift watering trough and nudged Cord's shoulder with her velvety nose, as though commiserating with him.

Cord hung his hat on the saddle horn and removed some dried beef from his saddlebag. He sat on a rock to eat while the horse rested her sore foot.

Damn Arista! Cord thought he had seen the last of him years ago. And now he had turned up and taken Faith as his captive. Cord planned to make certain that this time he would rid himself of Arista, once and for all.

Cord closed his eyes as a mental picture began to form. He could see Faith's silken brown hair, her soft brown eyes with the thick fringe of lashes, and her turned-up nose. He could almost taste the ambrosia of her rose-petal lips and feel the warm softness of her breath.

With a muttered curse, Cord sprang to his feet. He would walk and lead the horse behind him for a while. At least every step would bring him closer to Faith.

Faith stepped into the common room. No one else was there save Bianca, who was bent over a pot of chili that was cooking in the crude stone fireplace.

"Can I help?" Faith asked.

Bianca straightened and placed her hands on her ample hips. "What makes you think I need help, gringa?"

Faith sighed. "Never mind. I'm going for a walk."

"Don't wander too far away," Bianca admonished. "Supper will be ready soon."

Hopeful of finding a means of escape, Faith moved out onto the porch and took a good hard look at the small settlement. She could see nothing that might prove helpful. Her gaze drifted upward to the rugged mountain slopes. Unless some sort of additional secret pass existed, only a goat would be capable of traversing those mountains.

Faith turned and saw Consuela, Manuel's teen-aged daughter, walking along the path to the woods. On impulse, Faith hurried to her room to retrieve a small bundle, then ran back outside and along the path to join the young girl. She caught up with her at the edge of the woods.

"Hello, Consuela."

The girl flashed Faith a surprised smile. "Buenas noches, Senorita Jennings."

"I wanted to thank you for the clothes."

Consuela shrugged. "De nada."

"I would also like to give you this. If I may." Faith extended the bundle she had retrieved from her room.

Consuela's eyes grew round when she saw Faith's dark violet riding skirt and lavender silk blouse. Never had she owned anything so fine. "Oh no, senorita, I cannot accept it."

"Nonsense," Faith told the girl. "I hope you will consider it a trade for the clothing you gave me."

Consuela considered for a moment, then nodded. "Muchas gracias, senorita."

"Please, Consuela, call me Faith." Despite the circumstances, Faith couldn't help liking the young girl.

Consuela's smile grew broader. "I have another camisa and skirt you can have. I have outgrown them and you . . ." she looked at her own ample bosom, then at Faith's more modest one, "are not so big as me. Sí?"

"Sí," Faith replied with a laugh.

The two women walked along the path to the pool where Faith and Bianca had bathed.

"Aren't you afraid to come out here alone?" Faith asked.

"Why should I be afraid?" Consuela replied. "I am a very good swimmer."

"That's not what I meant. When Bianca and I were here yesterday, I caught Buck watching us."

Consuela nodded. "I do not like Senor Buck. Too many times I have felt his cold eyes on me."

The two women undressed and dove into the water. They swam for a while until they were tired, then settled down to the more mundane task of bathing.

Faith wiped the water from her eyes with her fingertips and turned to Consuela. "Do you know of another way out of Tierra Oro?"

Consuela's cheeks grew red and her dark eyes flashed fire. "So this is why you are kind to me. You wish me to betray my family and friends." Consuela scrambled out of the water. "You can take your gift back, gringa. I will tell you nothing."

"No. Wait." Faith followed the distraught girl onto the bank. "I didn't mean to upset you, and the clothes were not intended as a bribe."

Consuela turned her back on Faith and began to dress.

Faith began to slip into her own clothes. "I don't expect you to understand, but . . ." her voice broke slightly. "Oh, God! I just want to go home. I have people I love and who love me. They must be going crazy right now."

Consuela had a new light of understanding in her eyes when she turned to look at Faith. "I too would be sad if I were taken from my home and family. I would also try to escape. But I cannot help you. I cannot betray Arista."

"I know," Faith replied with a sigh. "Don't worry. I won't ask you again."

"You must understand. Arista has been very good to my family. If not for him, I do not know what would have become of us."

Faith's brows arched in surprise. "What do you mean?"

But Consuela would say no more. The two women returned to the village in silence. Consuela had given Faith no real information, but she had unwittingly confirmed Faith's suspicion. There was another pass out of the valley.

"Wait," Consuela cried when Faith would have walked past her family's cabin. "I will get the clothes I promised you."

Consuela hurried inside while Faith waited on

the porch. She had been waiting for less than a minute when she felt a strange prickling sensation. As though she was being watched. She turned around to see Buck standing at the end of the porch.

His mouth spread in a feral smile and even in the waning light of evening, Faith could see the evil gleam in his pale eyes. Without a word, Buck turned and walked away.

As soon as Consuela returned with the clothing, Faith hurried away to Arista's cabin. One thing was certain. She would be glad to see the last of Tierra Oro.

Chapter 19

Faith drew Dancer to a halt and gazed up at the sharply sloping mountainside. Arista had raised no objections when she had declared her intention to go riding alone, nor, as far as she could tell, had anyone bothered to follow her.

Sick and tired of her captivity—though she had been treated kindly—Faith was determined to find a way out of the valley. At least two guards were always on duty at the entrance to the mountain pass, and she could find no way past them, but if she could find another, less well guarded pass, she could simply ride away.

Faith could not believe that Arista didn't have a second means of exit from the enclosed valley. Consuela's reaction to the question practically confirmed it, but so far she had found nothing.

There had to be a way out. There just had to be! More determined than ever, Faith kneed Dancer into a walk and continued with her search.

She was so intent on her task that several moments passed before Faith became aware of an approaching rider. She glanced over her shoulder to see Buck racing toward her, his spurs digging into the sides of his lathered mount.

Faith's first thought was that Arista had sent Buck to check on her, but as he drew close enough for her to see the maniacal glow of his colorless eyes, she knew Arista had not sent him. Buck had been sent by his own lust.

Faith urged Dancer into a run as she bent low over the sturdy mare's neck. She didn't bother to look behind her. She could think only of escape. Escape from Buck. Escape from Tierra Oro. She could feel her heart pounding in her ears, matching rhythm with the rapid tattoo of Dancer's hooves. She could feel the horse's fluid motion beneath her as the pinto mare seemed to sense its mistress' need for haste and put forth an extra burst of energy.

Faith glanced up at last and felt her heart sink in her chest as she realized that all along, Buck had been riding abreast of her. She reached into her pocket and closed her fingers over the smooth bone handle of her knife. She would kill the evil Comanchero before she would allow him to touch her.

Then Buck's long arm snaked out to pull her from her saddle to his. Faith struggled against him, but Buck merely laughed as he held her in his viselike grip. Never loosening his hold, he slid from the saddle.

Faith was clutched tightly to Buck's chest, her arms pinned to her sides, her feet dangling above the ground. She spat into his face, but he appeared not to notice. "Filthy canaille!" she swore. "Release me immediately!" This order she followed with a kick to his shin, but Buck only grunted.

"Don't go acting all high-falutin' on me," Buck growled after she had stilled. "You're nothin' but a damn fancy puta and I'm just gonna give you what you been wantin'." He flung her to the ground.

Faith landed on her back and quickly tried to roll to her feet, but Buck was too fast for her. He dropped down to straddle her, one knee on either side of her waist.

"Hold still, little puta," he snapped. "Buck'll give you what you been cravin'."

Faith shuddered with revulsion as she slapped his filthy hands away from her breasts. Desperately she reached for her knife only to discover that her pocket was empty. The weapon must have fallen out when Buck threw her to the ground.

Buck's hands began to pull on Faith's blouse, ripping the delicate material in his haste.

Faith felt the gorge rise in her throat as the sour smell of Buck's unwashed body assailed her. She clasped his wrists in an effort to push him away. "Unhand me, you vermin!" she yelled. "Arista will kill you for this."

The warning gave Buck only a second's pause. "Hell," he declared as he shook Faith's hands loose. "I ain't scared of that half-breed Mex."

Faith curled her fingers into talons and began to claw at any part of Buck's anatomy she could reach. She could not, would not, allow him to violate her further.

Buck bellowed in pain as Faith gouged a long furrow in his cheek. "Bitch!" He cuffed the side of her head. "Be still."

Faith was left stunned and faint from the blow. Weakly, she tried to push Buck's hands from her, but he merely laughed.

"Nice breasts," he murmured as he brushed away the shreds of her blouse. "Not as big as I like 'em, but not bad." He pinched one nipple cruelly with his rough fingers.

Faith cried out and drew back a fist in preparation to deliver a blow to Buck's face.

"Go ahead and holler," Buck smirked. "I know you like it."

Faith's knuckles brushed the ground and she felt something hard and smooth beneath them. "Scum," she spat at Buck in an effort to distract him. "Bastardido!" Her fingers closed around the bone handle of her knife.

Laughing at her insults, Buck reached to pull up her loose cotton skirt.

The knife gripped tightly in her hand, Faith arched her arm upward, not knowing—nor caring—where the small, sharp blade would strike. She hoped only to inflict enough damage to make Buck release her.

She felt the blade slide in easily, all the way to the hilt, as though sliding into butter. She heard Buck gurgle and felt a warm, wet stickiness flow over her arms, chest and face. She saw the brief flash of disbelief in Buck's pale eyes as he released her to grab at the knife in his throat. Then he collapsed on top of her.

Faith managed to drag herself from beneath him. She knelt beside the still-warm corpse oblivious to her exposed, blood-covered breasts, and felt a shudder rack her body. My God! She had actually killed a man. A worthless man, to be sure, but a human being nonetheless. She had taken a life.

Faith rose to her feet. Still dazed and shaken, she did not notice Arista's approach. He rode his horse up to her and slid from the saddle. "Chica?" He grasped her shoulders. "What happened here?"

Eyes wide in her pale, blood-spattered face, Faith could only shake her head.

Arista released her and with the toe of his boot nudged Buck's body over. The handle of the knife still protruded from the dead man's neck. Arista retrieved it and wiped the gory blade on Buck's pants leg before turning to Faith. "Yours?"

She nodded.

Arista looked at the scene before him, taking in Buck's lathered horse, Faith's exposed breasts and the dead man at his feet. "It all becomes clear. Tell me, chica, are you harmed?"

DiAnna June

"No," Faith replied shakily. "I don't think so."

"Ah well," Arista sighed. "I never liked Buck anyway."

The nausea that continued to plague Faith could be denied no longer. She stumbled a few hasty steps away from Arista before her stomach erupted and heaved all of its contents onto the ground.

Arista was beside her in a flash, supporting her with his strong hands. "Better?" he asked when Faith had finished.

She managed a nod as he removed the silk bandana from his neck to wipe her mouth.

"Come on, chica." Arista slid his vest from his shoulders and draped it over Faith. "You can ride with me. I'll send some men back to fetch your horse and dispose of Buck."

Faith made no protest as Arista lifted her into the saddle in front of him. She wanted only to leave the grisly scene behind.

As Arista turned his horse toward the cabins, Faith squared her shoulders. She did not look back.

Chapter 20

Cord drew back on the reins as he approached the narrow entrance to Tierra Oro. He looked up at the guards who stood on the outcropping of rock. "Hola, Manuel."

"Cord!" Manuel's broad face split in an ear-to-ear grin. "I've been expecting you, amigo."

Cord waited as the short Mexican scrambled down the slope to stand in front of him.

"My woman is here?"

"Sí. She is at Arista's house, but I do not think Arista will be as glad to see you as I."

Cord shrugged.

"What took you so long?" Manuel demanded.

"Dorsey and Sykes held me up a little."

Manuel nodded in commiseration. "They are bad ones."

"They were."

It took a moment for Manuel to grasp Cord's meaning. When he did he guffawed loudly. "Good for you, amigo." He turned and called out to the other guard, "Rafael, it is our old friend, Cord McCamy. Let him pass."

Cord nodded his thanks to Manuel and rode into the valley. He needed no one to give him directions to Arista's cabin. He remembered. He remembered almost too well. He rode up to the porch. "Arista!" he called, "come on out."

Arista appeared on the porch almost immediately, as though he had been expecting Cord's summons. "So, McCamy, you have finally arrived."

"Where is she?"

Arista shrugged. "Who?"

That was it. The last straw. Cord lunged from his horse's back and into Arista.

Arista hit the porch with Cord on top of him, but not for long. Arista arched his shoulders in an attempt to throw Cord, and the two men rolled from the wooden porch to the ground.

Cord felt a sense of satisfaction as his knuckles connected with Arista's jaw, only to lose it seconds later when his opponent's fist thudded into his stomach.

Faith awoke refreshed. The blood had been scrubbed from her skin and hair the night before, and clean clothing lay folded on the wooden crate next to her bed. To her surprise, her knife lay atop the cotton skirt and blouse.

Vaguely aware of a commotion outside, Faith

dressed quickly, not bothering to wear shoes. What now? she wondered as she passed through the common room.

She stepped out onto the porch to find it crowded with people. More Tierra Oro citizens stood around on the ground, laughing, shouting and exchanging bets. Spying Bianca in the forefront, Faith pushed her way through the crowd.

Cord! Faith almost cried out to him as she saw him grappling with Arista. She pressed her hand to her mouth as she moved to stand next to Bianca. Cord was here! He had come for her.

Faith's joy at Cord's arrival was tempered by fear as she saw Arista produce a knife.

Bianca turned to Faith and patted the smaller girl's shoulder. "Do not fret, gringa. Men, they must have their battles."

Both men were on their feet. They circled each other warily as Arista brandished his knife.

Faith swallowed hard in an attempt to send her heart from her throat back to her chest where it belonged. Her hands gripped the porch railing as she leaned forward, her gaze riveted on Cord.

More bets exchanged hands as Cord leapt forward and threw himself onto Arista. The knife was dislodged from Arista's grasp and flew through the air to land in the dirt at the feet of Consuela, Manuel's daughter. With a wink at Faith, the girl scooped the weapon up and tucked it into the waistband of her skirt.

The muscles in Cord's neck and shoulders bulged beneath his bronze skin as he pinned his opponent to the ground. Cord's hand gripped

Arista's throat and he pressed a knee painfully into the downed man's chest. "Give me one good reason why I shouldn't kill you right now," Cord rasped.

Faith stepped off the porch and hurried forward. "Cord!"

Cord's eyes never left Arista's face. "Did he touch you, muñeca?"

Sensitive woman that she was, Faith understood the deeper meaning of Cord's question. She knew also that she held Arista's life in her hands. A hush fell over everyone as Faith shook her head. "No. I have not been harmed."

"Then maybe I'll let you live," Cord said as he released Arista's throat and stood up. "For now."

"How very generous." Arista's voice was heavy with sarcasm as he got to his feet. "Basta!" he called to the crowd. "Go home! It is over!"

The winners were counting their money while the losers grumbled direly beneath their breath as the crowd separated and began to move toward their homes.

At last Cord turned to look at Faith. She looked so damned beautiful with her hair unbound and shimmering in the morning sun. She was dressed simply in a low-necked camisa and cotton skirt and her feet were bare. It was her eyes, however, that captivated Cord. Her expressive brown eyes were aglow with love, joy and longing as she looked at him. He stretched a hand out to her and she ran into his arms.

Cord crushed Faith to him. He felt complete now. The empty space was filled. He slid his hands to the back of her head and gazed into her lovely face. She's mine, he thought possessively. All mine.

Faith smiled up at Cord. How wonderful to touch him again. To be held by him. She reached up and brushed a drop of blood from the corner of his mouth. The fire in Cord's eyes when he gazed at her began the now familiar stirrings deep inside her.

Cord smiled in understanding as he released her to slide an arm around her waist. He turned to Arista. "Once, a long time ago, I saved your miserable life, Arista. Do you repay me by kidnapping my woman?"

"It is not as simple as that," Arista replied as he rubbed his rapidly swelling jaw. "May I suggest we call a truce and go inside for a drink? Then I will explain."

Cord eyed him warily for a moment, then nodded agreement.

Inside, they found Bianca counting a stack of money. "Muchas gracias, Senor McCamy," she said happily. "I won much money today."

Arista appeared aggrieved. "Woman, you wound me. How could you have bet on McCamy?"

"Why not?" Bianca replied, unperturbed. "He won."

Chuckling, Cord took a seat at one of the tables and pulled Faith onto his lap. He never wanted her out of his sight or reach again.

Bianca fetched some glasses and a bottle of mescal, then she and Arista joined Cord and Faith at the table.

"Explain now. If you can," Cord demanded.

"Ah, McCamy, how long have we known each other?" Arista shrugged, then continued, not really expecting an answer. "First we were friends, then enemies, then strangers. Once, while we were friends, you saved my life. I saw a chance to repay you."

The muscles along Cord's jaw tightened. "By kidnapping Faith?"

"By saving her life!" Arista returned. "Montez did not pay me to kidnap Faith but to kill her. I took his money, but as you can see, your fair senorita is very much alive."

Faith stiffened on Cord's lap and he tightened his arm around her waist.

"Montez's plan was simple," Arista continued; "lure you away so I could kidnap Faith, bring her to Mexico and kill her. When you came looking for her, I was to kill you too. Your bodies were to be conveniently located and identified by Sheriff Hobbs, and Faith's inheritance would be Diego's."

"What about Coot and Sykes?" Cord snapped. "If you were to kill me, why were they out there gunning for me?"

"Were they?" Arista shrugged. "Perhaps Montez did not trust me completely."

"I wonder why," Cord drawled.

Faith squirmed on Cord's lap as his hand caressed the curve of her hip. She was beginning to feel a pleasant tingling warmth. "I believe him," she said suddenly.

Cord arched a skeptical brow as he looked at Faith. His lips curved upward in that special secretive smile that was his alone. "Why?"

Faith's hand slid along the outside of Cord's thigh. "I don't know. I just do."

Cord lightly caressed her cheek with his calloused fingertips before he returned his attention to Arista. "Why didn't you refuse the job?"

"I thought about it, but Montez would have hired someone else and you would both be dead now. Had I come to you and told you of his scheme, you would not have believed me. So I took Faith and brought her here. Where I knew you would find her."

"Maybe I believe you and maybe I don't," Cord conceded, "but I still don't trust you worth a damn."

Arista smiled. "And well you shouldn't."

"Gather your things, muñequita." Cord lifted Faith onto her feet. "We're leaving right away."

After Faith and Bianca had left the room, Arista took a drink of his mescal, then laughed. "I had thought to take Faith away from you, McCamy. To keep her here with me."

Arista held up a staying hand when he saw the angry green fire in Cord's eyes. "That was before I saw her eyes when she looked at you. I think that someday I would like to receive such a look from a woman. A look such as that would be worth dying for."

Both men rose to their feet when Faith reentered the room, a small bundle under her arm.

"Don't try to follow us," Cord warned as Faith joined him.

"The debt is paid, McCamy. I owe you nothing."

"Just stay out of my way, Arista. You'll live longer."

Neither man smiled as they parted company. And neither man was willing to turn his back on the other.

When she and Cord had gained the door, Faith paused and looked back. "Thank you," she said simply.

Arista sketched a bow. "Until next we meet, chica."

Despite the fact that Faith's mare, Dancer, had been prepared for departure, Cord lifted Faith onto his saddle in front of him. "I want you near me," he whispered in a voice that sent shivers down her spine.

Content in Cord's arms, Faith snuggled against his chest as he spurred his horse into a gallop. Neither of them looked back as they rode away with Dancer trailing along behind them.

Arista watched from the porch as Cord and Faith entered the pass and disappeared from sight. He briefly entertained the idea of sending men to detain them, but quickly dismissed the notion. At times, Cord McCamy could turn pure savage, and Arista could not afford to lose any of his men simply to satisfy a whim.

"So. The gringa is gone," Bianca said simply from the doorway. "I think I will miss her a little bit."

Arista continued to stare at the pass. He said nothing, but he couldn't shake the feeling that someday they would all meet again.

Chapter 21

"*I have missed you, muñequita,*" Cord said softly as they rode out of the mountain pass and into open country.

"And I you," Faith replied. They were still sharing his horse and she leaned her back against his chest and allowed her hand to rest on his thigh. "I knew you would come for me. What I didn't expect was your beard."

Cord pressed his lips to the top of her head and inhaled the delicate fragrance of her silken hair. "Do you like it?"

"I like *you*. Bearded or beardless."

Cord gripped the reins in one hand to caress the curve of Faith's waist and hip. "Good," he murmured as he leaned forward to lightly kiss her neck, "because I more than like you."

Faith tilted her head back against Cord's shoulder and her hands gripped his hard thighs as a strange curling sensation began in her stomach. His hand slid upward over her ribcage to pause maddeningly near her breast, and she moaned deep in her throat.

Cord's fingers gripped her blouse convulsively as he pulled her more tightly against him. He was aflame with wanting her. Her silken, fragrant softness, so near to him, so alive beneath his touch, was almost more than he could bear.

His hand moved upward to slide inside the low neck of her camisa. Slowly, and oh so gently, his fingers brushed the hardness of her nipple.

Faith squirmed in the saddle as a heated throbbing began between her thighs. She cried out softly as Cord's questing fingers warmed her sensitive skin and sent tremors of desire shooting through her body. She turned her head, her moist lips parted in invitation.

With a groan, Cord lowered his mouth to hers, his tongue thrusting boldly into her honeyed sweetness.

Faith felt almost giddy from the force of Cord's kiss. She arched her back, moaning as the heat between her thighs grew stronger.

Cord raised his head and their eyes met. His were ablaze with fierce green hunger. Hers glowed golden topaz with love and longing.

Cord gripped Faith's slim waist and with a swift fluid movement lifted her from the saddle and turned her to face him.

Faith sat astride Cord's thighs, the pulsing juncture between her legs pressed tightly against his male hardness. The rhythmic movement of the horse created a friction that sent their desire to almost unbearable heights.

Faith could feel the tightening of her stomach muscles as the building warmth within her grew to a raging flame. She gripped Cord's shoulders, her nails digging into his skin as she arched her neck backward and a cry escaped her lips.

Without a word, Cord drew his horse to a halt. He slid his hands beneath Faith's skirt to cup her buttocks and lift her. She twined her arms around his neck while her legs wrapped around his waist. Then they were kissing, their mouths seeking, probing, melding together.

Together they slid from the saddle to fall upon the soft green grass.

"You are mine, muñequita," Cord murmured huskily. "You have always been mine." With a few swift movements he divested Faith of her clothing.

Faith was vaguely aware that she was naked before Cord's heated gaze, but it had ceased to matter. Nothing mattered but her love for Cord and the all-consuming fire that raged within her. A fire only Cord could assuage. A need only Cord could meet. Her hands moved to unbutton his shirt, but, made clumsy by desire, her fingers refused to cooperate. With a frustrated cry, she gripped the sides of his shirt and tugged sharply. The buttons broke loose from their threads and flew to scatter in the tall grass.

Beyond caring, Faith knew only that Cord's bronzed chest was exposed to her view. She pressed her palms to the broad muscled expanse and moved them slowly over his tiny nipples and downward over his ribcage to his flat hard stomach.

Cord inhaled sharply as Faith's curious fingers reached his belt buckle. Struggling for control, he gritted his teeth and shrugged out of his shirt.

Cord moved back to sit on his heels and gaze down at Faith's nude form. Gently, he pulled her hands from his gunbelt and removed it himself. He laid it carefully within reach before he stood and quickly divested himself of his moccasins and pants.

Faith's heart fluttered rapidly in her chest as she looked up at Cord. He was magnificent. All smooth tanned skin, hard muscle and sinew, without a spare ounce of flesh. Her breath caught in her throat as her eyes fell on his throbbing manhood. He was the first man she had ever seen, but she knew in her heart that no other human could possible be his equal. She lifted her arms to him and he lowered himself into her embrace.

Then Cord was kissing her. Her lips, her throat, her breasts, all fell captive to the scorching heat of his lips. His hands caressed her gently. Her stomach, thighs and buttocks and even the warm secret place between her thighs.

Faith slid a hand between their bodies to boldly caress his manhood. She gasped sharply as the heat of him seared her palm. He was as hard as granite, as smooth as satin.

Faith cried out as Cord parted her thighs, one finger plunging deeply into her moist softness.

She arched against him as his mouth came down to cover hers, his thrusting tongue matching rhythm with his hand between her legs.

"Cord!" Faith's cry was filled with all the deep longing and hunger she felt.

"Shh, sweetheart, I'm here," Cord whispered thickly. "I know what you need. What we both need."

He moved over her and nudged her legs apart. He gripped her face in his hands and gazed into her eyes as, slowly, he entered her.

Faith felt a burning fullness between her legs and arched upward.

Cord's mouth descended on hers as he plunged forward, breaking the thin membrane that assured him he was her first.

Faith's cry of pain was muffled by Cord's ever deepening kiss. Then all thought of pain was forgotten as she felt the intensely pleasant fulfillment of their joining.

Cord raised his head to smile down at her. "You are truly mine now," he murmured. Then he was moving again, his hips working in a skillful rhythm that sent wave after wave of delicious pleasure surging through Faith.

She writhed beneath him, her arms encircling his neck, her hips lifting to meet his powerful thrusts. The pleasure was increasing, building, consuming her until she thought she would explode. Then she did. A magnificent, indescribable explosion of pure sensation as she clamped her legs around Cord's waist, her hips pressing upward against him as her neck arched back.

"I love you!" she cried out as Cord plunged into her one final time. A ragged cry escaped his lips as he threw his head back, his face tight with fulfilled passion. A last violent shudder racked his body and he collapsed onto his forearms, holding his weight from Faith as she grew limp beneath him.

Faith lifted a hand to gently caress his stubbled cheek. "I really do love you," she whispered hoarsely.

Cord turned his head to kiss her palm. "Ah, muñeca, I love you too. Beyond words. Beyond reason. We were meant to be together."

Darkness had fallen by the time Faith awoke. She lay alone on the grass, her nude body wrapped in a soft Indian blanket. She rolled onto her back and gazed up at the crescent moon and shimmering stars. The last she remembered, she had been lying in Cord's arms, his words of love echoing softly in her ears. She clutched the blanket to her breasts as she sat up.

Cord stood nearby. He had built a fire while Faith slept and she could see his features clearly in the flickering light. He had dressed once again in his shirt and pants. His gunbelt rested low on his hips. One corner of his mouth curved upward in a smile as he turned to Faith. "Hello, sleepyhead."

Faith's gaze fell on the black shirt he wore. Devoid of buttons, it hung open to display his magnificent chest. "So," she said softly. "It wasn't a dream."

Cord walked over to her and dropped to one knee. "No, muñequita," he agreed as he pulled her into his embrace, "not a dream."

Faith's arms encircled his neck. Rather than feeling awkward or embarrassed by what she and Cord had shared, she felt closer to him than ever. Making love with the bold, reckless McCamy brother had made her feel truly a part of him.

"I feel so close to you now," Faith voiced her feeling aloud.

"That is as it should be," Cord told her as he brushed the hair gently from her cheek.

Faith gazed up into the emerald pools of Cord's eyes. The tender emotions she read there caused her heart to catch in her throat. She laid her palm on his stubbled cheek.

Cord turned his head to lightly kiss her fingers. "Hungry?"

With a start of surprise, Faith realized that she was, indeed, very hungry. "Famished."

"How do beans and tortillas sound?"

"Right now, it sounds wonderful." Cord released her and Faith reached for her skirt. "I should get dressed."

"No." Cord's hand closed over hers. "I prefer you in your natural state."

Cord gripped the skirt and moved to toss it aside. As he lifted the garment, Faith's knife fell from the pocket. He stared at it for a moment, a strange, thoughtful expression on his face. He picked it up and gripped it lightly in his strong fingers. "Where did you get this?"

Faith shrugged. "I found it in an old trunk at the ranch. Why?"

Cord studied the knife for a moment longer. "Just curious," he replied as he handed it to her. "It's awfully small."

"Hey, don't insult my knife," Faith told him. "It saved my life."

Cord's brow creased in a frown. "Tell me."

"I think I would like to tell you." Faith suppressed a shudder as the memory of Buck's lust-crazed face filled her mind. "Will you hold me?"

Cord sat down next to her and pulled her into his lap. Silently, he enfolded her in his strong embrace.

As they sat together by the fire, Faith began to tell of her ordeal. She spoke haltingly at first, then faster as the story progressed until by the end her words were tumbling over each other in their haste to leave her mouth.

"Where was Arista?" Cord wanted to know. "Why didn't he protect you?"

"He arrived a few minutes after I had killed Buck." Faith pressed herself to Cord's hard chest. "It was so awful. I had actually killed a man and I was standing there all covered in blood and my blouse torn off, and, oh, Cord, I got sick. I couldn't help it."

Faith felt Cord stiffen. "Arista was there? He saw you?"

"Yes, I told you. He took me back to his house."

Abruptly, Cord set Faith aside and stood up.

Without a word, he began to walk toward the horses.

"Cord! Where are you going?"

"To do what I should have done in the first place. I'm going to kill Arista."

Drawing the blanket around herself like a cape, Faith scrambled to her feet. "But why? You've already given him a beating."

"Why?" Cord's eyes had turned to twin chips of green ice. "Not only did he allow your life to be in danger, he saw you. Damn it, Faith, he saw your breasts."

"For that you would kill him?" Faith asked, incredulous.

Cord's voice was edged in steel. "You are mine, Faith Jennings. Do you think I will stand for another man to see you? To put his hands on you? Let alone place your life in danger? I'll kill him like I should have killed Montez. Like I would have killed Montez if not for . . ."

Faith hurried forward and threw herself into Cord's arms. "It wasn't Arista's fault. I was in shock and didn't think to cover myself, and he had no way of knowing that Buck would assault me." She gazed up at him, her eyes wide. "Oh, Cord, I can't stand to be the cause of bloodshed."

"Damn it, Faith." Cord crushed her mouth beneath his own as they sank to the ground. He threw her blanket aside, and a moment later his clothes followed. This time Cord took her with a sweet, fierce possessiveness that seared her very soul and branded her for all time as his.

Faith accepted him with all the love and wanting she felt deep inside, enveloping him in her warmth and taking him for her own.

When Cord moved to lay beside her, Faith laid her head on his chest. "I'm still hungry," she teased.

"Don't change the subject," he said sternly. "I still plan to deal with Arista, but for your sake, I'll wait."

Faith lightly caressed Cord's hard stomach. "What do we do now?"

"Now, we go home and I kill Montez."

Chapter 22

Faith glanced over at Cord as they rode side by side across the dry Mexican countryside. Despite all the problems that lay ahead, she had never been happier. With Cord she had found a fulfillment, a completeness she had never dreamed possible.

They had risen early and eaten a simple breakfast. Afterward, Faith had sat cross-legged on her bedroll, content to sip coffee and watch Cord shave.

When Cord had removed the last of the lather from his face and turned to Faith, the look in his eyes had taken her breath away. The tin coffee cup had fallen from her hand, its contents soaking into the thirsty ground. The rest of the world had been forgotten as they came together beneath the early morning sky.

They had gotten a much later start than originally planned, but neither had complained. They had also decided it would be wisest to ride separate horses. Otherwise, they might never get home.

Cord felt Faith's eyes on him and gave her a reassuring smile. He didn't want to upset her, but something was wrong. He could feel it. It vibrated in the very air around him.

The terrain grew rockier and more treacherous as they entered a narrow canyon. Cord drew his horse to a halt and held up a hand in signal to Faith. He stared up at the steep canyon walls and felt a prickle along his spine. Here. The danger was here.

He dismounted and passed his reins to Faith. "Take cover behind those rocks at the mouth of the canyon," Cord instructed as he removed his rifle from the saddle scabbard.

Faith opened her mouth to protest, but Cord silenced her with a look. Without a word, she turned Dancer and rode toward the shelter of the rocks.

Once Faith and the horses had reached safety, Cord began to walk slowly forward, his rifle gripped lightly in his hands. After a few minutes he paused and looked upward. There, among the rocks.

A shot rang out, shattering the unearthly silence of the canyon. Cord threw himself to the ground and heard a second rifle slug strike the earth beside him. Raising himself up to a low crouch, he began to move along the base of the canyon wall.

"Damn it, McCamy!" a man's voice bellowed from the rocky ledge above. "Where's Luisa? What have you done with Luisa?"

Ross Fulton. Cord swore beneath his breath. He should have known.

"Where's my Luisa?" the ex-foreman bellowed again. "She was supposed to meet me in Cuervos."

Cord moved slowly along the canyon until he found what he was looking for. A way up. He felt a stinging sensation in his side as he began to climb the treacherous canyon wall, but he ignored the pain. Now was not the time for trivialities.

Faith stood beside the horses, the reins gripped tightly in her hand. What was going on? she wondered. Who or what was out there, and how had Cord known about it? She heard gunfire and stepped forward to peer around the cluster of boulders. She thought her heart would stop when she saw Cord drop to the ground, but he rose quickly and her breathing returned to normal. But a few moments later he rounded a curve in the canyon and disappeared from view.

Faith bit her lip, torn by indecision. Finally she realized she had only one choice. She ground-staked the horses and, holding her small knife—more for reassurance than protection value—made her way cautiously up the canyon.

Ross Fulton sat down on the ground within

his protective circle of rocks and began to reload his rifle. Goddamn that Cord McCamy! Where was he? Probably up to some no good injun trick. Well, he'd show that white savage a trick or two.

Fulton continued to mutter curses beneath his breath as he mopped the sweat from his reddened face. Once he had McCamy and the Jennings bitch out of the way he would find Luisa. He was convinced that his Luisa would be with him now if not for those interfering bastards at the Double J. He snapped his rifle closed and prepared to rise.

"Fulton."

Ross jerked around to see Cord standing above him. "McCamy!"

Cord held the rifle loosely at his side, the barrel pointed at the ground. "Give it up, Fulton. You haven't got a chance."

"Like hell!" The ex-foreman spun around, his finger depressing the trigger.

Cord dove, going into a roll as he raised his rifle and fired.

Faith froze when she heard the shots. Her eyes moved upward to the canyon rim. Where was Cord? She took a few panicked steps forward, then paused as a calm certainty descended over her. Cord was alive. She knew it. It was as simple as that.

Cord looked down at Fulton's still form and felt a great hollowness inside. Damn, but he was tired of the killing, of the seemingly endless trail of dead and dying he seemed to leave in his wake. He had found peace in only one place. In Faith's arms.

Faith watched as Cord climbed down the steep canyon wall. He moved as skillfully, as purposefully as a mountain lion. He dropped the last few feet and turned to Faith.

"Are you okay?" she asked.

He pulled her into his arms, almost crushing her with the force of his embrace. "I am now, muñequita," he replied softly. "I am now."

Chapter 23

Faith watched Cord surreptitiously from beneath her lashes as they drew their horses to a halt. It was nothing she could put her finger on, but something was wrong. Cord had not been himself since the confrontation with Ross Fulton. Now, here he was, stopping for the night, with at least a full hour left before dark.

Of course, Faith conceded, it was a lovely spot, with trees and grass and a shallow creek.

"Are you sure you're okay?" Faith asked as Cord dismounted.

Cord made no reply as Faith slid from her own horse, but she could see the tension in the tight set of his jaw.

Cord stood ramrod straight, one hand pressed to his side. He gazed calmly at Faith when she came to stand before him. "We'll make camp here."

Faith's eyes moved slowly over Cord, noting the stiffness of his stance and the hand pressed tightly to his side. Her eyes grew round with horror as she looked down and saw drops of ruby red blood drip slowly onto the toe of his moccasin.

"Cord!"

Cord gripped her chin between his thumb and forefinger and tilted her head back to gaze into her frightened eyes. Then his lips were on hers, his tongue moving sensuously in her mouth.

An almost desperate need consumed them both as they sank to the ground. Eager hands removed clothing as equally eager mouths melded and blended to send their passion soaring upward.

They made love as though there would be no tomorrow. Faith cried out as she arched against Cord, meeting his primitive need with an equal savagery.

"Faith," Cord groaned into her ear as he reached the heights of fulfillment. "Sweet Faith."

Faith clung to him, loath to release him even after they were both spent.

Cord raised himself onto his elbows and cradled her face in his hands. "You are so beautiful, and you're all mine. I'll be damned before I let anyone take you from me again. Ever." Having said his piece, he eased away from her and got to his feet. A moment later, Faith heard him splashing in the creek.

She stretched languorously, arching her back and lifting her arms over her head. With a sigh, she sat up, only to notice a strange stickiness on the front of her body. Faith looked down and felt herself grow pale. Blood was streaked liberally across her stomach and breasts. A great deal of blood. Cord's blood.

She turned quickly around to see Cord standing waist deep in the water. He was washing a wound in his side, turning the water a pale pink with his blood.

Faith was beside him in an instant, paying no heed to the iciness of the water. "Cord! Why didn't you tell me?" Her voice held a combination of accusation, concern and fear.

Cord turned to her, his face pale beneath his tan. "It was Fulton's first shot. Damn him. That first wild shot into the canyon."

When Faith pushed his hands aside to examine the wound, Cord caught her chin in his hand and tilted her head back to gaze into her face. "You're going to have to remove the bullet, Faith."

Faith saw the calm assurance in Cord's emerald eyes and nodded. "I know. I wish someone with medical experience were here, but for now, I guess I'm all you have."

Cord managed a smile. "You're more than enough."

"First things first," Faith said briskly. "Let's get you off your feet."

In a matter of minutes Faith had Cord

stretched out on a blanket in the shade of a tree and water boiling on the fire. She had donned her skirt and Cord's buttonless black shirt which she knotted beneath her breasts.

"Get the bottle of mescal from my saddle-bag," Cord instructed, "and my bowie knife."

Faith fetched the mescal for him, but eyed the huge knife with distaste. "I'll use my own knife," she announced as she retrieved the small weapon from her pocket. "Yours is too big for my hand."

"And yours is too damn small to remove a bullet," Cord returned.

Faith knelt beside him and placed a finger over his lips. "You worry about swallowing enough mescal to dull the pain, and I'll worry about the bullet," she said sternly, then added more softly, "trust me."

Cord did not appear pleased but he did at least seem less inclined to argue the point. He tilted the bottle of fiery liquid to his lips and drank deeply. "Get your knife," he instructed as he pressed the bottle into her hands. "Pour mescal over the blade and over my wound."

Faith took the raw liquor and did as she was bid.

Cord sucked his breath in sharply as the mescal was poured onto his open wound.

"Here." Faith passed him the bottle. "I have a feeling you're going to need this."

Cord tilted the bottle to his lips before he spoke. "Take your knife and follow the path made by the bullet until you reach it. Then dig it out."

Praying silently for a steady hand, Faith began to probe for the slug.

Perspiration rolled down Cord's pale face as he closed his eyes. His breathing was harsh, but otherwise he didn't make a sound.

Faith paused, thinking he had perhaps passed out.

"Go ahead," he said through clenched teeth, "you're doing fine."

Although she felt Cord's pain as her own, Faith set her jaw and continued with her task. She almost cried out with relief when she felt the tip of her blade touch the lead slug. She gripped the blood-slick knife even tighter as she began the delicate task of prying out the bullet.

She ignored the sweat that rolled into her eyes and the terrible fierce pounding of her heart to concentrate on the job at hand. She even managed to turn her mind from the quantity of blood that continued to seep from the wound. Cord was depending on her and she would not let him down.

After what felt like an eternity, Faith held the flattened, blood-covered slug in her hand. "It's out," she announced triumphantly.

Cord smiled weakly. "I knew you could do it, sweetheart."

"What now?" Faith asked.

But Cord had no reply. He was unconscious.

Chapter 24

"She is mine!"

Faith's head snapped up and she released her grip on Cord's shoulders. Why had he cried out? Had his fever worsened?

Shortly after he had fallen unconscious, Cord had grown feverish. And except to attend to the horses and build a fire, Faith had not left his side. She had spent the hours since dusk alternately bathing his body with cool cloths and attempting to hold him down when he thrashed about.

Cord's eyes flew open. Glazed with fever, they stared through Faith. "Damn it, Fierce Hawk! Their blood was mine!"

He was delirious, Faith decided as she placed a cool compress on his forehead. She had heard that fever sometimes had that effect on its victim.

Cord flung his arms wide, and Faith, fearing he would reopen his wound, spoke soothingly to him as she checked his bandage. She sighed with relief when she saw no sign of further bleeding. Damn it! She hated the feeling of helplessness. If only she had more medical knowledge, then perhaps she could arrest the fever that racked Cord's muscular frame.

Cord began to speak again, unintelligible mutterings in Spanish and English.

Frightened for his well-being, Faith stroked his brow and murmured comforting words in an effort to calm him.

"Angelique!" Cord's eyes blazed fever bright as he cried out. "I promised Angelique."

Faith was taken aback. Was Cord speaking of Angelique Jennings—Faith's mother? What could he possibly have promised her mother?

Lost in his own fevered world, Cord continued to speak. After a moment it dawned on Faith that he was no longer speaking English, or even Spanish. Her eyes widened in astonishment. He was speaking Comanche! She was sure of it! And even more surprising, Faith realized she could understand him. Not every word, but enough to know what he was saying.

Faith closed her eyes as a series of images began to flash through her mind. Not brief and incomprehensible as before, but vivid and full-blown. A violent throbbing began in her temples as her head was literally flooded with a montage of scenes.

Faith opened her eyes to gaze into Cord's face. His breathing was less labored. She lay a hand to his cheek and saw that he was cooler to the touch. "Oh, Cord," she said softly, "why didn't you tell me?"

With a sigh, Faith lay down beside him and rested her head on his chest. Her weary mind awhirl with discovery, she fell into a deep sleep.

Dawn had broken over the eastern horizon by the time Faith awoke. Yawning, she rose to her knees and placed a hand on Cord's brow. Thank God, his fever had broken. His skin was cool and damp with perspiration, his breathing deep and even, his sleep natural.

Faith kissed Cord lightly on the cheek before she rose to her feet and moved to throw more wood on the fire. Cord would be hungry when he finally woke up, she decided as she began to search through their supplies for coffee and dried beef.

She was opening Cord's saddlebag when she felt someone watching her. Expecting to find Cord awake, she turned around. Caught unawares, she was totally unprepared for the sight that met her eyes.

Standing on the creekbank was an Indian. His black waist-length hair was unbound except for the red bandana tied around his head. He wore a calico shirt, fringed buckskins and moccasins. In one hand he held the reins to a magnificent palomino stallion, in the other hand a rifle.

Her breath caught in her throat, Faith stared at the unexpected visitor. She closed her eyes and reopened them slowly as a crashing pain, like a dam bursting, began in her head. Then, with a cry, she began to run.

Her bare feet skimmed lightly over the dried grass and her hair flew out behind her like a silken banner as she ran—straight into the wild-looking Indian's arms.

Faith threw her arms around his neck and pressed her cheek to his shoulder as he dropped the rifle and reins to return her embrace.

She tilted her head back to smile into his ebony eyes. "Fierce Hawk," she said softly, "I'm so glad you're here."

PART TWO
— Little Shadow —

Chapter 25

Cord awoke to a dull throbbing in his side and the delectable smell of roasting meat in his nostrils. He opened his eyes slowly and gazed upward into the endless blue sky. "Faith?"

"Over here."

He turned his head and saw her kneeling by the fire. She was slowly turning a rabbit on a spit while Fierce Hawk sat nearby and cleaned his rifle.

Cord didn't so much as raise a brow in surprise. It was as though the unorthodox scene that greeted him was an everyday occurrence.

Faith rose to her feet and hurried to Cord's side. "How are you feeling?"

"I've been better," Cord returned drily.

Faith removed the bandage and examined his

wound. "It's healing nicely," she informed him. "Those herbs Fierce Hawk used really did the trick."

"How long have I been out?" Cord asked as he struggled to a sitting position.

"Lie still. About twenty-four hours."

"Where are my pants?" Cord demanded as he threw the blanket aside.

"Cord, will you please lie still?"

"No."

Despite Faith's admonishments and Fierce Hawk's amused expression, Cord insisted upon donning his pants and joining the two of them at the fire.

"You are feeling stronger?" Fierce Hawk asked as he passed Cord a portion of the meat.

Cord merely grunted.

Faith regarded Cord with a worried frown. She had never attended a gunshot victim before, but she was quite sure that he shouldn't be up and about yet. "I really think you should rest," she told him.

Cord's expression softened. "Trust me, muñeca. I've survived worse."

Faith was far from satisfied but she knew that further argument would prove futile. Reluctantly, she nodded.

"I believe," Fierce Hawk announced suddenly, "that Little Shadow has recalled her past."

Cord appeared unsurprised. "I assumed as much when I saw the two of you together."

"I don't remember everything," Faith said. "It's all fragmented and in need of sorting out." She looked at Fierce Hawk. "You were there."

Her eyes moved to Cord. "And so were you. Will the two of you help me to put all the pieces together?"

The two men exchanged glances.

"What is it you wish to know, Little Shadow?" Fierce Hawk asked.

"Everything! Why do you call me Little Shadow? How did my mother and I end up in the Comanche village? Why do I have memories of Cord being there? Tell me everything."

Cord felt a wrenching deep inside as he looked into the soft brown depths of Faith's eyes. The moment he had both dreaded and anticipated had arrived. By helping Faith recall her past, would he also be helping her to recall the pain and grief of that long-ago time? He turned to gaze into the fire as his face took on a faraway expression.

After a moment, he began to speak. "Matthew and I were only six years old when Matthew was struck with a fever. He was so sick that my parents were certain he was going to die. Mom was afraid I would catch the sickness too, so in an attempt to protect me, she sent me to the Double J to stay with Jeremiah, Tom and Angelique." Cord turned to Faith, his green eyes intensely bright in his pale face. "That's how it all began."

Six-year-old Cord was happy at the Double J. Of course, he missed his parents and brother, but his own home in Sonria couldn't begin to compare with the delights of the ranch.

Cord's father was a banker and, although a

kind man and good father, he wore a suit and tie every day instead of the cowboy boots and chaps that Cord so admired. Angelique was soft and sweet like his own mother, but she spoke with a French accent that was totally captivating to a young boy. She could also bake exotic French dishes and delicate pastries guaranteed to tempt the palate of a growing boy.

Jeremiah and Tom always had a few spare minutes for Cord too. Time to teach him rope tricks, lassoing and the all-important proper horse grooming.

The best part of the ranch, to Cord's young mind, was the corral and the beautiful horses. Cord loved all the horses and was forever begging Emily for sugar lumps and apples to feed them.

Cord had been with the Jenningses for a week when Angelique, fearing he would fret overmuch for his brother, decided to take the young boy on a picnic.

Angelique was huge with her advanced pregnancy, and Tom worried for his wife's safety.

"Don't be silly, darling," Angelique had chided her husband. "We will go only as far as the creek and we will take the buggy. We will even take a ranchhand along as a guard if it will make you feel better. What could be safer?"

Still uneasy, but unable to deny his beautiful young wife anything, Tom Jennings had relented.

The day of the picnic dawned bright and clear, Angelique, Cord and their escort Jim headed for the creek with their food-laden basket. They spread a blanket on the creekbank and dangled their feet in the clear cool water as they ate.

Cord was delighted. He had never seen a grown woman go barefoot before. As a matter of fact, he had never seen any grown-up like Angelique before. So happy and carefree. So willing to spend her time playing games or telling stories.

Angelique had just finished laughing at a remark Cord had made and turned to offer Jim another pastry when the man suddenly collapsed.

Cord froze and his eyes grew huge when he saw the arrow protruding from Jim's back.

Angelique clasped Cord's hand and struggled to her feet as swiftly as her rounded belly would allow, but it was too late.

They were surrounded by Comanche.

"He blames himself," Fierce Hawk said quietly.

Faith looked over at Cord's sleeping form. "He shouldn't."

Despite his protestations that he felt fine, Faith had finally convinced Cord to return to his bedroll. The loss of blood had left him weaker than he cared to admit.

Faith peered up at the night sky, the luminous moon and brightly twinkling stars. "It was no one's fault, not really."

Fierce Hawk grunted. "Your mother took Wind Rider for a picnic, therefore he feels he is to blame."

"He was a child."

Fierce Hawk merely nodded.

Faith looked at her newly remembered friend. Her eyes roamed lovingly over his dark, impassive face, hawklike nose and obsidian eyes. How could she have forgotten someone as dear to her as Fierce Hawk? And how on earth could she have forgotten her mother?

"Tell me about my mother."

"My people called her Hair-Like-the-Golden-Sunset," Fierce Hawk replied. "She was a beautiful woman. A strong woman. What more could you need to know?"

"More, Fierce Hawk. A great deal more."

Fierce Hawk was the first-born son of Brother-of-the-Eagle and Brother-of-the-Eagle's chief wife, Summer Sky. He was only a child when his father and the raiding party returned to the village with Angelique and Cord.

Fierce Hawk was proud that his father had been the one to capture the woman with hair the color of fire, and even more pleased when Brother-of-the-Eagle took the flame-haired woman as a second wife.

Cord was turned over to Long Knife, another member of the raiding party. Long Knife's wife, Rain Flower, had not been blessed with children and was more than happy to adopt the young boy.

Angelique was weary and homesick and longed desperately for her husband, but she knew her only hope of survival was to adapt as quickly as possible to her new surroundings. To keep herself sane, she concentrated on the forthcoming birth of her child.

Summer Sky was a small woman with huge brown eyes and a shy smile. She spent a great deal of time with the newly christened Hair-Like-the-Golden-Sunset, teaching her all she would need to know to make Brother-of-the-Eagle a good wife.

As the days slowly turned into weeks, a friendship slowly blossomed between Angelique and Summer Sky. Each woman had been surprised to discover qualities to admire and respect in each other.

Brother-of-the-Eagle was away from the village most of the time. When he was home he treated both women kindly, but Angelique could never bring herself to consider Brother-of-the-Eagle as her husband. Thomas Jennings was Angelique's husband. No one else. At least her ever-increasing stomach kept the Indian brave from making any sexual advances. But what if they weren't rescued by the time the child was born? Angelique refused to think about it. She would deal with the situation when and if it arose.

"When you were born, my father adopted you as his own," Fierce Hawk told Faith. "You are my sister."

"Adopted stepsister," Cord spoke up as he rose to a sitting position. "A distant relation at best."

Faith moved to sit cross-legged on the ground

next to Cord. "I'm proud to claim Fierce Hawk as my brother."

"What about me?" Cord cupped Faith's chin in his hand and looked into her eyes. "You have shared my blankets and I have proclaimed you as my wife. By Comanche custom we are married. Will you accept that?"

"Yes," Faith agreed without hesitation, "but as soon as everything is settled, I want a ceremony performed by the minister in Sonria."

Cord chuckled deep in his chest. "Fair enough."

Fierce Hawk rose silently to his feet. "Will you be strong enough to leave tomorrow, Wind Rider?"

Cord nodded. "I see no reason to wait."

Leave? Tomorrow? This was news to Faith. "Are we going home?"

"Not yet," Cord told her. "Fierce Hawk and I have some business to attend to first."

"Where?"

Cord's eyes met Fierce Hawk's briefly before he replied. "Devil's Crossing."

Chapter 26

The sky was heavy with stars and the sun still slept when Faith, Cord and Fierce Hawk set out for Devil's Crossing. Fierce Hawk rode ahead while Faith and Cord followed at a more leisurely pace.

Cord gazed up at the sky for a moment as they rode, then turned to Faith with a bittersweet smile. "Nights like this remind me of our childhood with the Comanche. It was not an unhappy time. In fact most of the memories are good ones."

Life for young Comanche boys was an idyllic existence. Their days were spent in games of horseback riding and hunting as they learned skills necessary for survival in the harsh and often brutal land. Late at night, the young men and boys of the tribe could often be found racing their ponies across the moon-washed plains.

Cord was homesick at first and grieved for his parents and twin brother, but as is the way of the very young, he adapted quickly. Only Angelique's steadfast influence kept Cord from completely embracing the Comanche way of life.

In due course, Angelique gave birth to a daughter. Brother-of-the-Eagle called the baby Topsannah, the Comanche word for flower, but Angelique named her Faith. To the young woman who had been so cruelly taken from her home and husband, her newborn daughter was a symbol of her faith. Faith that she, her child and Cord would all someday return home.

As for Cord, it was love at first sight. He took one look at the tiny, squalling, scrap of humanity known as Topsannah Faith and lost his heart.

The attraction soon became mutual. Faith loved her mother, but it was Cord she adored. The sight of the young boy brought gurgles of happiness to her lips as she eagerly lifted her chubby arms to him. On days when she was fretful, only Cord could soothe her. As soon as Faith learned to walk, she followed Cord everywhere, her short, plump legs working furiously to keep up with his longer stride.

As time passed, it was common to see Cord walking through the village with Faith on his shoulders, her sticky fingers twined in his hair, or to see her sitting in front of him on his Indian pony as he raced across the plains in a boyhood game. To Fierce Hawk, Faith gave a generous share of her love and devotion. To Cord, she gave her heart.

The people of the tribe began to call Faith "Little Shadow" for the way she followed closely behind her beloved Cord. Soon, everyone except Angelique forgot she had ever been called anything else.

Angelique never let the children forget who they really were and where they came from. She reminded Cord often of his family in Sonria and told Faith all about her father, grandfather and the Double J.

Angelique never forgot and she never lost faith.

Faith and Cord's reminiscence was cut abruptly short when Fierce Hawk turned his horse and rode back to join them. With a grunt and a gesture the Comanche warrior conveyed his message. They had reached their destination.

Devil's Crossing was a handful of adobe huts clustered together on the dry, parched flats. No trees nor even large cacti existed to offer shade to the village's few inhabitants. The only source of water was a town well. The only source of commerce, a crude cantina.

Faith turned from her position at the window of the adobe hut Cord had procured for them. The dwelling consisted of one room, about ten feet by twelve feet. The floor was hard-packed dirt, and the open windows had no covering. The door was a makeshift affair of gray warped boards on leather hinges. The furnishings consisted of a bed, a mattress and a rickety table with an oil lamp perched in the center.

"Why are we here?" Faith asked.

Cord sat on the bed, his back against the headboard, his legs stretched out before him on the mattress as he polished his six-shooter. "Because I'm going to kill Montez."

Faith moved to sit on the edge of the mattress. "Here?"

"Here, is a way station for half the gunslingers, bounty hunters, bank robbers and general lowlife of West Texas." Cord slid fresh cartridges into the chambers of his pistol and laid it within reach on the bed beside him. "Just before I left to search for you, Paco told me that Diego had gone into hiding. I can spend weeks tracking him, or we can spend a few days here and find out where he is."

Faith stretched out beside Cord and laid her head on his chest. "Do you have to kill him?"

Cord wrapped his arms protectively around her. "What do you think?"

Faith sighed. She knew there was no way to talk Cord out of killing Diego, but despite the fact that the scheming Montez deserved to die, the thought of his death by Cord's hand disturbed her. "I guess I'm just a little homesick."

"For where?" Cord asked in a strangely toneless voice.

"The Double J. Where else?"

Cord relaxed perceptibly. "I thought you might be homesick for New Orleans, or Paris or even New York City."

"Oh, no," Faith stated emphatically. "I had never felt at home anywhere until I came to Texas. I never want to leave."

Cord tightened his embrace. "I'll never allow you to leave me muñequita. You are mine."

"Where were you all the years we were apart?"

"A lot of different places."

Faith snuggled closely against him as he began to stroke her hair. "Did you ever think of me?"

"Only every day," Cord admitted. "Sometimes, late at night, I would look up into the sky and think, 'The same moon and stars shine for my Little Shadow. She is beneath the same sky as I.' It made me feel closer to you."

"I feel cheated that we were separated for so long."

"You were a child," Cord reminded her. "Jeremiah wanted the best possible life for you and he felt you would be better off with your Aunt Nicole. He lost his wife, son and daughter-in-law to Texas. He didn't want to lose you too. He was also afraid that the Double J might stir painful memories for you. Memories best left forgotten."

Faith tilted her head back to look into Cord's face. "Is that why you didn't tell me everything when I first arrived? Were you afraid the memories would upset me?"

"Emily and I went into town and talked it over with Doc Fogarty before you arrived. He told us that it would be best to keep quiet and let you remember on your own."

"I'm glad I remember," Faith said softly. "Even the bad part about Maman. It's better to remember than to have that awful blankness in my mind."

Cord held Faith tightly as she continued to talk. "I can see Maman as she looked that day. So young and beautiful. I see her now whenever I close my eyes."

It was a beautiful Indian summer day and eight-year-old Faith was sulking as only a child of that age can. Fierce Hawk and Cord had ridden out with the hunting party earlier in the week, and their refusal to take "Little Shadow" along had come as a blow to the young girl.

"You are older now," Angelique reminded her daughter as they walked side by side to the river. "Too old to follow Cord and Fierce Hawk everywhere."

Faith made no reply. Even though her mother had explained many times that she, Faith and Cord were not truly Comanche, it still bothered Faith that Angelique steadfastly refused to call her daughter Little Shadow or to refer to Cord as Wind Rider. After all, Cord had earned his name just as the other young braves had.

Angelique knelt by the river to fill her buckets, and Faith dropped to her knees beside her. "I wish my real father would come for us and take us home," Faith sighed wistfully. To her, the declaration was the equivalent of wishing on a star, for she had known no other life than that of a Comanche, and no other father than Brother-of-the-Eagle, whom she called "Ap," the Comanche term for father. To her young mind, Tom and Jeremiah were mythical creatures who inhabited some vague faraway land her mother called the Double J.

"We will go home someday," Angelique declared softly as she got to her feet, "but for now, we must return to the village. The men will be arriving soon and there will be much work to do."

They heard the noise before they reached the village. A confusion of gunfire, horses and screams. The air was thick with the acrid stench of spent gunpowder and dust stirred up by the charging horses.

Angelique and Faith rounded a bend in the path and came upon a scene of pure horror. Men on horseback rode helter skelter through the village gunning down every Comanche in their path. Faith screamed as she saw Fierce Hawk's mother, the gentle Summer Sky, shot down, the baby in her arms torn from her grasp and tossed aside like so much refuse. Old Gray Horse, the ancient white-haired brave who had spent many long hours telling stories to Faith and the other children, attempted to usher a group of toddlers to safety, but collapsed as a bullet pierced his heart.

"White men," Angelique breathed. She

dropped her buckets of water and ran forward into the midst of the marauding band. "No! Stop it!" she screamed. "You can't do this! It's murder."

A man leapt from his saddle and clutched Angelique by her upper arm. "Well, well, well," he drawled evilly. "Looks like we got us a white squaw here."

"Unhand me at once, filthy vermin," Angelique snapped. "My husband will kill you for this."

"I ain't askeered of no injun." The man laughed as he flung Angelique to the ground.

"Run, Faith!" Angelique screamed as she hooked her foot around the man's ankle and knocked him off balance. The man landed on his back in the dust with a force that shook the ground.

Terrified for the first time in her life, Faith ran to their tipi and ducked inside. Angelique scooted in behind her and clutched her small bone-handled knife in her hand. "Be a good girl and, no matter what happens, do not cry. Remember, Faith," she whispered. "I love you."

"Oh, Maman! I love you too. Where are Ap and Fierce Hawk and Wind Rider?"

Angelique backed up, placing Faith protectively behind her as the flap of their tipi was flung open and the same white man who had attacked Angelique moments earlier stepped inside.

"Whore!" he rasped. "I'll show you what a

white man feels like between your legs."

Angelique stabbed at him with her knife, but the man clasped her wrist and squeezed cruelly until the small weapon fell from her grasp. "Just for that, as soon as I'm through with you, I'll have a turn with that little half-breed bastard of yours."

Angelique fought like a wildcat, but her strength was no match for the vicious gunman. In an attempt to help her mother, Faith launched herself at the man, kicking, biting and scratching, but her mother's attacker merely backhanded the young girl with such force that she was knocked from her feet. Faith lay, half dazed, at the rear of the tipi while her mother was savagely raped.

When the man was finished he got to his feet, a satisfied smile on his face. "Well, little half-breed," he leered at Faith, "I reckon you're next, but first I better dispose of my leavings."

Angelique groaned softly as she turned her head to face her daughter. The agony and despair in her mother's eyes froze Faith's heart with fear.

With no more thought than he would give to stepping on an ant, the man drew his pistol and shot Angelique Dumont Jennings between the eyes.

The man took a step toward Faith. "Come on, little half-breed, and I'll pleasure you before you die."

Faith opened her mouth to scream, but no sound would come out.

"Aieee!" The cry shattered the stillness of the tipi as Wind Rider ran and launched himself at Angelique's murderer. The man was knocked to the tipi floor, and Cord made short work of slitting his throat. When Cord noticed Angelique's lifeless form, he took savage satisfaction in parting the man from his scalp too.

Cord unfolded a blanket and draped it over Angelique before he turned to Faith. "Are you all right, Little Shadow?"

Faith's eyes were as huge as saucers in her pale face as she gazed at Cord. His hands and chest were covered with blood from the dead man, and the still-dripping scalp dangled from his belt. It was just one more horror piled on top of the countless horrors the young girl had witnessed that afternoon. Stunned beyond comprehension by all that had passed, Little Shadow fainted.

When Faith regained consciousness she was outside, lying on a blanket beneath the late evening sun. Her mother's tipi was gone, as was her mother's body and that of the attacker. Faith sat up and saw that the carnage of the afternoon had been cleared away. The men had returned too late to save the majority of the women and children, but at least they had killed their white attackers.

Cord and Fierce Hawk approached her, and Faith silently reached for Cord. Already, the events of that day, along with everything that had passed previously in Faith's life, were receding into a safe and comfortable blankness.

Cord knelt before her and stretched out his hand. In his palm lay Angelique's small bone-handled knife. "It is all that is left of your mother," he said.

Silently, Faith tucked the knife in her belt.

Cord lifted the young girl into his arms and turned to Fierce Hawk. "Little Shadow and I are leaving. We are going home."

"You are home," Fierce Hawk returned. "My father has lost both his wives today. Summer Sky and Hair-Like-the-Golden-Sunset have gone to the Great Spirit, as well as my infant brother. He will not allow you to take Little Shadow away."

"I have no choice. Hair-Like-the-Golden-Sunset is dead, and I must fulfill her wish to reunite Little Shadow with our true people."

"We are your true people, Wind Rider, but I think I understand how you feel." Fierce Hawk gazed thoughtfully out over the plains. "What of Long Knife, your father?"

"I have spoken to him. He is not pleased, but like you he understands."

"Take care, my brother," Fierce Hawk said solemnly, "and take care of my sister. I will speak to Ap."

With Faith held firmly in his arms, Cord turned and walked toward his horse. They were going home.

Cord gazed out the window of the Devil's Crossing hut as he gently stroked Faith's silken hair. She had drifted into slumber with her head on his shoulder, one arm draped loosely across his waist. She looked so beautiful, so vulnerable, that Cord had no desire to disturb her.

He kissed her lightly on the temple. He knew she was reliving the pain and grief of her mother's violent death, but he also felt that she was coping with the return of her memory with admirable aplomb.

Cord knew how she felt. He had been dealing with memories of his own.

Angelique sat cross-legged on the ground in front of her tipi as she watched Faith play with the other young children. She saw Cord approach and signaled to him.

"Good morning, Hair-Like-the-Golden-Sunset," he greeted her.

Angelique nodded, her expression serious. "Cord, could I speak to you for a moment?" She spoke English, as she always did whenever she was alone with Cord or Faith.

"Of course." Cord dropped to the ground to sit beside her.

"Lately," Angelique began, "I have been having some strange feelings. What some would call a premonition." She paused for a moment before continuing. "I will never see Tom or the Double J again."

Cord frowned. "You have had a vision?"

"No. I speak only of my feelings." Angelique smiled sadly. "I want to ask a favor of you, Cord. A very important favor. One I want you to consider carefully."

Cord nodded. He had never before heard such a sad, resigned note in Angelique's voice.

"Faith is my only child and I love her more than life itself," Angelique said. "And you, Cord, have been like a son to me. If something should happen to me, I want you to take care of Faith. I know you love her and I know you will always do what is best for her. I won't ask you for miracles, but if someday the opportunity arises, please take Faith and return home. To our true home. Go back to the Double J. To Sonria."

"I promise you that I will always take care of Little Shadow," Cord said with all the solemnity of his fifteen years. "But I think you are wrong. Nothing will happen to you. You, Faith and I will someday return home together."

The conversation was brought to an abrupt halt when Faith spied her two favorite people. She left her playmates and hurried over to leap into Cord's lap. "Wind Rider," she squealed. "I have not seen you all day."

"Such a long time," he teased as he tugged one of her long braids.

"Faith." Angelique clasped one of her daughter's hands. "There is something I want you to remember."

"Yes, Maman?" Faith's expression grew serious. She knew by the tone of her mother's voice that she was speaking of something important.

"I want you to remember that you can trust Cord. No matter what happens, you can always trust Cord."

Faith turned first to Cord, then to her mother.

"Yes, Maman," she agreed.

Angelique nodded, satisfied. Two weeks later she was dead.

After Angelique's death Cord had been determined to fulfill his promise to take Faith home. He had been only six years old when he and Angelique had been captured, so had only a vague idea of where Sonria and the Double J were located. But the Comanche had taught him well. As long as he knew the general direction in which to ride, he was confident of finding the way.

Cord's hunting and tracking skills were well honed, so he and Faith ate well during the journey. He could ride endlessly all day, then lead the horse on foot after darkness fell. Their passage was swift and silent, and they left no sign to mark their path.

Cord's only concern was for Faith. Always a happy, talkative child, she had grown strangely silent since her mother's death. She would eat the food Cord gave her, drink the water, ride, walk and sleep, but she made no sound. She would only stare at Cord with wide, blank eyes until he sometimes wondered if she even recognized him.

They arrived on Jeremiah's doorstep late one evening. Despite some trepidation on Cord's part, Jeremiah had taken one look at the weary young travelers and cried out with joy. "She is the image of Tom," Jeremiah had exclaimed as he reached for Faith.

Taken from the familiar comfort of Cord's arms, Faith began to scream. She looked at the man who was her grandfather and saw only a white-skinned stranger. Hysterically she struggled against him and hurled Comanche curses at his head. Hurt and disappointed, Jeremiah relinquished his only grandchild to Cord's care. Cord held her, murmuring soft Comanche phrases until she drifted into sleep.

When Cord and Jeremiah were finally able to talk, Cord was sent reeling by the news that his parents had moved away. They had given their son up for dead and returned East.

Jeremiah had to cope not only with a granddaughter who was frightened of him, but with the death of a daughter-in-law whom he had loved as his own child. To add to his sadness, his son, Tom, had died of snakebite the year before while out on one of his frequent searches for his beloved Angelique.

Emily and Jeremiah tried to make friends with Faith, but she would allow no one except Cord to come near her.

Finally, at a loss, Jeremiah had taken the two young people to New Orleans. Faith had looked at Nicole, who with her auburn hair and soft gray eyes was so much like Angelique, and allowed her aunt to care for her.

After a few days, Faith began to speak, broken phrases in Comanche and English. Careful questioning by Cord and Nicole soon revealed that Faith's memory was gone—locked away in the deep recessess of her eight-year-old mind.

DiAnna June

Once Faith was settled in with her aunt, Jeremiah had personally escorted Cord to his new home. Cord, remembering his promise to Angelique, had not wanted to leave Faith, but Jeremiah had convinced him that for the time being Faith would be better off with her Aunt Nicole.

Jeremiah had decided something else as well. A decision he told no one about. He would not allow Faith to return to Texas. He loved his granddaughter too much to allow her to return to a place that held so many terrible memories. Memories best left forgotten.

The McCamy family had been overjoyed to see their long-lost son, but Cord found himself no longer comfortable in their presence. For one thing, he had acquired younger sisters during his absence. Sisters who were complete strangers to him. He felt awkward sleeping in a bed and eating meals in a formal dining room. Even the clothing he was expected to wear felt stifling and uncomfortable to him.

He also missed Faith. He felt guilty about leaving her with Nicole even though he knew it was the best place for her. But as badly as he wanted to see her, he would not journey to New Orleans. He was a part of her past. A painful past he had no wish to resurrect for his "Little Shadow."

For his parents' sake, Cord stayed with them for three years. On his eighteenth birthday, he shook hands with his father, kissed his mother goodbye and headed west. To find his destiny.

Chapter 27

Cord had changed clothes. Gone were the famil- iar moccasins, buckskin pants and worn faded shirt. In their place he wore high-heeled boots, black pants, black shirt and black silk bandana. With his black Stetson on his head and gleaming revolver at his hip, he presented the very image of a dangerous gunslinger.

"Why can't I go with you?" Faith demanded as Cord headed for the door of their hut.

"Because the Devil's Crossing cantina is no place for you," Cord explained patiently, "or any other woman."

"But, your wound," Faith reminded him. "Are you certain you're up to this?"

"It's almost completely healed and you know it." An edge of exasperation was beginning to creep into Cord's voice. "Just wait here and be patient. Fierce Hawk will be outside if you need anything. I won't be long."

Faith watched him leave, then turned and sat down on the bed. She had been waiting for Cord most of her life. She could wait a little longer.

The interior of the cantina was cool and dimly lit. No tables or chairs graced the earthen floor. Rough-hewn benches provided the only seating. The bar was a haphazard affair of warped boards, and the only liquid refreshment available was fiery pulque.

Cord cast a wary eye about the room as he entered. Two Mexicans straddled one of the benches, playing poker with a dog-eared pack of cards. A large-bellied gringo dozed on a bench in the corner, his legs stretched out in front of him, his head against the wall. The hat the man had placed over his face did nothing to muffle his loud snores.

The bartender dozed behind the bar where a plump senorita sat with a bottle in her hand. She smiled lazily as Cord approached.

"Parker?" Cord asked her, ignoring the sour stench of her unwashed body.

The senorita's gaze raked Cord's form boldly, but when she saw no flicker of interest in his green eyes she shrugged. "In the corner, senor. Sleeping it off."

Cord seized a chipped earthenware pitcher of water from the bar and approached the sleeping man. Carefully he removed the revolver from the man's holster and tucked it into his own belt.

He removed the man's hat and dumped the entire contents of the pitcher onto the man's face.

"What the hell?" The rudely awakened man jumped to his feet, his hand automatically dropping to his empty holster.

"Hello, Parker."

The man's eyes narrowed in his beefy face. "McCamy!" he spat as he cast his glance about the room. The cantina's other inhabitants had mysteriously disappeared. Having anticipated a confrontation between Parker and the newcomer, they had wisely vacated the premises. Parker turned back to Cord. "What are you doing here?"

"I need information." Cord returned the disgruntled Parker's gun to him. "And you're going to give it to me."

Parker swiped at his lips with the back of his hand. "First let me get a drink," he grumbled, "then I'll see what I can do."

Cord nodded toward the board structure that dominated one wall of the small cantina. "The bar's open."

Parker ambled behind the bar and uncorked a fresh bottle of pulque. He drank deeply and wiped his mouth on his sleeve before addressing Cord. "What is it you need to know?"

"I'm looking for Diego Montez."

Parker's hand trembled visibly as he tilted the bottle to his lips again. He sat down heavily on a bench before turning one red-rimmed eye to Cord. "I've heard some talk. None of it good."

Cord grasped the bottle and pulled it from Parker's grip. "Suppose you tell me what you've heard."

Fierce Hawk stepped inside the door of the adobe hut. "Are you all right, Little Shadow?"

"Yes." Faith smiled at the tall Comanche. "I'm fine. Just a little worried about Cord."

"Do not worry for Wind Rider," Fierce Hawk said as he moved forward. "He can take care of himself."

Faith stood up and walked to the window. She gazed out into the inky night blackness for a moment before asking the question that had plagued her since the return of her memory. "Where is Ap?"

"Brother-of-the-Eagle is nearby. A few days' ride from here," Fierce Hawk answered solemnly. "Someday, I will take you to him, but not now. Times are not good for the Comanche. A great unrest sweeps the land, and our father has much to do to prepare our people." Fierce Hawk joined Faith at the window and laid a comforting hand on her shoulder. "Rest assured, my sister, that you are always in his heart and mind."

"As he is in mine," Faith replied. "Tell me, Fierce Hawk, have you a wife and children?"

"No. I have not yet met a woman who enflames my soul—as you enflame Wind Rider's." Fierce Hawk gripped Faith's shoulders and turned her toward the bed. "Go to sleep, Little Shadow. It may be hours before Wind Rider returns. I will be nearby." He turned and walked away to disappear into the darkness beyond the door.

With a weary sigh, Faith stripped out of her clothes and crawled into bed. She leaned forward to blow out the lamp before sinking back into the pillows. In moments, she was asleep.

Faith sat up with a start, blinking rapidly in the darkness as she felt the mattress move beneath her. "Cord?"

"Shh, muñequita, it's only me." Cord slid beneath the covers and pulled her into his arms. "We've never made love in a bed before."

Faith pressed herself against him and was not surprised to discover that he was as naked as she.

"Your wound?" Faith asked, but her arms were already twining about his neck, her lips blazing a fiery trail along the column of his throat.

"To hell with my wound," Cord growled as his mouth captured hers.

Faith moaned deep in her throat as Cord's tongue plunged into her mouth. He tasted of pulque, tobacco and sweet hot desire.

Their hands and mouths roamed at will, seeking and giving pleasure as, together, they discovered anew the delights of their shared love and passion.

When their desire had reached a fever pitch, Cord rolled to his back and pulled Faith on top of him. "Take me inside you, muñequita," he groaned. He positioned Faith astraddle him and thrust his hips upward, enveloping himself in her warmth.

Faith cried out as bolt after bolt of sheer pleasure surged through her. She arched her spine and threw her head back. Her nails dug furrows in Cord's shoulders as he plunged deeply within her. Moaning softly, she began to move her hips in a sensual rhythm that drove Cord almost to the brink.

With a savage growl, he grasped Faith's waist and turned over, pulling her beneath him for the final few thrusts that would send them both flying to the pinnacle.

When it was over, Faith snuggled, breathless, in Cord's embrace.

"I love you, Faith," Cord said simply.

"And I love you, Cord. I always have and I always will."

Content and sated, they slept.

Chapter 28

Immaculately attired in a black Spanish-style suit with silver trim, Diego Montez paused in the entranceway to peruse the crowded room. Despite the lackluster decor of the hotel dining room, it was apparently a popular spot, for every table was occupied.

After a moment, Diego spied the party he was seeking. He approached their table and shook hands with both men. "Senor Rothschild, Senor Montgomery. It was good of you to meet me."

"Happy to oblige," Montgomery boomed in his overloud voice. "Join us, won't you?"

The heavy-jowled Englishman had his napkin tucked into his shirt collar and was using his knife and fork to energetically attack the thick steak on his plate.

"Would you care to order?" Rothschild asked politely.

Diego shook his head. "No, thank you." The smell of rancid grease that permeated the air effectively robbed him of his appetite. He sat down in the empty chair as Rothschild shrugged his thin shoulders.

"You caught us just in time, old chap." Owen Montgomery waved his knife in the air to emphasize his words. "We're leaving for New Mexico in the morning. We have a lead on some property there."

"What about my ranch?" Diego asked.

"Lovely place. Just lovely," Montgomery mumbled around a mouthful of steak.

"As we have already explained to you, Senor Montez," Rothschild said primly, "your ranch is not large enough to satisfy our clients."

"Combined with the Double J, it should be more than adequate," Diego returned.

"Quite, quite," Montgomery agreed, "but as of yesterday, you did not own the Double J, and it is our understanding that the woman who does own it has no desire to sell."

Beneath his cool exterior Diego was seething with suppressed outrage. Surely McCamy and the Jennings bitch were dead by now. If he could only stall these two English buffoons for a few more days. "I will be the Double J's owner very soon," Diego said in a carefully controlled voice. "After all, I am the rightful heir."

"So you say, old man." Montgomery patted his thick lips with his napkin. "But we haven't the time to dilly dally. Our clients, being of the nobility and all, will brook no delays on our part. They have a desire to own an American cattle ranch, and we have been entrusted to find the best available property in the minimum amount of time."

"My property is the best," Diego insisted.

"I say, you're beating a dead horse, aren't you, my good man?" Rothschild sniffed. "We cannot pay you for a ranch you don't own."

"I'll have the ownership papers by the end of the week," Diego promised rashly.

"Well, why didn't you tell us that straight off," Montgomery boomed. "That's a different story entirely."

"I'll tell you what we'll do, Montez," Rothschild offered. "Owen and I will just pop over to New Mexico and give the property there a good look. We'll return here by the middle of next week. If, as you say, you own both ranches, then we will be more than happy to talk business."

"Capital idea, simply capital." Montgomery nodded enthusiastically. "I say, would you gents care for dessert?"

"I've grown quite fond of American apple pie," Rothschild said. "Why don't we have a slice?"

Montgomery signaled for the waiter, and Diego reluctantly agreed to join the men for dessert.

"Did Senorita Alvarez accompany you?" Montgomery asked as he forked himself a huge bite of pie. "Wonderful girl, just wonderful."

Rothschild's eyes lit up. "Yes. Quite an enjoyable piece. The best I've had in America so far."

"The girl or the pie?" Montgomery queried.

Both men laughed raucously at their joke while Diego smiled thinly. The other restaurant patrons turned to frown disapprovingly at the guffawing Englishmen.

Diego rose to his feet. "If you gentlemen will excuse me, I have business matters to attend to."

"Of course, of course," Montgomery said. "We'll see you next week."

"Please tell Miss Alvarez that we send our regards," Rothschild said.

The comment sent both Englishmen into new and louder gales of laughter. They slapped each other on the back merrily as Diego made a hasty exit from the dining room.

Diego was barely able to contain his rage as he mounted the stairs to his room. Montgomery and Rothschild were nothing but ignorant buffoons, hirelings of upper-crust English nobility. The only thing that kept him from killing the two fools was the fact that, at the moment, they controlled a healthy amount of their employer's money. Money that Diego lusted for. After the sale of the ranches had been completed, perhaps he could arrange a convenient "accident" for the two Englishmen.

He entered his room and slammed the door shut behind him. With quick jerky movements, he removed his jacket and tossed it onto the bed. He poured himself a drink from the bottle on his dresser, then crossed the room to gaze out the window and into the dusty street below.

Diego knew he had been drinking too much lately, but he didn't care. Godforsaken place. Who could blame him for turning to the bottle? He would be glad to leave America and all things American far behind.

He continued to gaze moodily out the window as he refilled his glass. What did it take to rid himself of that one small thorn in his side, Faith Jennings? Surely this time he had pulled it off.

The bitch should have died in the first attempt his hired guns had made on her life. Instead, thanks to that damned guard dog McCamy, she had only received a scratch and Diego's men had been found dead. The recipients of Comanche justice. And then McCamy had had the unmitigated nerve to threaten *him*. With a knife, no less.

When Diego had then turned his attention to ridding the world of one Cord McCamy, every attempt had backfired.

Diego congratulated himself on one major achievement despite the McCamy brothers' interference. He had lured Ross Fulton to his side, thanks to Luisa. Poor Ross had believed Luisa's lies as easily as Luisa had believed Diego's.

The latest takeover plan—Diego's last desperate gamble—was bound to pay off. He was certain of it. He had been assured that the mysterious "Arista" was very good at this sort of thing. And to be on the safe side, Diego had put Dorsey and Sykes on McCamy's trail too. Not to mention his ace-in-the-hole, Ajax Killian, who was ready, willing and eager to do his part. For a price, of course.

Diego had a veritable army of hired killers in his employ. He was taking no more chances.

With a muttered curse, Diego set the whiskey aside and retrieved his jacket. The raw liquor had done nothing to dampen the fires of his anger. He needed something or someone on which to vent his rage.

He placed his flat-brimmed hat on his dark head and exited his room, in search of whichever unfortunate prostitute he chanced to find first.

Chapter 29

"Wake up, sleepyhead." Cord bent to kiss Faith's slightly parted lips. "I've brought breakfast."

Faith opened her eyes and smiled up at Cord. "Did you say breakfast? I'm starved."

With a laugh, Cord straightened and delivered a pat to Faith's temptingly rounded derriere. "Then get out of bed before it gets cold."

The ancient bed creaked and groaned as Faith slid from beneath the covers. Cord had salvaged a couple of rickety chairs from somewhere and had placed them at the hut's wobbly table. He offered a seat to Faith, then took the other for himself.

Faith took a bite of the fluffy, delicately spiced eggs and still-warm tortilla. "Where on earth did you get this? It's delicious."

"From Senora Garcia, an old woman at the edge of town. She makes a fairly decent living by cooking for the drifters who pass through Devil's Crossing." Cord pushed his empty plate aside. "She's a little strange, but a damned fine cook."

Faith polished off the last of her eggs. "When do we leave here?"

"Tomorrow if things go as well as I expect."

Faith sighed happily. "It will be wonderful to be home again. I bet Emily and Paco have been frantic."

"It will only be wonderful after Montez is dead," Cord informed her.

"What could he have hoped to accomplish by this latest fool scheme of his?" Faith wondered aloud.

"Our deaths, sweetheart."

"Well, it seems like an awful lot of trouble to me. Why didn't he just ride onto the ranch and shoot us both?"

"Too many witnesses," Cord replied. "He would've had to kill everyone on the ranch to escape detection. Even Leroy Hobbs couldn't cover up that many murders."

"Diego certainly is hell-bound and determined to own the Double J," Faith said. "And only he knows for what sinister reasons."

"I wish I could have talked to Jeremiah just once more before he died," Cord said. "He was wary of Diego from the first moment they met. Perhaps he could have shed a little more light on the situation."

"Granddad was a good judge of character. Oh!" Faith's eyes grew round and she sat up straighter in the splintery chair. "With everything that's happened, I completely forgot. Did you know that several pages are missing from Granddad's appointment book?"

"No. Do you think it means anything?"

"I don't know." Faith released a frustrated sigh. "I do know that Granddad was very meticulous with his notebook. It just doesn't make sense for an entire week's worth of pages to be missing. Especially since it was the week just before his death."

Cord turned his head to gaze thoughtfully out the window for a moment before turning back to Faith. "Jeremiah knew he was dying."

"What?"

"Doc Fogarty told him. Jeremiah's heart was simply worn out. He knew his time was short, so maybe he had personal reasons of his own for disposing of those pages."

"I didn't know."

"Jeremiah didn't want you to know."

Fierce Hawk arrived a few moments later. He stood in the doorway and motioned for Cord to join him outside.

Cord brushed a kiss on Faith's cheek. "I'll be back soon."

The two men carried on a quick, mumbled conversation outside the door, then Cord hurried away.

Fierce Hawk entered the adobe hut. "Good morning, Little Shadow."

"Good morning. Where was Cord going in such a hurry?"

Fierce Hawk merely shrugged.

Faith shook her head. She should have known she would receive no answers from the Comanche warrior. "Have you eaten?"

A barely perceptible smile tugged at the corner of Fierce Hawk's mouth. "Yes. I had my meal early. While some still slept."

Faith laughed softly. "Do you think we could go for a walk? I'm growing heartily sick of this house."

Fierce Hawk hesitated for a moment, then nodded. He motioned for Faith to proceed out the door ahead of him.

There wasn't much to see in the village of Devil's Crossing. Just dust and adobe dwellings. A couple of tired-looking dogs, a few mangy burros and more dust. Still, Faith enjoyed being outside.

The noonday sun had reached its zenith by the time Faith and Fierce Hawk arrived at the end of the dusty, rutted lane that wound through the village. A small adobe house reposed there, set slightly apart from the other buildings, with the word *alimento*, Spanish for food, scratched above the door.

"This must be where Cord bought breakfast," Faith said. She reached into her skirt pocket and withdrew some coins. "Why don't we go in and buy our lunch while we're here?"

"Go ahead, Little Shadow," Fierce Hawk said. "I will wait here."

Faith stepped inside the doorway, then paused, blinking in an effort to adjust to the dim light. "Senora Garcia?"

Faith strained her eyes in the darkness until she saw a very plump gray-haired woman seated at a wooden table. "I would like to buy some food."

"Sit, child, sit." Senora Garcia motioned to an empty chair across the table. "Drink some water. It is very hot, is it not?"

"Yes, ma'am," Faith agreed as she took the offered seat. "My husband bought our breakfast from you this morning. You're a wonderful cook."

"Gracias." The woman passed Faith a tin cup of water. "Your husband is Senor McCamy?"

At Faith's affirmative nod, Senora Garcia smiled broadly. "Senor McCamy is very handsome, very virile. He will give you many beautiful babies."

Faith was at a loss as to how to reply to the older woman, but fortunately Senora Garcia didn't seem to require one. Without warning, she reached across the table and seized one of Faith's hands in her plump fingers.

"Do not fret, child," she said. "I am but a harmless old woman."

Faith had stiffened at the contact, but now she relaxed. Senora Garcia certainly appeared harmless enough. "Are you a fortune teller?"

The old woman shrugged. "Sometimes God gives you a gift. Sometimes he gives you more than one. I have received two such gifts. My talent for cooking is one. Second sight is the other."

"What do you see?" Faith asked as Senora Garcia studied her palm. Faith had never been certain whether she believed in such things or not, but she did try to be open-minded about it.

Senora Garcia frowned in concentration. "You have suffered much, child, but you have also known much happiness. One thing balances the other. Sí."

"Sí," Faith agreed.

"Now your heart is filled with happiness and love, but you must beware, for a dark shadow looms on the horizon." Senora Garcia looked deeply in Faith's eyes. "You are loved by many, but you are also deeply hated by one who covets what you possess. I am afraid that more trouble awaits you."

Despite the heat of the day, Faith felt chilled. Everything the elderly woman had said had hit very close to home.

Senora Garcia released Faith's hand and rose laboriously to her feet. She moved to her corner work table and wrapped several tortillas in a cloth. "For your meal," she told Faith as she placed the package in her hands.

Faith stood and passed the woman some coins. The money instantly disappeared into the pocket of her voluminous apron.

Faith turned to leave, but Senora Garcia laid a staying hand on the younger woman's arm. "Be careful, child. Stay close to your husband, listen to him, and the evil cannot harm you."

Faith nodded, mumbled her thanks and hurried out the door. The conversation with the elderly cook and fortune teller had left her with a decidedly odd feeling.

"What took so long?" Fierce Hawk demanded.

"Senora Garcia wanted to talk for a while. That's all."

Fierce Hawk merely grunted, but the look he gave her was piercing.

Cord was waiting for them when they returned to their small adobe dwelling. He pulled Faith into his arms and kissed her gently before turning to Fierce Hawk. "Tomorrow," he said, "we head for home."

Chapter 30

Nicole de Beauharnais entered the lobby of the posh San Antonio hotel in a flurry of lavender silk. Vibrantly beautiful, with auburn hair and alabaster skin, she gave scant notice to the men who turned to watch her passage.

Nicole had eyes for only one person, the man who had just descended the elegantly curved staircase. She hurried forward and clasped the visitor's hand. "It is so wonderful to meet you at last," she exclaimed, "but come along. We must hurry."

She tugged the man in the direction of the exit. "We haven't much time."

Emily Stubbs gazed out the door at the eerily silent ranchyard. "What do you think?" she asked her two companions.

Paco and José exchanged glances. "I'm not sure," Paco replied. "All of the ranchhands appear to have left during the night."

"Montez is behind it," José declared. "He has to be."

Emily nodded grimly. "Whatever it is that's going on, it doesn't look good for us."

"Paco and I turned all the horses loose from the stables and upper corral," José said. "We'll play hell catching them, but if trouble's coming, I don't want the horses in the middle of it."

"Paco." Emily turned to the handsome young vaquero. "You'll find plenty of guns and ammunition in the ranch office. I suggest you bring all the firepower you can carry into the parlor." She turned to look out the door once again. "I think we had best be prepared. I have a feeling that time is not on our side."

Diego Montez tossed back yet another shot of whiskey, then slammed the empty glass onto the table top. The strong liquor had done nothing to lessen his determination or his anger.

He cursed softly beneath his breath as he thought of Cord McCamy. If not for the fiery-tempered fast gun, Diego would now be the owner of two huge cattle ranches.

Impatiently, Montez sprang to his feet and consulted the antique gold timepiece in his pocket. Damn it all! Time was running out.

Fierce Hawk boosted Faith into the saddle. "Won't you reconsider and come with us?"

Faith asked him.

"No. It is time I returned to my people." He gave Faith's hand a brief squeeze. "Remember, my sister, I will never be far away."

Cord galloped up to join them. He drew his horse to a halt and leaned down to clasp Fierce Hawk's hand in farewell. "Good-bye, old friend."

"Until next we meet, my brother," Fierce Hawk returned.

"Let's ride," Cord said as he turned to Faith. "We can't afford to waste time."

PART THREE
Faith

Chapter 31

Cord drew his horse to a halt and dismounted. He signaled for Faith to remain behind, then continued on foot to the top of the hill.

They had ridden onto Double J land in the predawn hours and had arrived on the low hill overlooking the ranchhouse just as the first rays of sunlight were beginning to streak the sky.

Cord took cover behind a clump of trees and observed the scene below him for several moments before returning to Faith. "Something's going on down at the ranchhouse," he informed her. "It's too damn quiet."

As though to belie Cord's words, a sudden volley of gunfire erupted from the direction of the house.

Cord hurried back up the hill and took another look. "Damn," he swore, "the house is surrounded by gunmen. They must have been inside the stables when I looked before." He slid down the rise and swung into the saddle. "Just lean down low in your saddle," he told Faith as he reached out to grab her reins.

Cord clasped the reins to both his horse and Faith's in one hand and removed his rifle from the saddle scabbard with the other. "Stay low," he snapped as he spurred the horses into a run over the crest and down the hillside.

They charged headlong through the ranch-yard, Cord firing his rifle one-handed as hot lead whizzed past them from all sides.

Cord did not pause when they reached the courtyard but rode through the gate, right up to the French doors of the parlor. He leapt from the saddle and threw an arm around Faith to lift her from her horse and into the house.

"Cord, Dona Faith!" Paco exclaimed. "Welcome home."

José was more practical. He tossed a loaded rifle into Faith's hands as he said his hellos.

"Remind me to give you both a big hug later," Emily told them as she wearily moved to reload her rifle. "If we live that long."

"How long has this been going on?" Cord asked as he knelt by the front window and shot at a man who had taken cover behind the watering trough.

"Since yesterday morning," Paco replied, then ducked as a bullet pinged off the window frame near his head. "We've managed to hold them off so far, but I *am* grateful for reinforcements." Paco grinned as he turned and began to fire into the ranchyard.

"What do they want?" Faith asked as she joined Emily and José at the courtyard windows.

"To kill everyone," Emily answered with a sigh, then turned and fired several rounds at a man who was attempting to climb over the courtyard wall. The man clutched his shoulder as he fell back. "Winged him," Emily crowed triumphantly.

"Apparently Don Diego's ultimate solution is to simply murder us all," José explained as he reached for fresh ammunition. "Then, with the help of Sheriff Hobbs, he can move right in."

"Where are the ranchhands?" Cord asked as he fired out the window at a man who was making a bold dash for the house. The slug caught the gunman between the eyes and lifted him off the ground before he collapsed.

"Your guess is as good as mine," Paco said. He moved to reload his rifle. "They all seem to have disappeared."

For a while, no one spoke. They were all too busy reloading and firing to make conversation. Finally, as the morning and afternoon began to fade away into evening, there came a lull in the fighting.

"What do you think?" Paco asked Cord.

"I estimate less than a dozen men left out there," Cord replied. "They're probably behind the stables regrouping and making plans."

"Who wants coffee?" Emily asked as she struggled to her feet.

"Everyone, but I'll make it." Faith gestured to

the wingback chair near the fireplace. "Rest for a while. The shooting could start up again any minute."

"She's right," José agreed as Faith ducked into the kitchen. "We need a plan."

"I think we have a few minutes," Cord replied. "They're probably as tired as we are."

Faith returned and began to pass out steaming mugs of bitter black coffee. "How's the ammunition holding up?" she asked.

"So far, so good," José replied, "but we can't keep this up forever."

"Well, it's a cinch the sheriff isn't going to send help," Emily declared. "Old Leroy is firmly in Diego's back pocket."

"Montez is a damn yellow coward," Paco snarled. "He's hiding somewhere in safety, while his hired guns do the dirty work." He caressed the stock of his rifle. "What I wouldn't give to have the slimy bastard in my sights."

"Cord told me about your cousin Luisa," Faith said. "How is she?"

"Recovering," Paco replied. "Tia Rosa took her home a few days ago." He slammed his fist into the window frame. "When I think of all that Montez has done to you, Dona Faith, and to my cousin and to everyone else, I long to feel his evil throat between my hands."

"I have to admit, I'm ashamed that he is my cousin." Faith took a sip of her coffee. "It's hard to believe that the son of Granddad's sister could turn out so bad."

"But your Great-aunt Hannah didn't raise him," Emily reminded her. "Who knows what kind of notions he picked up from his kinfolk in Spain."

Faith merely nodded. God! When would it all end? What could make a man so greedy he would go to such lengths? Why was Diego so obsessed with the Double J? She turned to gaze at Cord and a great surge of love filled her heart as he felt her eyes on him and winked.

Faith couldn't resist smiling despite their circumstances. She rose to her feet and moved to lay a hand on Cord's shoulder. In spite of the apparent temporary cease-fire, Cord had not moved from his spot by the window. He turned his head to kiss her fingers.

"What you got to smile about?" José groused as he noted the exchange between the couple. "We could all be dead soon."

"No," Cord said firmly. "We won't die today, but Diego's hired guns have seen their last sunrise."

"You have a plan, amigo?" Paco asked.

Cord shook his head. "Not a plan. An option. The only one left open to us."

Darkness was beginning to fall when Paco and Cord slipped away from the house. All evening the two sides had halfheartedly exchanged occasional gunfire, but even Diego's hired killers appeared to be losing their enthusiasm for the fight. Partially due, no doubt, to their ever decreasing numbers. Of the original fifteen gunmen, only six remained alive.

Cord motioned for Paco to circle around one side of the stables while he took the other side.

The plan was simple: sneak up on the opposition and take them by surprise. Cord rounded the corner of the stables. He melted back into the shadows when he heard someone approaching.

The gunman started to walk past Cord without even seeing him. With silent, pantherlike speed, Cord reached out and grabbed the man by the shirt collar. Before the man had time to draw his gun or cry out, Cord used his knife to quickly and silently cut the man's throat. He stripped the gunman of his weapons and tossed them into a watering trough, then wiped his knife blade clean on the dead man's shirt. He then rolled the body out of sight into the shadows.

Cord continued to the other side of the stables. A man was there, hunkered down on his heels, his head drooping forward as he snored softly.

Cord eased forward and removed the man's revolver. He tossed the weapon aside, then had the man pinned, a knife to his throat, before the hapless gunman could even open his eyes.

Paco appeared around the opposite end of the stable building and Cord signaled to him.

"I got one of the bastards," Paco whispered as he joined Cord.

"This one makes three." Cord increased the pressure of the knife and the gunman's eyes rolled in fear. "How many more?" he asked the captured man. "Tell me and I might consider letting you live."

"Th . . . three," the man stammered. "Me and Shorty Wiles and Luther Bedlow was supposed to keep guard while Ajax, Coot and Tyson got some shut-eye."

"Coot Sykes?" Cord asked.

The man nodded, then flinched as the knife bit into his neck.

"Are all three of them in the stables?"

The man answered in the affirmative. He opened his mouth to speak further, but Cord removed the knife and gave the man a swift punch to the jaw. The talkative gunman was rendered instantly unconscious.

"Coot Sykes," Cord spat with disgust. "I should have killed him when I had the chance."

"Well, amigo," Paco grinned, "sometimes life gives you a second chance. Then it is up to you to make the most of it."

Cord nodded. "I reckon you're right." He slid his knife into his boot and pulled his .44 from his holster. "Ready, amigo?"

"As I'll ever be," Paco replied. "Have you a plan?"

Cord grinned. "Sure. We go in shooting and kill us a few bad guys."

"Yeah," Paco sighed. "That's what I figured."

The two men quickly barred the doors on one end of the stables, then positioned themselves at the other entrance. At a signal from Cord, Paco kicked the door open.

"Come out with your hands up!" Cord called.

"Like hell!" came Ajax Killian's reply as a hail of gunfire erupted from within the stables.

277

Paco and Cord threw themselves to the ground, six-guns blazing as they returned the outlaw's fire.

Ajax and Coot dove into an empty stall, but the third man, Tyson Macgregor, was younger and less experienced. He charged toward Paco and Cord and managed to crease Paco's shoulder with a bullet before he fell, dead, onto the stable floor.

"Coot! Ajax! Give it up!" Cord called out.

Coot's answer was to run from the stall as he fired his revolver at Cord. He quickly joined Tyson on the stable floor.

"Okay, okay!" Ajax cried. "Hold your fire. I'm comin' out."

Cord and Paco rose to their feet as Ajax, his hands raised above his head, slowly made his way toward them.

"Drop the gun, Killian," Cord told him.

"Sure thing, McCamy." Ajax reached for his gun. As his hand dropped to the butt of the revolver, he suddenly wheeled around, drew and fired.

Cord had been expecting just such a trick. He drew and fired. His bullet lodged in Killian's throat, sending him flying backward as his gun discharged harmlessly into the ceiling.

"Are you okay?" Cord asked Paco.

"Never better," Paco said with a grin.

"Come on," Cord told him. "Faith will patch up your shoulder. I happen to know she does a pretty good job on bullet wounds."

As though summoned by Cord's words, Faith

appeared from the shadowy darkness to throw herself into his welcoming embrace. "Thank God, you're unharmed."

"Oh, muñequita." Cord smiled. "I should have known you would end up out here."

Suddenly, Cord saw a flicker of movement off to his right. He pushed Faith behind him and turned swiftly, revolver in hand. "Hold it right there!"

"Put that dadblasted gun away, boy!" Max, the wizened old cook, hobbled out of the darkness to join them. He was followed closely by two other ranchhands.

Cord noticed that all three men were limping.

"Where have you been?" Paco demanded.

"Where we been? We been walking! That's where we been!" Max returned.

"Walking?" Faith asked the men.

"Yep," Max affirmed. "Took us all day to get here."

The ranchhand's story was a simple one. Two new men, recently hired by Ross Fulton, had turned out to be hirelings of Diego Montez. In the middle of the night they had drawn their guns on the men in the bunkhouses and forced them to leave the ranch. Max, Ramon and Calvin, not easily intimidated, had ridden only a short distance from the ranch, then decided to circle back.

"It happened while you was up at José's cabin," Max told Paco. "They didn't know about you two. I reckon they expected Miss Emily to just hightail it out of here when she found everybody missin'."

The three ranchhands had waited for morning, then took a circuitous route across the rangeland. They were on their way to the ranchhouse when they were bushwhacked by some of Killian's men. Luckily the three men had not been killed, but they had been left without their horses and guns. They had once again slept out in the open for the night. When morning arrived, they had started home on foot.

"It sure takes a lot longer on foot than it does on horseback," Max lamented.

"Would you men like to come inside for a bite to eat?" Faith asked.

"Nope. I can fix us up somethin' in the bunkhouse," Max replied. "Since we missed out on all the fun, I reckon we'll stay out here for a while and bury these boys."

"Thanks, Max," Cord said. "But don't bury the one on the far side of the stable. He's not dead, just unconscious."

Max nodded. "I reckon we can lock him up in the shed."

Cord, Faith and Paco adjourned to the house. While Faith bandaged Paco's shoulder, they filled Emily and José in on all that had occurred.

Emily sighed heavily. "I sure hope Montez waits awhile before he tries to kill us again. I'm getting too old for all this gunplay."

"Don't worry, Emily." Cord stepped forward and placed a reassuring hand on the housekeeper's shoulder. "I have a feeling that this was the last stunt Diego Montez will ever pull."

"I hope you're right," Emily said as she allowed Cord to help her to her feet. "What are we going to do with the man Max locked up in the shed?"

"I'll send Calvin into town tomorrow to wire the federal marshal. It would be a waste of time to turn him over to Hobbs."

Emily nodded her agreement. "Makes sense to me."

When the others had left the room to seek their beds, Cord pulled Faith into his arms and began to kiss her. A soul-stirring kiss that ignited a fire in her blood and turned her knees to water. "Let's go to your room," he murmured against her lips.

"Our room," Faith corrected as she gazed into his emerald eyes. "You have shared my blankets and I have proclaimed you as my husband. Will you accept that?"

Cord laughed softly as he lifted her into his arms. "Only until we can visit the minister in Sonria."

Although weary to the point of exhaustion, Cord and Faith were happy simply to be alive and together after all that had occurred.

Faith caught sight of herself in the mirror as Cord carried her into the bedroom. Her long silky hair was snarled and tangled, and her eyes had dark circles beneath them. "Oh no! I look terrible," she cried.

Cord kissed the tip of her nose as he laid her gently on the bed. "You look beautiful to me."

Faith reached for him and he lowered himself

to lie beside her.

Slowly they removed each other's clothing until they lay naked, limbs entwined. A cooling breeze blew through the open window to caress their passion-warmed skin as they discovered anew the secret delights of each other's bodies.

They came together as man and wife. A sharing of love, commitment and need that forged an everlasting bond. A bond built on a lifetime of love.

Chapter 32

"What happens next?" Faith asked. She and Cord were seated at the table in the courtyard enjoying a late breakfast. Due to the excitement of the day before, almost everyone at the Double J had risen later than their accustomed hour.

Cord pushed his empty coffee mug aside. "I deal with Montez."

Faith's brows rose in surprise. "You know where he is then?"

Cord shrugged. "Maybe."

Faith pushed her plate aside. She was no longer hungry. "What are you planning to do?"

"What I should have done in the first place," Cord replied. "I'm going to kill the bastard. It's the only way to make certain you'll be safe from him."

Faith's expression grew sad as she gazed out across the ranchyard. "So much death."

Cord's features hardened and his emerald green eyes grew dark. "Maybe you should get used to it. Violence and death seem to have a habit of following me. No matter where I go."

"No!" Faith left her chair to fly into Cord's arms. She knelt between his knees and pressed her face to his hard chest as she encircled his waist with her arms. "Please don't say that. You know it doesn't have to be that way. None of this has been your fault. You've been protecting me. If it's anyone's fault it's mine."

"No, sweetheart." Cord gently caressed her hair. "You're not to blame and neither am I. The blame rests entirely on Don Diego Montez. All the deaths, all the pain and anguish can be attributed directly to him. But even if the fault isn't mine this time, you don't know the kind of life I've led for the past ten years. You don't know about the things I've done. The men I've killed."

"And I don't care!" Faith tilted her head back to look into his face. "I love you, Cord McCamy, and you love me. Together we can build a new life, and that's all that matters."

"Shh, muñequita. I know." He pulled her into his lap. "I'm sick of all the killing too, of the bloodshed and endless violence. But you have to understand, I can't allow Diego Montez to live. Not after all he has done. To you. To me. To untold numbers of innocent people. I would be less than a man if I didn't stop him. For good."

"I understand," Faith told him. She placed a hand on his cheek. "But it doesn't make it any easier."

"Nothing worthwhile is ever easy." Cord turned his head to kiss her palm. "I want to be selfish. To just take you and ride away into the hills and make love to you for the rest of our lives. But how can we begin a new life together while Diego lives? His shadow would always haunt us. No matter where we go."

Suddenly the words Senora Garcia had uttered in Devil's Crossing returned to Faith. "Stay close to your husband, listen to him," the old woman had said.

"I guess you're right." Faith sighed and kissed him lightly on the cheek.

"After all this is over with, why don't we give ourselves a proper wedding here at the ranch?" Cord said, deftly steering the conversation to a happier topic. "We can honeymoon in California."

"Sounds wonderful. I'd love to visit California."

"But would you like to live there?"

"Live there? In California?" Faith was stunned. She had assumed they would live on the Double J.

"I have a horse ranch in California," Cord told her. "Only a day's ride from the Pacific Ocean. It's kind of small right now, but I have plans. It's a beautiful place, Faith. Lots of green grass, fresh water, and the finest horseflesh west of the Mississippi. I have a house too. I built it myself.

It's not fancy, but it's plenty big enough for the two of us and however many children we eventually have." His deep green eyes searched her face for some sign of what she might be thinking. "I would like for us to live there, at least part of the time."

Faith rose to her feet and walked over to the courtyard wall. She looked at the ranchyard, her eyes touching on the stables, the barn, the corrals, sheds and bunkhouse. She thought of Emily, Paco, José and Max. She loved the ranch, but the ranch was only a place. Her love for it could not begin to compare to her love for Cord.

"When I first returned to the Double J, for the first time in my life I felt like I had come home," Faith said carefully. "I felt that this was where I was meant to be and I never wanted to leave here again. But during the past few weeks, I've discovered something very important. I've discovered that where I live doesn't matter. What matters is who I live with. As long as I am with you, I am home."

Cord walked up behind her and placed his hands on her shoulders. "You're sure?"

Faith turned to face him, her soft brown eyes aglow with love. "Very sure."

"I want you to be happy, muñequita," Cord said as he pulled her into his arms. "We'll stay in California for a while. If you like it as much as I think you will, we can divide our time between here and there." He lowered his mouth to kiss her.

"Hola! Cord, Dona Faith!" Paco called out as

he entered the courtyard gate.

Cord's head jerked up. He had scarcely touched Faith's lips with his own when Paco interrupted. He turned such a fierce scowl on the vaquero that Paco halted in his tracks.

Faith looked at the expressions on the two men's faces and began to laugh. Cord looked so darkly forbidding that Paco appeared ready to run. "Stop it, Cord!" she admonished between laughs, "or Paco will think you're serious."

"I am serious," Cord snapped, but one corner of his mouth began to twitch upward in amusement.

Paco grinned, clearly relieved. "I just came to tell you and Dona Faith that José and I have corraled all the horses and Calvin has ridden into Sonria to wire the federal marshal."

"Thanks," Cord said.

Paco turned to leave but Faith stopped him. "Paco, after all we've been through, don't you think you could drop the 'Dona' and just call me Faith."

"I do not think . . ." Paco began.

"Especially," Faith interrupted him, "since you are now my ranch foreman. If you'll accept, of course."

Paco's grin grew broader. "Of course I accept," he replied. "Thank you, Dona . . . er, thank you, Faith."

"No thanks are necessary. You're the best qualified for the job. You've earned it."

"I'll go into Sonria this afternoon and see if I can find the ranchhands who were scared off,"

Paco said eagerly, "but right now I'm going to go tell José I'm his new boss."

After Paco had left, Cord turned to Faith and eyed her speculatively for a moment. "That was a smart move."

Faith laughed softly as she threw her arms around Cord's neck. "I know."

Chapter 33

Cord slid an arm around Faith's waist as they walked out of the stables. He paused suddenly and looked out toward the road. "Someone's coming."

Faith lifted a hand to shade her eyes from the noonday sun and peered into the distance. A dust cloud could be seen moving steadily closer to the ranch. "Who do you suppose it is?" she asked.

Cord stepped in front of her and lowered his hand to the butt of his holstered .44. "Could be trouble."

They watched silently as a huge carriage drawn by six lathered horses rolled up the lane and into the ranchyard. It was closely followed by a lone man on horseback.

The driver brought the ornate coach to a halt directly in front of them. Without a word, he jumped down, opened the door and put the steps in place.

As soon as the driver moved out of the way, a woman appeared in the carriage doorway. She was a small woman, dressed in champagne silk with gold lace trim. An elaborate hat was perched atop her carefully coiffed auburn curls, and diamonds glittered from her fingers and ears. Despite what had surely been an arduous journey, the woman appeared as fresh and as beautiful as if she had just stood up from her dressing table.

"Aunt Nicole!" Faith rushed forward, her arms spread wide in welcome.

Nicole de Beauharnais stepped down from the carriage and into her niece's embrace. "My darling Faith," she cried. "How I have missed you. I have so much to tell you."

Faith clasped her aunt's hand and led her to where Cord was patiently waiting. "Aunt Nicole, I would like you to meet my husband, Cord McCamy."

"Husband? Ah, ma petite. I think you have much to tell me too. Oui?" Nicole kissed Cord on the cheek. "Such a handsome one you are, Monsieur McCamy. I think I shall like having you for a nephew."

Cord smiled. "I think under the circumstances, ma'am, you can call me Cord."

"And you must call me Nicole. Oui?"

Cord glanced over Nicole's head at the carriage and a scowl darkened his handsome face. "What are you doing here?"

Faith followed the direction of Cord's gaze and saw Matthew alight from the carriage. Matthew? How on earth had he gotten together with Nicole?

"Did I hear correctly?" Matthew asked as he joined them. "Are congratulations in order?" He kissed Faith's cheek in a brotherly fashion, but she could see the light of disappointment in his emerald green eyes. Eyes so much like Cord's.

Matthew moved to shake Cord's hand, and Faith was struck anew by the twin brothers' uncanny resemblance.

"Well," Matthew said simply, "I guess the best man won."

"As usual," Cord returned.

Before anyone could speak again, a third passenger stepped down from the carriage. He was tall, dark and classically handsome. His raven hair was touched with gray at the temples and his eyes were a dark and vibrant blue. He walked over to stand by Nicole, but before she could introduce him to her niece, the lone horseman, who had followed the carriage into the yard, rode up to Cord. "Pardon me," he said, "but where might I stable my horse?"

Cord directed him to the stables.

"As soon as you are through Monsieur Rollins," Nicole called to the horseman, "please join us in the house."

Arms linked, Nicole and Faith moved toward the house. The blue-eyed stranger followed closely behind them, but Cord and Matthew held back.

"When did you and Faith get married?" Matthew demanded.

"While we were in Mexico."

"Mexico?" Matthew scowled, but try as he might, he could not manage the same degree of menace as his twin. "What were you doing in Mexico?"

"It's a long story," Cord replied. "How did you end up with Faith's aunt?"

Matthew sighed. "I'm afraid that's a long story too."

The two brothers, never particularly close despite the fact that they were twins, eyed each other silently for a moment. Finally Cord nodded toward the house. "Come on. Let's get this over with."

Nicole and Faith were seated on the parlor sofa, while the stranger had taken one of the wingback chairs. Emily bustled about happily as she poured coffee and chattered nonstop to Nicole.

Matthew settled himself into a vacant chair, but Cord preferred to stand, one arm draped over the corner of the fireplace mantel.

"Now," Faith said to her aunt. "Can you tell me what's going on?"

Nicole sighed. "Of course, darling, but first there is someone I would like you to meet." She gestured to the tall blue-eyed stranger. "This is your cousin. Diego Montez."

Faith's eyes grew round and she was left

speechless as the man rose to his feet and bowed low over her hand. "At last we meet, Cousin Faith," he said.

Faith's eyes flew first to Cord, whose forehead was creased in a frown, then to Matthew who was smiling in a satisfied manner.

"You're not Diego," she sputtered as she turned back to the handsome man. "I've met Diego."

"No, my sweet," Nicole said. "You met the man who has been posing as Diego."

"If that don't beat all," Emily exclaimed, a note of disgust in her voice. "We were almost murdered by an imposter."

"His real name is Francisco Vasquez," said a voice from the doorway.

Everyone turned to see the horseman standing in the door. He was a short man with a sun-creased face and permanently bowed legs. His appearance labeled him as a saddle tramp, but his eyes shone with a keen intelligence.

"This is John Rollins," Matthew said as the man stepped into the room. "A Texas Ranger."

"Every lawman in the United States, France and Spain has been looking for Vasquez," Rollins explained. "He's a murderer, thief and con artist."

Faith was elated to discover that she was in no way related to the evil man who had tried to kill her. "So, you are the real Diego," she said with a broad smile. "I can't tell you how happy I am to meet you."

"And I you." Diego squeezed her hands as his

eyes crinkled in a smile. "My American cousin."

Cord stepped forward. "I'd like to know how the four of you got together."

"Diego," Nicole said, gazing at him fondly, "I believe the story begins with you."

"I've prepared enough lunch for everyone," Emily interrupted. "Why don't we go to the dining room and we can talk while we eat."

Everyone took a seat around the huge dining room table while Emily placed trays of bread and cold meat at the center of the table. She added a large pot of coffee and a pitcher of lemonade, then plopped into the empty chair next to Matthew. "This I gotta hear," she explained.

While everyone helped themselves to food, Diego began to speak.

"As you know, I have lived in Spain for most of my life. I have been content, but I have always been aware of the ranch, here in Texas, left to me by my parents. It has been managed successfully by my business managers and solicitors, and each year I have received a report and profit-or-loss tally, but other than that, I had given it little thought. Until a year ago.

"For a while now, I have had the urge to visit the place of my birth. Perhaps it is due to the fact that I have reached middle age and have no family of my own." Diego shrugged. "Whatever the reason, I decided I should journey to America."

Diego looked around at all the patiently listening faces and smiled a bit ruefully. "I met

Vasquez on the ship to New York. I have never believed myself to be naive or gullible, but he proved to me that I am just that. Vasquez was very friendly and very knowledgeable about America. I was alone, bored and curious about this country. We soon became almost constant companions. Like most con men, Vasquez was an excellent listener. I'm afraid I told him every detail of my life in Spain and of my property here in Texas."

"You are extremely lucky he didn't murder you on the spot," Faith exclaimed.

"Believe me, dear cousin, he tried," Diego sighed. "Once we were in New York, he stated his intention of accompanying me to Texas. At the time I was delighted. We journeyed to St. Louis and boarded a paddle wheeler for New Orleans. This was also Francisco's suggestion. He said it was a part of America that I should not miss. The boat was marvelous. There was gambling, drinking and entertainment. I must say that I enjoyed myself immensely. There was only one problem. Vasquez did not intend for me to reach New Orleans. Not alive anyway."

It had been very late at night and Diego had not fared well at the gaming table. The liquor he had consumed had affected him more strongly than usual. He felt groggy and his thinking was muddled. He stumbled out on the deck and leaned against the rail. He gulped huge breaths of air, hoping to clear his head, but the dizzy feeling merely increased. He tried to turn his head when Francisco walked up beside him, but his eyes seemed to be mesmerized by the dark swirling water of the Mississippi. He felt a push and then he was floating. The dark water soon engulfed him.

Diego awoke to find himself lying on a rough pallet in a dimly lit room. His head throbbed almost unbearably and his lungs felt on fire. He heard a door open and turned his head painfully on the rough blankets.

Diego saw a young boy enter the room. He was a painfully thin child in ragged knee britches, tattered shirt and bare feet. He set a bucket down by the door, then turned to look at Diego. When he saw Diego looking back at him, his eyes grew round and his mouth fell open. "Maman! Maman! Come quickly!"

An equally thin woman of indeterminate age hurried into the room. She saw Diego and bustled over to kneel beside him. "So, monsieur, you are awake. Are you in much pain?" The woman, like the boy, had a thick French Creole accent.

"Water?" Diego managed to croak.

The boy hurried to him with a dipper of water. Diego managed a few sips, then blessed darkness claimed him again.

As the days passed, Diego's moments of lucidity grew into hours of consciousness. He was soon strong enough to sit up and eat the pitifully thin fish stew his hostess provided. He was also able to think clearly enough to realize that his "friend" Vasquez had drugged him and thrown him overboard. At the time, he could only guess at Vasquez's reasons.

The woman's name was Claudette Bujold. A widow, she and her son, Charles, spent all their waking hours trying to make a living from their small plot of land by the river. Fish provided the majority of their sustenance and it was Charles's habit of early morning fishing that had saved Diego's life.

While fishing from the rickety dock behind their one-room shack, Charles had spied what appeared to be a man floating downriver on a log. Without hesitation, Charles had dove into the river. Diego was unconscious, his forehead bleeding. Only his coat sleeve tangled in the branches of the fallen tree had kept his head above water. He had been in the river for several hours. His skin was dangerously chilled and he had swallowed a lot of the muddy water.

Possessed of a wiry strength, Charles had somehow managed to free Diego from the log and pull him ashore.

Diego had lain unconscious in the Bujold shack for days. Racked with fever and delirious from his head wound, he had been patiently nursed back to health by Claudette and Charles.

When his strength began to return, Diego wanted to send a message downriver to Nicole and Faith. He had never met them, but had gotten their New Orleans address from Jeremiah in a letter.

Claudette explained that she had no horses, wagon or boat for transportation. The Bujolds' nearest neighbor was almost a full day's walk, and she knew of no way to send a message.

Diego stayed with the woman and her son for over three months, until he was strong enough to walk. Then early one morning he set out on foot to find a way to New Orleans.

"And do you know what this dear sweet man did?" Nicole exclaimed. "He arranged to have cows, chickens and pigs sent to Madame Bujold. Along with two horses, a wagon and a small boat for Charles. He filled the wagon with foodstuffs and cloth and opened an account for Claudette in a New Orleans bank."

Diego blushed profusely. "It was little enough payment in return for my life," he said gruffly.

"I can understand that Vasquez wanted you out of the way," Cord said thoughtfully. "But why didn't he just empty your bank accounts and run? Why stick around and cause so much trouble?"

"Greed," Matthew replied. "He had made arrangements to sell the Montez ranch, but apparently the party wouldn't buy unless the Double J was part of the deal."

"He met two Englishmen aboard the riverboat," Diego explained. "They claimed to be searching for ranchland on behalf of some wealthy British clients. I paid no attention to them, but I did notice Vasquez conversing with them on several occasions. At the time, I thought nothing of it."

"The Englishmen are using the names Owen Montgomery and Wilbur Rothschild," John Rollins interjected. "Their aristocratic clients have put out a reward for them. Seems the two men are nothing but con artists. If it wasn't so damned tragic, it would be funny."

"You mean Vasquez is a con artist who was taken in by a couple of con artists?" Faith asked.

Rollins nodded. "Exactly."

"When Diego arrived on my doorstep," Nicole said, "I didn't know what to think. After all, Faith, you had mentioned in your letter that Diego was in residence at the Montez ranch. It took a while, but I had my New Orleans attorney check his story. When I found out that he was indeed the real Diego Montez, I wired Matthew immediately."

"Why didn't you let me know?" Faith asked.

"I thought Matthew would inform you," Nicole replied.

Matthew shrugged. "I wanted to be one-hundred-percent sure before I told you. Sorry."

"Has Vasquez given you a very hard time, my pet?" Nicole asked Faith.

Faith and Cord began to laugh, while Emily rolled her eyes.

"I believe," Faith said, "I will allow Emily to tell you about it. She is a much better storyteller than I."

"We set out for Texas immediately," Nicole said. "Of course I didn't have to come along, but I was so worried about Faith that I couldn't stay put."

"Matthew met us in San Antonio," Diego explained. "While awaiting our arrival, he made the acquaintance of Senor Rollins, who was very interested in our story."

"That is how we all ended up traveling together," Nicole said.

"I aim to find Vasquez," John Rollins announced. "And them two English sidewinders too. Does anyone here have any idea where Vasquez might be?"

No one spoke. After a moment of silence, Cord rose to his feet. Without a word, he turned and left the room.

Chapter 34

It was after midnight by the time everyone had left or retired. Diego had chosen to continue his journey and spend the night at his own ranch. John Rollins, hoping that Francisco Vasquez had left behind some clue to his present whereabouts, had accompanied Diego.

After Faith fell asleep, Cord, feeling restless, wandered out into the courtyard.

A barn owl hooted in the distance, and Cord could hear the horses stirring about inside the corral. The moon hung round and full in the night sky. A good night for riding free and wild across the plains.

Cord wandered over to the fountain and struck a match to his cheroot.

"You know where he is, don't you?"

Cord did not bother to turn around. "Where who is?"

"Don't be obtuse." Matthew walked out of the shadows to stand by Cord's side. "You know where Vasquez is."

"Maybe," Cord conceded.

"Then you have to tell Rollins."

"Why?"

"So he can arrest him, damn it!" Matthew exclaimed. "That's why."

"No."

"No?"

Matthew grew livid with outrage. "You promised me that you would try to do this legally, Cord. That we would deal with this matter within the law."

Cord dropped his cheroot and ground it beneath the heel of his boot. "All bets are off, brother. I never promised to stand idly by while some lowlife con artist tries to kill my woman."

"It's over, Cord. Let the law deal with it."

"The law is your problem," Cord snarled as a muscle along his jaw began to twitch in anger. "Vasquez is mine. And for your information, it's not over. Not by a long shot."

"How does Faith feel about this?" Matthew asked in desperation.

Cord rounded on him, a hard gleam in his emerald eyes. "If you know what's good for you, you'll leave Faith out of it."

"Aha!" Matthew cried. "Faith doesn't approve."

"Don't push me, Matt." Cord's voice had

grown low and dangerous. "I know you wanted Faith, but she doesn't want you. She's mine."

"We're getting a bit off track here," Matthew snapped in exasperation. "We were discussing Vasquez."

"Drop it. It's between Vasquez and me now. His blood is mine."

Matthew could not suppress the cold chill that surged through him at Cord's words. "My God! You really are a savage sometimes, aren't you?"

Cord merely shrugged and turned to walk away.

"Cord!" In his anger Matthew could not resist one final dig. "You never did tell me the details of your wedding."

Cord paused, but did not turn to look at his twin. "We were married Comanche style. How else would 'savages' wed?"

This time when Cord walked away, Matthew remained silent.

Cord entered the bedroom and stood silently for a brief span of seconds as his eyes caressed Faith's sleeping form. She looked so damned beautiful that Matthew was forgotten, and Cord felt his tension and anger slip away.

Faith's magnificent silken hair was spread out like a fan on her pillow, providing the perfect frame for her exquisite face. Her lips were parted slightly and the light bed covering had fallen to her waist to leave her firm, coral-nippled breasts exposed.

Cord swiftly removed his clothes and slid into bed beside her. He pulled her into his arms and gently kissed her awake.

Faith's eyes flew open and automatically she slid her arms around his neck. "Cord," she murmured sleepily.

"I love you, muñequita," Cord said as his lips began to blaze a fiery trail along her neck.

Faith moaned deep in her throat and slid her hand across the crisp golden hair of his hard-muscled chest. "Oh, Cord. I love you too."

The moon shone through the open window, bathing their bodies in a golden light as they came together in a great surge of love and burning passion.

Faith writhed beneath Cord, lifting her hips in welcome of his slow and gentle thrusting. Their joining was spiritual as well as physical. A melding of body, mind and soul. They came together in affirmation of future dreams and fulfillment of yesterday's promise.

Cord rolled onto his back and Faith snuggled against him, her head on his shoulder. "You can wake me like that anytime," she teased.

"We have to talk," Cord said.

Cord's voice held such a serious tone that Faith sat up in bed. She drew her legs up beneath her and turned to face him.

The pale moonlight etched the hard angles of Cord's face, softening his features and making his expression unreadable.

"You're going after Vasquez," Faith said softly.

"Yes." Cord left the bed and began to dress.

"Now?"

"It's now or never." Cord shrugged into his shirt. "I should have already been on his trail, but I didn't want to leave you with only Paco, Emily and José for protection. Now, Nicole, Matthew and Diego are here, and Paco has brought back most of the ranchhands. You should be safe until I return."

Faith rose to her knees. Her eyes glowed softly in the pale light. "Do you really have to go after him?"

"You know the answer to that."

Faith reached out and laid a hand on his shoulder. "Can you at least wait until daylight?"

Cord strapped his gunbelt onto his hips with the ease of long practice. "If I wait any longer, Matthew will probably do something foolish. Like set that Texas Ranger on my trail."

"Oh God! Cord, I . . ."

"Shh, muñequita. I know." Cord reached for her and hugged her tightly to his chest. "I'll hate every second I'm away from you, but this is something I have to do."

Her face pressed to Cord's neck, Faith nodded. She could find no words to say.

Cord leaned back and cupped her face in his hands. "I'll be back." He kissed her then. Not a good-bye kiss, but a kiss that spoke of better days to come. "Trust me," he whispered. Then swiftly and silently, he was gone.

Faith laid the currycomb aside and gave Dancer an affectionate pat on the neck. The pinto mare snorted softly and nudged Faith's shoulder with her velvety nose. "Sorry, girl. I'm fresh out of sugar lumps."

Faith was exhausted. After Cord had left, she had been unable to sleep. She had lain awake until daylight, then had taken Dancer for an early-morning run. She left the stall and turned just in time to see Nicole enter the stables.

"Good morning, pet," Nicole called cheerfully. "Why so pensive this morning?"

Faith closed and latched the stall gate. "Cord left last night."

"Left?" Nicole asked in surprise. "Whatever for?"

"He went after Vasquez."

Nicole frowned. "I thought it was John Rollins' job to capture Vasquez."

Faith shook her head. "Not to Cord's way of thinking."

Nicole sighed heavily. "That is the way of men. You must not worry for him, darling. I am certain he will be fine."

"I know," Faith agreed, and for the first time noticed that her aunt was wearing a riding habit. "Are you going for a ride?"

"Oui." Nicole blushed charmingly. "I am going to Diego's ranch for lunch."

"Diego's, huh?" Faith noted her aunt's pleased expression and flustered manner. "Why do I have the feeling that there is more between you and Diego than meets the eye?"

Nicole laughed softly. "Diego and I have grown quite close over the past few weeks. Nicole Montez has a nice ring to it. Oui?"

"Oh, Aunt Nicole! You're getting married? How wonderful." Faith hugged the older woman. "When?"

"We have not yet set a date," Nicole replied. "But rest assured, pet, you will be the first to know."

"Senora de Beauharnais," Paco called from the doorway. "Your horse is saddled and José and Ramon are waiting to escort you."

"We will talk later," Nicole promised. She kissed her niece's cheek and hurried away.

Faith watched her aunt leave the stables. Nicole had always been a cheerful person, kind, loving, spontaneous, outgoing and never depressed. Yet Faith had never seen her look happier. Never before had Nicole's soft gray eyes held that very special sparkle. Faith thought it was wonderful that Diego and her aunt had fallen in love. They were both very unique individuals.

Paco was waiting outside when Faith left the stables.

"Are you certain my aunt will be safe?" Faith asked him.

"Sí. José and Ramon are well armed, but I do not think any of Vasquez's hired killers are still alive to cause trouble."

"You're probably right," Faith conceded. "Do you have time to go to the office with me? I'd like to go over the payroll records with you."

"Of course," Paco agreed.

"How is Luisa?" Faith asked as they crossed the ranchyard.

307

"It is very kind of you to ask, considering all the trouble Luisa caused you."

"You musn't think I blame your cousin," Faith hastened to assure him. "She was Vasquez's victim just as I was."

"You are a very understanding woman," Paco said with deeply felt sincerity. "And to answer your question, Luisa's condition is much improved."

"That's good news." Faith opened the office door and led the way inside. "Please let me know if there is anything I can do."

"Cord has gone after Vasquez alone, hasn't he?" Paco asked suddenly.

Faith nodded, then stooped to retrieve the ledgers from the bottom desk drawer.

"I wish mi amigo had allowed me to accompany him." Paco took the ledgers from Faith's hands and placed them on the desk.

"So do I," Faith said, "but Cord felt that this was something he must do alone."

They sat side by side at the desk and began to go over the accounts. They were only halfway through the first ledger when they were interrupted by a knock on the door.

Faith looked up to see John Rollins standing in the doorway.

"Excuse me, Miss Jennings," the Texas Ranger drawled as he removed his hat. "Your housekeeper said I would find you here."

"It's Mrs. McCamy," Faith corrected automatically. "How may I help you?"

Rollins walked into the room. "I found some

items at Senor Montez's home that he and I thought might have come from here. We think Vasquez took them from your grandfather."

Paco and Faith exchanged glances.

"Show me," Faith said as she turned back to the law officer.

Rollins set his saddlebag on the desktop and unbuckled the catch. First he removed a small portrait miniature and placed it in front of Faith. The painting depicted a man, woman and young blue-eyed boy.

"Senor Montez and his parents when he was a child," Rollins explained. "Turn it over."

Faith looked at the back of the small portrait. Written in a woman's neat script were the words. "To my brother Jeremiah with much love, Hannah."

"Why would Vasquez steal this?" Paco asked as he examined the portrait.

"Because it's a picture of the real Diego, who has blue eyes. Vasquez has black eyes," Rollins said. He removed a small bundle of envelopes and tossed them onto the desk. "Letters from Senor Montez to Mr. Jennings. Vasquez most likely needed them for the handwriting. Using those, he probably developed a reasonably good forgery of Diego Montez's signature."

Rollins reached into the saddlebag once again and removed a sheaf of papers. "Last, but not least," he announced as he handed the papers to Faith.

"Oh, my," Faith gasped. John Rollins had given her the missing pages from Jeremiah's appointment book. She studied them carefully. The first page said only, "meeting with Diego, one o'clock." The second page contained the names of Owen Montgomery and Wilbur Rothschild along with the names and addresses of their clients in England. On the third page Jeremiah had written, "contact Pinkerton Detective Agency about investigating phony Diego."

"Granddad was wise to him from the start," Faith exclaimed.

The remaining pages outlined Jeremiah's continuing efforts to investigate Vasquez.

"Apparently Mr. Jennings tried to contact the Rangers," Rollins said, "but unfortunately the message was intercepted by Sheriff Hobbs."

Tucked away within the thin stack of papers was an envelope addressed to Faith and Nicole in New Orleans. Inside was a letter Jeremiah had written to them explaining the situation.

"Vasquez must have sneaked in here during Jeremiah's funeral and taken these things," Paco said. "Too bad El Patron died before he told anyone of his suspicions."

"Why would Vasquez keep these things?" Faith asked. "It would have been much safer for him had he burned them."

"Francisco Vasquez suffers from an affliction that strikes most successful criminals," John Rollins replied. "Overconfidence. He was so certain of not being caught that he had just tossed these things into a desk drawer."

"I thank you, Mr. Rollins, for returning these

items to me," Faith said. "Would you care to stay and join us for lunch?"

"No, thank you, ma'am," Rollins declined. "I'm in a bit of a hurry. I've got some hard riding to do if I'm gonna catch up with your husband before he reaches Vasquez."

John Rollins noticed the astonishment that registered briefly in Faith's eyes. "I didn't get to be a Texas Ranger for my looks alone, ma'am." He laughed. "I have a few brains too." Still laughing, he left the office.

Chapter 35

Francisco Vasquez, alias Diego Montez, peered out his hotel room window and into the dusty main street of El Paso. Nothing, damn it! He had received no word at all from Sonria.

After Luisa's nearly fatal beating, Francisco had opted to remove himself to El Paso. There, from the relative comfort of his hotel room, he continued with his evil plot. He had planned to remain in El Paso until he heard word of Faith Jennings' and Cord McCamy's deaths, but so far no news had arrived.

Montgomery and Rothschild would return at any time, and Vasquez was growing increasingly restless. The Englishmen were expecting him to have the deed to the Double J, but he had nothing.

Surely Hobbs had reported the deaths of Jennings and McCamy by now. And Vasquez had no doubt that Ajax Killian and his hirelings had cleared the Double J of all inhabitants. So why hadn't the long-awaited telegram arrived?

Francisco knew that if things had not gone as planned, he had only to cross the border into Mexico to evade the law. And he was finally beginning to consider that things might not have gone as smoothly as he had hoped. In fact, he had begun to realize that things may have gone very badly indeed.

Swearing beneath his breath, Vasquez checked his pocketwatch. He should have been a wealthy man by now, safely tucked away on a ship bound for London. Instead, he was sweltering in a seedy hotel room awaiting word from the asinine buffoons it had been his extreme misfortune to employ.

Vasquez poured himself a stiff drink and began to carefully weigh his options. He had begun to lean toward a decision to make a hasty retreat into Mexico when he was interrupted by a soft rapping on his door.

He rose slowly to his feet. "Yes?"

"Let me in. It's me, Leroy."

Vasquez eased the door open a few inches and peeked outside. Standing in the hallway was none other than the intrepid Sheriff Leroy Hobbs.

Francisco threw the door open and quickly scanned the empty corridor before he pulled the heavy-bellied sheriff inside. "What are you doing here?" he snapped.

Leroy removed his hat and began to twist it nervously in his hands. His eyes appeared frightened in his red and sweating face. "All hell's broke loose in Sonria," he gasped. "We got to get outa Texas."

Francisco's eyes narrowed shrewdly. "Have a seat and calm down, Leroy. I'll pour you a drink and you tell me what happened."

Sheriff Hobbs clasped the whiskey glass in trembling hands. "Much obliged," he mumbled and tipped it to his meaty lips. He tossed the fiery liquid off like so much water.

"Now, Leroy," Vasquez said calmly. "Tell me why you're here."

"The real Montez showed up in Sonria," Leroy said. He held his glass out for a refill. Vasquez automatically obliged. "Along with a Texas Ranger, and that ain't all. McCamy and that Jennings woman are still alive. They came back from Mexico and killed Ajax Killian and all your men. They've wired the federal marshal too." Hobbs signaled for yet another refill, but this time he was ignored.

Vasquez surged to his feet and began to pace. "You're quite correct, Leroy. Our only option is to flee." He turned and studied the trembling sheriff thoughtfully for a moment. "Tell me, does anyone know you're here?"

"No," Leroy mumbled as he stared morosely at his empty glass.

"Did you tell anyone?"

Leroy shook his head.

"Were you followed?"

"'Course not," Leroy snorted. "Could you pass me that bottle?"

"Certainly, help yourself." Vasquez handed him the whiskey. "If you'll give me a moment to pack, we'll be on our way."

Leroy was so involved in filling himself with more whiskey that he failed to notice the small two-shot derringer that Vasquez removed from a valise.

"Are you quite certain you weren't followed, Sheriff Hobbs?" Francisco queried.

"As sure as sure," Leroy replied and took another gulp of whiskey.

"Excellent." Vasquez smiled. He pressed the derringer's barrel to Leroy's forehead and pulled the trigger.

Hobbs never knew what hit him. He merely slumped over into a silent, lifeless heap.

"Fool," Vasquez muttered. He replaced the derringer and dropped it into his valise. He then removed a .44 revolver and checked the load before tucking it into his jacket. After a final check of the room, he stepped over the lifeless remains of Sheriff Leroy Hobbs and opened the door.

Since daybreak Cord had occupied the ladderback chair on the sidewalk in front of the El Paso General Store, directly across the street from the hotel entrance. Cord knew that Vasquez was inside the hotel. He had also witnessed Sheriff Hobbs' furtive entrance. Sooner or later they would have to come outside. Cord was a very patient man.

In the late afternoon Cord received his reward, when Francisco Vasquez walked out of the hotel. Vasquez stood on the sidewalk for a moment as he cast his glance warily up and down the street.

The streets and sidewalks of El Paso were teeming with people and horses, but as Cord rose to his feet, the crowd—as though sensing trouble—began to scatter.

Cord walked slowly and deliberately across the dusty street. He paused a few feet in front of Francisco. "Vasquez."

Francisco whirled around. His face drained of color and his eyes widened in fear when he saw Cord standing in the street.

At that moment, Cord had become the man feared by so many. The cold, ruthless gunslinger his reputation spoke of.

"Time to die, Vasquez." Cord's hand dropped to his holster.

"You!" Vasquez roared. He hurled his valise at Cord and began to run along the sidewalk.

Cord easily sidestepped the heavy bag. He drew his six-shooter and began to follow, but unlike his prey, Cord did not run. His contempt was too great to hurry.

Vasquez fumbled for his revolver as he hastened up the suddenly deserted street. He pulled it free of his jacket and turned to fire at Cord. Francisco's hands shook with fear and outrage, so his shot flew wild. Cord kept walking toward him, without so much as a break in stride.

In desperation, Vasquez fired another wild shot and ducked into a saloon.

The bar patrons, having heard the commotion, swiftly sought cover.

Francisco looked desperately around the barroom but could see no solution to his dilemma. Every decent hiding place was occupied. After a second's hesitation he bolted for the stairs at the back of the room.

Revolver in hand, Cord pushed his way through the saloon's batwing doors. He crossed the room to the foot of the stairs.

Vasquez gained the upstairs hallway and turned to fire at Cord again. Cord dove to the side, and the bullet hit the large plate-glass window in the front wall. The glass shattered outward, its jagged, glittering shards flying into the street and scattering on the boardwalk.

One of the saloon girls screamed, but Cord ignored her as he rose to his feet and began to advance up the stairs.

With absolutely no pretense of bravery, Vasquez turned tail and raced down the hallway.

When Cord reached the upper floor, Vasquez was nowhere to be seen. He made his way slowly along the dimly lit corridor, pausing to look into each room he passed.

When Cord came to a locked door, through which he could hear a muffled sobbing, he knew he had found the right room. He took a step back, kicked the door open and walked inside.

Vasquez stood in the middle of the room. He

held a very frightened, half-dressed woman in front of him. One arm was around her waist, the revolver barrel pressed to her temple. "Get lost, McCamy," he snarled. "Leave me alone or the bitch dies."

"You'll never learn, will you, Vasquez?"

"I mean it, McCamy! Get the hell out!"

The woman sobbed harder.

"Be very still, little lady," Cord said calmly. He raised his revolver, cocked, leveled and pulled the trigger in one smooth motion.

The shot caught Vasquez directly between his eyes and threw him backward against the wall. He pulled the woman with him, and as he slumped to the floor, she fell atop his body.

With a terrified scream, she rose to her hands and knees and backed away from Vasquez's body. Her eyes almost wild in her pale face, she backed up against the wall and began to swipe at the splatters of blood on her cheek with her hands. "Oh, mister! What if you had missed?" she sobbed.

Cord removed the empty shell casing from his gun's chamber and walked over to look down on the remains of Francisco Vasquez. "I never miss."

He reholstered his revolver and turned slowly toward the door. "I've been expecting you."

Sheriff Ezra Brimley stepped into the room. "Damn it all! I should of known it was you, McCamy, as soon as I heard the shootin'." He turned to the girl. "You okay, Molly?"

"Yeah, sheriff." She rose shakily to her feet. "I

just gotta wash this blood off me."

Molly paused when she reached the door. "Thanks, mister. You saved my life."

As soon as Molly left the room, Sheriff Brimley turned back to Cord. "Well, McCamy, you want to tell me what happened?"

Cord nodded in the direction of Francisco's corpse. "Take a look for yourself."

Sheriff Brimley bent to take a closer look at Vasquez. "Yep. Got a wanted poster on him just this morning. Francisco Vasquez, A K A Hector Calderone, A K A Rafael Santini. He's wanted for murder, robbery, kidnapping, extortion and about a dozen other crimes." Brimley straightened and turned to Cord. "Looks like you have a reward coming."

"Keep the reward, Ezra. With my compliments." Cord turned to leave, then paused. "Do you remember Leroy Hobbs?"

"That poor excuse for a man?" Brimley snorted. "Sure I remember him. What about him?"

"He went up to Vasquez's room a couple of hours ago and never came back down. You might want to check it out." Before Brimley could reply, Cord left the room. He walked down the stairs and across the saloon, ignoring the curious stares that turned his way.

Cord had taken only a few steps along the boardwalk when he was brought up short by the sight of John Rollins walking toward him.

The Texas Ranger halted when he reached Cord. "I see you're alone, so I guess that means

Vasquez is dead."

Cord shrugged. "Could be you're right."

"Well, damn." Rollins removed his hat and mopped the perspiration from his brow. "I guess I'll head on out after them two English dudes, Rothschild and Montgomery." He grinned. "Unless, of course, you got a score to settle with them."

"Nope," Cord assured him. "They're all yours. I'm going home."

Thoughts of Faith uppermost in his mind, Cord continued on his way.

Chapter 36

The moon, so round and full when Cord had left for El Paso, had dwindled to a mere half. Still, it provided enough light for Faith to recognize the approaching rider.

Alone in her room, Faith had awakened suddenly from a sound sleep. Cord was on his way home. She had known it. She didn't understand how, but it was as though she could feel him drawing nearer.

Without hesitation, she had left her bed and dressed hurriedly in her riding clothes. She had slipped quietly out to the stables, saddled her sturdy pinto mare, and as though guided by some invisible magnetic force, had ridden to Mustang Creek.

Cord saw her as he approached the creek. She

stood near the water, her form silhouetted by the shimmering starlight, her unbound hair aglow with silver moonbeams.

He had been expecting to find her there. At first he had tried to dismiss the feeling as mere wishful thinking, but as he had drawn nearer to home, the feeling had grown from expectation to certainty. Faith awaited him at Mustang Creek. He knew it.

Cord rode Bright Star through the icy water of the creek to where Faith waited on the opposite bank. "Muñequita," he said softly as he slid from the saddle and drew her into his embrace.

Faith slid her arms around Cord's neck and tilted her head back to accept his kiss.

As the thirsty desert absorbs the rain, so did Faith absorb the essence of Cord's love. She had been too long without his kiss, his touch, his presence.

Cord crushed Faith to his chest as his lips covered hers and his tongue delved into the sweetness of her mouth. He couldn't get enough. He would never get enough of her.

No words were necessary. They communicated with their minds, their hearts, their touch. Each knew what the other wanted, what the other needed.

They made love on the soft grass of the creekbank. Joined together beneath the endless Texas sky and the muted half-moon light.

Their joining was fiercely sweet, savagely gentle. A joyous renewal of vows spoken by the heart, of lovers too long denied.

Afterward, they lay, limbs entwined, upon the ground.

"It's over now, isn't it?" Faith said softly.

"Yes, muñequita." Cord gently stroked the curve of her waist and hip. "It's all over now."

Faith sighed as she snuggled against him. "Why don't I feel more relieved?"

"Because, sweetheart, the price was too high." He raised himself on his elbow to gaze into her face. "But, God willing, this is the end. We'll never be separated again."

Faith placed her hand on Cord's cheek. His two-day beard stubble felt rough to her palm. "That reminds me." She smiled. "I have a wedding to plan."

Chapter 37

The wedding to unite Faith and Cord in holy— and legal—wedlock took place in the courtyard of the Double J ranchhouse. Reverend Maywood of Sonria performed the brief ceremony while Nicole acted as matron of honor and Matthew filled the role of best man. Emily, Diego, Paco and José were the only guests.

Faith was beautiful in the white lace wedding gown and veil that had belonged to her mother. Cord chose to wear his black shirt, pants and vest.

The wedding was simple, but the celebratory fiesta that followed was a more elaborate affair. All of the Double J ranchhands attended as well as the neighboring ranchers and the majority of Sonria's citizens.

Nicole hired a small Mexican band, and lively music filled the air as the guests danced beneath the golden glow of festive lanterns. Children tried their luck at the pinata José had fashioned for the occasion, while their parents helped themselves to Emily's sumptuous buffet.

The fiesta continued into the wee hours of the morning until even the ever-energetic Emily was forced to plead exhaustion.

"Happy?" Cord asked. He slid an arm around Faith's waist as they watched the last of their guests depart.

Faith glanced down at the plain gold band that graced the third finger of her left hand, then smiled up at Cord. "Beyond my wildest dreams."

Before Cord could kiss her as he wished to do, Matthew approached them.

"You're a lucky man, Brother," Matthew said as he kissed Faith's cheek.

Cord scowled. "Is that all you wanted?"

"No." Matthew grinned, unperturbed. "I have something to tell you both. I'm going to Europe."

"Europe?" Faith frowned. "Why?"

"I received a wire this morning from John Rollins," Matthew explained. "He caught up with Montgomery and Rothschild in Laredo. He contacted their English clients and it turns out they're looking for a legitimate American representative. Rollins suggested me, so I'm off to London to meet with them."

"Matthew! That's wonderful." Faith hugged

her brother-in-law.

"Congratulations, Matt." Cord shook his twin's hand. "Is it what you really want?"

"Yes. Yes, it is," Matthew replied. "Obviously it's a good move, but more than that, I think the trip will do me good. Who knows, it may turn into an adventure."

"Nicole has friends in London," Faith told him. "You should have her give you letters of introduction."

"I'll do that," Matthew agreed. "Are you two still planning to go to California?"

"We leave in three days," Cord answered.

Matthew nodded. "I leave on Friday." Once again he kissed Faith's cheek, then gave Cord's shoulder a brief squeeze. "Be happy," he said simply, then turned and left.

Cord bent to kiss his wife only to again be interrupted, this time by Nicole.

"My darlings," Nicole exclaimed as she embraced each of them in turn. "I know you will be very, very happy."

"Thank you," Faith said and kissed her aunt's cheek.

"Diego and I have decided to be married tomorrow," Nicole told them. "A small ceremony at Reverend Maywood's home. We have also decided to live here on Diego's ranch. It is past time for both of us to settle down."

"I'm so happy for you," Faith told her.

"Diego Montez is a lucky man," Cord said.

"And I am a very fortunate woman." Nicole fairly bubbled with happiness. "All I need now are a few grandnieces and nephews to make my life complete. I shall expect the first one within a year's time."

Cord grinned. "I promise to do my part."

As soon as Nicole left them, Cord and Faith were approached by Emily Stubbs and Paco Lopez, who offered their congratulations to the newlyweds.

"Do not worry," Paco said. "I will take excellent care of the Double J while you are in California."

"With my help," Emily added.

Faith laughed. "I know, and we won't worry."

Finally no one else remained in the courtyard.

"Alone at last," Cord sighed as he pulled his wife into his arms. "Have I told you today how beautiful you are?"

Faith gazed up into Cord's emerald green eyes and felt her heart swell with love. She could not imagine a happiness any greater than what she felt at that moment. "Only a dozen times," she replied.

Cord smiled. His special secretive smile that tugged one corner of his mouth upward. "I love you, Mrs. McCamy."

"And I love you, Mr. McCamy. With all my heart."

A chill night breeze blew across the courtyard and a coyote howled his lonely song in the distance. But Cord and Faith paid no heed as hand in hand they sought the privacy of their bedroom.

YESTERDAY'S PROMISE

They were together in the wildly beautiful land they loved, and the bright future of California beckoned them.

Destiny was fulfilled. Each had found a home in the other's heart.

Their journey was over.

Night Wind's Woman

By Shirl Henke

OUR STORY SO FAR . . .

Proud and untameable as a lioness, Orlena had fled the court of Spain and a forced marriage to an aging lecher. But in the savage provinces of New Spain, the golden-haired beauty was destined to clash with another man—one whom her aristocratic blood dictated that she loathe, one whom her woman's heart demanded that she love . . .

Half white, half Apache, he was a renegade who attacked when least expected, then disappeared like the wind in the night. He would take his revenge against the hated Spaniards by holding hostage the beautiful Orlena.

We pick up the story, on the trail, as Night Wind takes Orlena back to the Apache camp . . . .

Orlena cursed the plodding, foul-tempered little beast that smelled even worse than she did. After three days without a bath, she was filthy. The hot, parching days in the sun had wind-blistered her delicate golden skin until it peeled painfully; the cold night air drove her to seek the most unwelcome body heat of her captor.

As if conjured up, Night Wind reined in his big piebald stallion alongside her. He inspected her bedraggled condition, finding her distressingly desirable in spite of burned skin, tangled hair and torn boy's clothing. In fact, the shirt and pants outlined her flawlessly feminine curves all too well now that she had discarded the binding about her breasts.

Orlena watched his cool green eyes examine her and felt an irrational urge to comb her fingers through her hair in a vain attempt to straighten it. Instead she said waspishly, "Why do you stare at me? To take pleasure in my misery?"

He chuckled, a surprisingly rich sound, vaguely familiar. Indeed the eyes, too, seemed familiar, but that was only because in his swarthy face such an obviously white feature stood out.

"Look you ahead. Relief for your misery is at hand, Doña. Your bath awaits." He gestured to a dense cluster of scrub pine and some rustling alders. They ringed a small lake of crystal-clear water fed from some underground spring.

Orlena's first impulse was to leap into its cool,

inviting depths, but her reason quickly asserted itself. She fixed him with a frosty glare and replied, "A lady requires privacy for her ablutions. Also some clean clothes to wear afterward."

"Unfortunately for you, my men and I travel light. We have no silk dresses in our saddlebags."

"Then you should not have abducted me," she snapped as her burro skittered, smelling the water.

"You should not have worn your brother's clothes and my men would not have taken you by mistake," he replied evenly as he dismounted by the water's edge.

Her eyes narrowed. They were back at the original impasse. "Why did you want Santiago?"

His face became shuttered once more as he considered his plan gone awry. "I did not plan to kill him," was all he would say.

Or ransom him either. Orlena was certain of that much. His motives regarding both of them centered on Conal in some way. Before she could argue further he strode over to the burro and swept her from it, tossing her into the deep clear water. At first she shrieked in shock as her blistered, sweaty body met the icy cold water. But when she began to swim, the cold became refreshing. However, her clothes and boots were a decided impediment. With a couple of quick yanks she freed the boots and tossed them onto the bank.

Night Wind watched her glide through the water like a sleek little otter. He was surprised that she could swim. He had expected her to flounder and cry out to be rescued from drowning. Smiling grimly to himself, he shed his moccasins and breechclout and dove in after her.

"Ladies do not know how to swim, Lioness," he said as he caught up with her in several swift strokes.

She gasped in surprise, then recovered. "Conal taught Santiago and me when we were children."

His face darkened ominously. "He has taught you much—too much for a Spanish female of the noble class."

"Some Spaniard has taught you also—too much for an Apache male of the renegade class," she replied in a haughty tone as cold as his expression.

He reached out and one wet hand clamped on her arm, pulling her to him. "Come here. Take off your clothes," he whispered.

Her eyes scanned the banks. As if by prearrangement, the Lipan and Pascal had vanished downstream. She could dimly hear them unpacking the animals and making camp, but a thick stand of juniper bushes and alder trees provided complete privacy. She jerked free and kicked away from him, but he was a stronger swimmer. In a few strokes he caught up to her, this time grabbing her around her waist.

"You will drown us both if you are not sensible," he said as he struggled with the shirt plastered to her body.

"I told you the last time you asked me to disrobe that I would never do it for you," she gasped, flailing at him. Blessed Virgin, she could see through the water! He was completely naked! "No!" The cry was torn from her as he finally succeeded in freeing her from the shredded remnants of her shirt.

"You are burned and filthy. If you do not cleanse your skin properly you will become ill," he gritted out as he began to unfasten the buttons on her trousers. She continued struggling. "I am not going to rape you, little Lioness," he whispered roughly.

"I do not believe you," she panted. "You only waited, tricked me—"

He silenced her with a kiss. It was most difficult to remain coldly rigid with her lips closed when she was gasping for breath and flailing in the water. The hot interior of his mouth was electrifying as he opened it over hers. His tongue plunged in to twine with hers in a silent duel. Orlena pushed at his chest ineffectually as he propelled them effortlessly toward the bank where shade from an overhanging alder beckoned.

The sandy soil was gritty and full of rocks away from the water's edge, but an uneven carpet of tall grass grew out of the water and up the gently sloping bank. He carried her dripping from the water and tossed her on it. Before she could regain her breath or roll up, he seized her sagging, loose pant legs and yanked, straightening her legs and raising her buttocks off the ground. Unbuttoned at the top, the trousers slid off with a whoosh, taking with them the ragged remains of her undergarments.

He looked down at her naked flesh, sun and wind burned, covered with scratches and bruises. Orlena shivered as the dry air quickly evaporated the cold water from her skin. She tried ineffectually to cover herself with her hands as she rolled to one side, unable to meet his piercing gaze. He reached down and scooped her into his arms again.

"Now, I am going to let you swim for a few moments while I get some medicine from my saddlebags. I do not think it wise to try to escape with no clothing. You are already burned enough!" With that he tossed her back into the icy embrace of the water and strolled off, heedless of his own nakedness.

Orlena fumed as she treaded water, watching him carry off the last remnants of her clothes. He was right. Where could she go in the mountain wilderness, naked and afoot? In only a moment he returned, leading the big black-and-white stallion. He took something from the buckskin pouch on what passed on an Apache mount for a saddle and waded back into the shallows. "Spanish ladies seem to set great store by this," he said mockingly, holding up a piece of what looked to be soap—real soap! "It is not the jasmine scent you favor, but it is all I could find for our unplanned bathing." He held out the soap for her inspection. The unspoken command was in his eyes as he waited, waist-deep in the water, for her to come to him.

Orlena warred within herself. She could not out-run him and had nowhere to go, yet she hated to let him humble her by begging for the soap—not to mention having to expose her nakedness once again to his lascivious green eyes in order to reach the bribe. She treaded water, careful not to let her breasts bob above the surface.

"Toss it to me. I can catch quite well."

He smiled blackly. "Allow me to guess. Conal taught you. No, Doña Orlena, you must come to me—or stay in the lake until that lovely little body turns blue and freezes at nightfall." With that he sauntered toward the shallows, tossing the soap casually from hand to hand.

"Wait!" Orlena was growing cold already and the sun was beginning to arc toward its final descent beyond the mountain peaks to the west.

He turned with one arched black eyebrow raised and said, "I will meet you half way, but you must do as I command. I have already given my word not to take you against your will. Unlike your Spanish soldiers, the word of a Lipan is never broken."

That a savage could talk to her thus made bile rise in her throat, but she was trapped in the freezing water, hungry, naked, completely at his mercy. "I suppose I must trust your Apache honor," she replied through chattering teeth. Was it only the cold that made her shiver?

Very slowly she swam toward him. Very slowly he walked across the smooth lake bottom toward her. Orlena watched the sunlight filtering through the trees trace a shifting design on his bronzed skin. His arm and chest muscles rippled with every step he took. He had taken off the leather headband along with his other apparel and his wet black hair hung free, almost touching his shoulders. Without the band, he seemed less Apache, more white, but not less dangerous.

"Come," he whispered, watching her, knowing what this was costing her Spanish pride. Waiting for her, touching her without taking her, was exacting a price from him as well. He observed the swell of her breasts swaying as she moved through the clear water. Darkened almost bronze by soaking, her hair floated like a mantle, covering her as she touched bottom and rose from the water.

He reached out and drew her to him, unresisting at first, until he pushed back the wet heavy hair from one pale shoulder. "No," she gasped, but it was too late. He had one slim wrist imprisoned. Slowly he worked a rich, sensuous lather against her collarbone, moving lower, toward her breast. When his soap-slicked fingers made contact, she forgot to breathe. The tip of her breast puckered to a hard rosy point and the tingling that began there quickly spread downward. When he released her wrist, Orlena did not notice. His free hand lifted the wet hair from her shoulder and he spread the lather across to capture her other breast, gently massaging both of them in rhythm. She swayed unsteadily in the water. Although it was still cold, Orlena Valdiz had become hot. Night Wind cupped her shoulders and then worked the sensuous, slick suds down her arms.

She stood glassy-eyed and trembling in the waist-deep water, studying the rippling muscles beneath the light dusting of black hair on his chest. It narrowed in a pattern that vanished beneath the water. Just as her eyes began to trespass to that forbidden place, she felt a jolt as he reached that selfsame location on her! Quickly and delicately, he skirted the soft mound of curls and lathered over her hips, then around, cupping her buttocks.

"Raise your hair and turn," he commanded hoarsely, maneuvering her like a porcelain doll into shallow water. He could feel the quivering thrill that raced through her as he performed the intimate toilette. His own body responded, hard and aching, but he ignored his need and massaged the delicate vertebrae of her back, down past her tiny waist to the flair of hips and rounding of buttocks. "Now, kneel so I can wash your hair."

Like a sleepwalker she responded to his slight pressure on her shoulders and knelt with her back to him. He lathered the masses of hair, massaging her scalp with incredibly gentle fingers. Orlena imagined her maid back in Spain performing this familiar ritual, but this was not Maria and she was far from Madrid, alone in a foreign land, the prisoner of a savage!

His voice, low and warm, with its disquietingly educated accent, cut into her chaotic thoughts. "Lower your head and rinse away the soap."

Orlena did so, working all traces of the lather from her hair. Then she rose from the water, eyes tightly closed against the sting of the soap, and began to squeeze the excess water from her hair. Night Wind watched the way her breasts curved as she raised her arms above her head. Her waist was slim, her skin pale; she was so fragile and lovely that it made his heart stop.

He had used many white women over the years, but none had any more claim on him than to assuage his lust, more often to please his masculine pride. A despised Apache could seduce a fine white lady, have her begging him to make love to her. Make love! Those other times had been more acts of war than love to Night Wind. Never had he played a waiting game, balancing gentleness with iron authority. Never before had he taken a white woman's virginity. And it was still far too soon, he knew, for that to occur unless he forced her. The feelings she evoked were dangerous and he did not like them. The anger betrayed itself in his voice.

"Now, I have bathed you. You will bathe me."

Orlena's eyes flew open and she blinked in amazement. "Surely you jest, but it does not amuse me!"

"So, I can play lady's maid to you," he said in a quiet deadly voice, "but you will not be body servant to a dirty savage."

She reddened guiltily, recalling her thoughts of Maria a moment earlier. He held out the soap in one open palm, waiting once more.

"No! I will not—I *cannot*." She hated the way her voice cracked.

"Yes, you will and you can—else the young deer Broken Leg is now roasting will not fill that lovely little belly tonight."

Ever since her first temper tantrum with the bowl of beans and the water gourd, she had learned the power of hunger and thirst over human pride. She had not been fed all the following day, only given water, until they camped last night. By then the mush of bean paste had actually been palatable. Now the fragrance of roasting meat wafted on the evening breeze. She salivated and her stomach rumbled. They had broken their morning fast at dawn with cold corn cakes and water, but she had eaten nothing since.

"I have clothes for you, in Warpaint's saddlebag," he motioned to the horse grazing untethered nearby. "Or, you can stay here all night, freezing and starving."

With a remarkable oath she had overhead a Spanish sailor use, Orlena stalked over to him and grabbed the soap.

Forcing her hands to remain steady was nearly impossible as she flattened her lathered palms against his sleek dark skin and began to rub in small circles across his chest, then down the hard biceps on his arms. His chest was lightly furred with curly black hair. Trusting the steadiness of her voice only slightly more than that of her hands, she said curiously, "All the other men are smooth-skinned. Why do you—."

"You may think me a savage, but I am half white," was the stormy reply. Then he added in a lighter tone, "You have never seen any man's bared chest before, have you, Lioness?"

She stiffened at the intimacy of his voice, hating herself for her stupid words. "Of course not!"

"Then how did Conal teach you to swim—fully clothed?"

A small smile warmed her face as she recalled being a little girl with a toddler brother, cavorting in the pond at the villa in Aranjuez. "In fact, we all wore light undergarments. I was a child and never thought on it. But I do not remember him furred as are you."

He frowned. "Conal's hair is red. It would not show as easily as dark hair. Body hair is considered ugly among my people."

She looked up suddenly. "Then the Apache must think you uncomely indeed," she said with asperity.

"No. The Lipan accept me as one of their own," he replied with an arrogant grin, adding, "Woman, red or white, have never found me unattractive."

"Well now you have met the first one who does," she hissed.

"Liar," he whispered softly, watching as she lowered her eyes and busily applied herself to the disconcerting task he had set her.

Orlena felt the steady thud of his heart, angry at its evenness when her own pulse was racing.

Night Wind was having a far more difficult time looking calm than the furious, golden-haired woman before him could imagine. Lord, her small rounded breasts arched up enticingly as she raised her arms to lather him. Intent on winning this contest of wills with her, he clenched his fists beneath the water to keep from caressing the impudently pointed nipples. Smiling, he watched how she bit her lip in concentration as she was forced to touch his body. She kept her eyes fastened on her busy hands, not looking up into his face.

Orlena could feel him shrug and flex his muscles as he turned, allowing her such casual access to his body. She thought she knew it well from lying wrapped in his arms the past nights. She was wrong —how much different this was, with both of them naked, slicked by the cool water and warm sun.

"Turn so I may wash your back." She tried to emulate his command and was rewarded with a rich, low chuckle. When he did not move at once, she added, "You do not, for a surety, fear to turn your back on a mere female?"

"Not as long as my knife and any other weapons lay well beyond your reach," he replied with arched eyebrows. Then kneeling in front of her he added, "It will be far easier for you to wash my hair than me yours."

His thick, night-black hair was coarse and straight, shiny black as a raven's wing. She worked a rich lather into it, finding the massaging motion of her fingertips on his scalp soothing. Angry with herself, she shoved his head under the water abruptly, saying, "Rinse clean."

He came up coughing and splattering her with droplets. "You try a man's patience overmuch, Lioness." Then a slow smile transformed his face as he said with arrogant assurance, "Wash below the water, also, as I did to you."

She dropped the soap with a splash, but he quickly recovered it in the clear water. When he handed it to her silently, she moved around him and began with his back. Touching his tight, lean buttock made her quiver with a strange seeping warmth in spite of the cold water. She finished quickly, forgetting to breathe as he turned around to face her again.

His eyes burned into her as he took her wrist and began to work her small, soapy palm in circles around his navel, then lower, beneath the water. When she touched that mysterious, frighteningly male part of him, she could feel its heat and hardness.

In spite of his best resolution, Night Wind let out a sharp gasp and his hips jerked reflexively when he closed her soap-filled little hand around his phallus. Orlena jumped back, jerking her hand free. At first she was uncertain what had happened, but then she realized what it was, and a small smirk curved her lips.

So, he is not as indifferent to me as he would pretend. On a few occasions when she escaped her *dueña*, she had seen animals mate in their stables. Always the male's staff had seemed an ugly, threatening thing to her. But those were merely horses and dogs. This was different . . . frightening, yes, but not ugly. . . .

She dragged her thoughts from their horrifying direction. Blessed Virgin, what was happening to her? She surely had not found the naked body of a man pleasing! And a savage at that! Like mares and bitches, women had to subject themselves to male lust in the marriage bed. But she knew well from her own mother's plight what the consequences were—a swollen belly and an agonizing childbirth. She backed away from him, clenching the soap unconsciously in her hands.

Night Wind struggled with his desire for her, but at last let her go, deciding the game had been played out long enough for now. Then he realized that she continued slowly backing away from him, all the spitting fury and innocent sexual awakening of moments ago evaporated. Her face was chalky, and she wrapped her arms protectively about her body as if warding off a blow.

"I did not intend to frighten you, Lioness," he said softly. "I gave my word not to force you, and I will keep it."

"I see evidence to the contrary," she spat, but refused to look at his lower body, clearly outlined beneath the water.

One long arm shot out and grabbed her wrist, prying the soap from her fingers. "We are both clean enough," he said gruffly, pulling the shivering woman behind him as he splashed to the bank.

Feeling her resistance, he released her in the shallows and said, "I have cloth to dry you and an ointment for your burns."

"And what of the small matter of clothing? You have destroyed the pitiful remnants of Santiago's shirt and trousers."

"I have more suitable garments—women's clothing with which to replace them," he replied reasonably, ignoring her as he pulled a long cloth from the piebald's saddlebag and tossed it at her.

Orlena dried herself carefully with the rough cotton towel, wincing at its abrasion on her tender skin. In a moment he returned from another foray into his pack with a small tin. "Pascal says this is a miracle cure for sun and wind burn. It will serve until the women of my band can tend you."

She eyed him suspiciously. His hair and chest were still wet but he had slipped on a pair of sleek buckskin pants and his moccasins. He held out the ointment like a peace offering. "Come here." A smile played about his lips. "After all, I need not repeat the rest of the sentence. You are already rid of your clothes."

"You promised me women's clothing," she replied with rising anger, but still she clutched the towel protectively in front of herself.

He waited until she approached, warily, then commanded, "Raise your hair first so I may treat your shoulders.

Still holding the towel draped around herself with one hand, she lifted her hair up with the other. Santiago's thin shirt had been ripped on the brushy shrubs and trees as they rode and her skin was both scratched and sunburned. His fingers were calloused, yet warm and soothing as he spread the salve on her skin with surprising gentleness. The sting evaporated magically, but she did not voice her appreciation, only turned to let him minister to her throat and arms, then her hands.

When he tipped up her chin to touch her wind-burned cheeks and nose, she was forced to meet his eyes. Again a sense of recognition niggled, then vanished as she observed his reaction to her.

"Ah, Lioness, you are too delicate for New Mexico. You should have stayed in Spain," he said with what almost sounded like regret in his voice.

She looked at him oddly, puzzled and afraid. Of him . . . or of herself? She honestly did not know.

THE QUEEN OF WESTERN ROMANCE

MADELINE BAKER

When Lacey Montana began her lonely trek across the plains behind her father's prison wagon, she had wanted no part of Matt Drago. Part Apache, part gambler, Matt frightened Lacey by the savage intensity in his dark eyes, but helpless and alone, she offered to tend Matt's wounds if he would help find her father. Stranded in the burning desert, their desperation turned to fierce passion as they struggled to stay alive. Matt longed to possess his beautiful savior body and soul, but if he wanted to win her heart, he'd have to do it Lacey's way.

__2918-9 $4.50

Cassie Edwards

When Passion Calls

"A SENSITIVE STORYTELLER WHO ALWAYS TOUCHES READERS' HEARTS!"
— *Romantic Times*

Heartbreakingly lovely, Melanie Stanton had long been promised to Josh Brennan. But marriage was the last thing on her mind until Josh's twin Shane returned to the family's Texas spread. Raised by the Chippewa, Shane was as wild as the untamed frontier, as savagely virile as Josh was weak. Shane's intimate caresses aroused a white-hot desire Melanie had never known in Josh's arms. Their love was forbidden, but Melanie knew that when passion calls, the heart must obey.

__2903-0 $4.50